Sarah's Fortune

Sarah's Fortune

Mary Street

ROBERT HALE · LONDON

ISBN 0 7090 6867 0

Robert Hale Limited
Clerkenwell House
Clerkenwell Green
London EC1R 0HT

2 4 6 8 10 9 7 5 3 1

Typeset by
Derek Doyle & Associates, Liverpool.
Printed in Great Britain by
St Edmundsbury Press, Bury St Edmunds, Suffolk.
Bound by Woolnough Bookbinding Limited.

One

My future prospects looked bleak indeed.

I had become accustomed to luxury these last three years, for I had lived in comfort at Kilburn Hall, with no exacting duties, as companion to my aunt, Lady Kilburn.

Now, this was at an end. My aunt had died, the funeral had taken place, and I had to find a new situation for myself.

I was offered a home at Kilburn Parsonage, living with my sister and her husband. After one week, it was clear this could not continue. The parsonage was not large and I too often had the feeling of being in the way: though I was fond of Arabella, her Henry was too stiff and pompous for my taste.

I was pleased when fair weather allowed me to escape out of doors.

One day, I was taking a solitary ramble in the grounds of Kilburn Hall, pondering my future without enthusiasm, miserably aware how few were my choices, when my thoughts were interrupted by a man's voice.

'Good day to you, Miss Holroyd! May I join you?'

'Mr Foster!' I turned to greet him. After civilities, I accepted his condolences and we talked of my aunt as I adjusted my pace and fell into step beside him.

Mr Foster had business with my uncle, Sir Nicholas. I first met him at Kilburn Hall when my cousin Thomas had invited his own friends for sport and I had wondered at him being there, for Mr Foster did not shoot: he seemed awkward and lost amidst the noisy, high-spirited bucks.

He was thirty years old, disabled, with a vacant look which could mislead others into taking him for a simpleton. But he was shrewd enough to comprehend my cousin's friends did not please me, and the smile in the steady brown eyes taught me he would willingly assist my escape from their attentions.

I had begged him to indulge me at backgammon. We had some animated conversation and that was the beginning of an odd friendship.

'I had not known you were in Leicestershire, sir?'

'I arrived last night. There is a matter which I put off when your aunt was taken ill, but now I wish it settled. I was surprised to learn you had quitted the hall so soon?'

'That was my brother-in-law's doing,' I said.

Henry had been quick to point out the irregularity of a single female remaining at the hall with two gentlemen, even an uncle and cousin. Henry was a stickler for propriety.

My companion laughed at my prim expression. 'He means well, I do not doubt.'

'Indeed he does,' I said gloomily. 'I fear I do Henry less than justice, for he has been kind enough to offer me a home, and I cannot feel the present situation is agreeable to him. Well, I shall not impose on him for long, if I can help it.'

I hesitated, wondering how much I should reveal. Mr Foster was a gentleman of substance, with estates in Derbyshire and any number of genteel acquaintance. He could assist me. So I went on, 'I have determined to seek employment. Do you know of any lady requiring a young female companion, sir?'

He stopped, teetered a little, steadied himself and brought his crutch forward, holding it with both hands. 'I do not,' he said. 'And I doubt you would find such employment agreeable.'

'Much would depend upon the disposition of my employer,' I

6

agreed. 'I may hope for a lady with my aunt's amiable qualities, but I cannot afford to be too nice in my notions.'

'Are you necessitous?' he asked curiously. 'Has your uncle made no provision for you?'

'No indeed, and why should he? I am no relation of his, merely one of his wife's nieces. He has been generous to my family, but he has no particular obligation to me. And at this present,' I went on, 'I suspect his means are limited. My cousin Thomas is rather extravagant, you know.'

'I do know,' said Mr Foster grimly. 'His period of mourning should curb his excesses for a while. What of your family? Had you no thought of returning home?'

'I could do so, but I do not wish it.'

My home was in Northampton: we were poor relations to the Kilburns, a large family living in a small house, and we were cramped and noisy and continually bumping in to each other. I had not been unhappy but I had been uncomfortable, for I was one who liked to maintain order in my life.

My very brief stay at the parsonage had brought back feelings of being stifled, feelings I had forgotten when I lived at the hall, but which were familiar from earlier times. But even the parsonage was preferable to returning home.

Home had been bad enough when I was accustomed to nothing better, attempting to pacify Mama when she was angry, attempting to scold the maids into better habits, attempting to curb the pranks of my young brothers and teach them their letters.

Even attempts to keep my own property in order were frustrated by those who would turn over the contents of my drawers when they needed bootlaces or handkerchiefs, and never could I sit down to write a letter without having to search high and low for an inkwell and a penknife.

My Aunt Kilburn had but one child, my cousin Thomas, and she wished for a daughter. After a succession of miscarriages, she had the happy thought of adopting my sister Arabella.

We, the poor relations, could not afford to refuse. Arabella had left us at ten years old; she returned briefly, to attend service when Papa died, and we did not see her again for another two years, when she came to pay a longer visit.

I was then seventeen: she was one-and-twenty and recently engaged to her Henry. He also was a Kilburn, a nephew of my uncle, but no kin to us. The living at Kilburn had been saved for him and became his as soon as he was ordained. When he found himself in need of a wife, his fancy alighted on my sister and everyone agreed it was a very good match for her.

Only my aunt repined. At the parsonage, Arabella would be no more than half a mile away, but Aunt Kilburn did not know what she would do without her.

By way of a solution, Arabella had returned home to look at her sisters and determine which would take her place. She came with a purse full of guineas and bought treats for us and, I confess, I admired this sister-stranger, softly spoken, elegantly dressed, who was not above helping me with patching and darning.

So I was flattered and pleased to be chosen and since I was never a favourite with Mama, she agreed to part with me.

'She may regret your absence, though,' Arabella had said. 'I have seen how much you do, Sarah, and it pains me she has so little value for you. Well, our sisters will have to bestir themselves now. Harriet could certainly do more and Emily is not too young to be useful.'

She paused, brooding on what she had seen. 'I was young when I left but I confess I do not remember such disorder! Has it always been so?'

'There are three more of us,' I said, for the younger children had been born after she left. 'Our papa has died, and the older boys come home only when they are on furlough.' I sighed. 'Mama cannot exercise authority as a man does.'

'It is improper in me to criticize Mama,' said Arabella, 'but I mislike the way she contradicts everything you say. She would do better to support you. Indeed, I have misgivings about removing you, for they will be sorely tried without you.'

'Mama is of the opposite opinion,' I smiled. 'They may get on better without me!'

'As to that, we shall see. Well, you will find everything very different at Kilburn.'

As indeed I had. I was startled when we passed through acres of parkland before coming to formal gardens where the hall was situated, and I was awed by the hall itself, granite, with lead roofs, mullioned windows and the main entrance fronted by a columned porch.

Arabella had given me very necessary lessons in how to conduct myself and how to make myself presentable. My aunt had provided me with gowns which were becoming to me. I had been waited upon, with a fire in my room and hot water for washing and clean towels every morning.

I took pleasure in having my comfort thus regarded; I enjoyed the delicate fare served at table; I was impressed by the spaciousness and elegance of the rooms and amazed by the beautiful furnishings and ornaments. It had been easy, all too easy, to become accustomed to luxury.

All this came to an end when my aunt died. Now, there was nothing for me to do at Kilburn: my uncle had confessed he did not know what to do with me and only Arabella and her Henry had spared me a return to Northampton.

Mama had written to say I might return: I believe my uncle thought I should go. Had I the smallest hope of effecting improvement, I would have been less dismayed by the prospect, but experience had taught me I would be frustrated.

These unbecoming sentiments I kept to myself. But I thought if Mr Foster would exert himself a little on my behalf, he might assist me to find a good situation.

So, by way of explanation, I told a small part of it.

'We are a large family, too large for our house, and one more makes too much difference in cramped surroundings. Besides, one day I must earn my bread for my portion is wholly inadequate. My aunt,' I added with a smile, 'had the good sense to

9

attach Sir Nicholas, but Mama was not so prudent in her marriage.'

Papa had nothing. He had been a captain in the regulars, dashing and impecunious when Mama married him, and later, wounded and discharged from service. Such income as we had came from Mama's modest fortune, and we had received occasional presents of money and clothing from our wealthier relations.

I faltered in the middle of explaining this, for Mr Foster looked even more vacant than usual. I knew he was by no means foolish but I could not be certain I had his attention. I would have dropped the subject, had it not been for my urgency.

'So you see,' I said, 'I must find employment. I am not sufficiently accomplished to teach children, or old enough to be engaged as a chaperon. But as a genteel companion for an elderly lady, I might find a situation. It would be a kindness, sir, if you hear of one, to recommend me.'

'A kindness!' He gave a mirthless laugh. 'To find employment for you with an elderly tyrant? I think not!'

'I would not expect—'

'I will tell you what you may expect! You may expect to run pointless errands, exercise overweight lap dogs, hunt high and low for every trifle that has been mislaid, fuss around her with shawls and screens and cordials and heaven knows what else. You may expect to have blame heaped upon you constantly, be cavilled at for doing the wrong things, for doing things in the wrong way, for being forgetful, or for being too slow. You would not believe how it is possible to be so consistently in the wrong as paid companions are! You find that diverting?'

'Excessively diverting in the way you express it.'

'You would find the reality something savage,' he said drily. 'In any case, your appearance is against you.'

'Indeed?'

I confess I was offended. Since I had been at Kilburn, my figure and complexion had improved, and I had learnt to take pains, paying particular attention to dress, deportment and the arrangement of my hair. My features are good and though I wished my eyes were blue rather than grey, I knew my pale hair was the envy of several ladies in the neighbourhood.

Now I spoke stiffly. 'I was not aware there was anything in my appearance to offend?'

'You are quite beautiful,' he said calmly. 'And there is much in that to offend a woman seeking a companion! No lady will employ a female to outshine her in every particular.'

'Oh!' Never had it occurred to me I could be disadvantaged for such a reason. I felt a sudden lurch of fear. 'What is to become of me? There seems to be nothing I am suited for.'

We had been walking through a grove: now, Mr Foster indicated a sycamore which had a circular bench built around the trunk. 'I am a little fatigued,' he said. 'I think we could discuss this matter more comfortably if we sat down.'

When we were seated, he gazed upwards into the leafy canopy. He looked vacant again, but I had the impression that his mind was very busy indeed. I waited in the hope that he would produce a notion which I had not thought of and it seemed he had, for he said, 'I hope I may persuade you to give up this idea, in favour of a different situation.'

I waited again, but he did not elaborate. At last, I said cautiously, 'What situation did you have in mind, sir?'

He abandoned his contemplation of nature and turned to look directly at me and never in my life had I been more astonished than when he said, 'I would like to be married, Sarah. Will you do me the honour of becoming my wife?'

'Can you be serious?' I demanded.

He flushed, a deep crimson, and I saw that he had mistaken my surprise. I said quickly, 'Forgive me! I have no wish to offend. Indeed, I have a very good opinion of you. But sir, this can only be impulse – you cannot have given it proper consideration!'

'You are mistaken. I have given it a great deal of consideration. This is not a sudden whim, in fact I came to Kilburn Hall expressly

11

for the purpose of making my proposals. What I have heard of your situation encourages me to hope that I do not press my suit in vain.'

I was silent, too amazed even to know what I was thinking or feeling. At last I said lamely, 'I had not expected to marry.'

'If you can overlook my obvious disadvantages, you will easily comprehend your situation will be much improved.'

'I – my family—'

'You will find me at least as generous as your uncle.'

I felt my colour rise. 'I meant my birth! Mama was genteel, but she married beneath her. I told you Papa was a captain in the army, and so he was, but I have not been wholly frank! His birth was humble; he was a gamekeeper's son, which is hardly a connection you could wish for. Gentlemen in your situation look for ladies with birth and fortune to recommend them.'

'Well, ladies of birth and fortune can marry where they choose: they do not choose to marry ill-favoured cripples.'

I winced at his slighting description of himself, but I said nothing. It was too painfully accurate.

The lines around his mouth relaxed, and he smiled. 'I am very sensible that I am by no means a prepossessing gentleman. Lands and fortune I have, and an heir I must have, therefore I must marry a wife. Since I am unlikely to attach any lady with romantic notions, I am obliged to look for a lady who cannot afford to have romantic notions.'

'There are any number of those,' I pointed out.

'Indeed there are,' he agreed. 'So why should I not try my fortune with one I find most pleasing? I understand you have no attachment to any other gentleman?'

'I have not.'

'Very well! I do not expect you to be in love with me, but I would point out our marriage would be of material benefit to you and your family.'

'I am very sensible of it,' I admitted.

In my uncle's library were many engravings of gentlemen's

country residences and I had seen one of Foster Leigh House. Situated in Derbyshire, not far from Ashbourne, it looked a fair prospect. Now, I was entranced by a vision of myself as mistress of a fine house.

'Of course, if you find my infirmities repulsive—'

'No, indeed,' I said absently. 'I am accustomed to such.'

'I beg your pardon? How so?'

I shook away my vain imaginings, returning my thoughts to Mr Foster. 'Papa was wounded in action, disabled before I was born; have I never mentioned it? I was raised with such infirmity daily before my eyes. Your condition raises no repugnance in me, sir.'

'I had not known that. It is, perhaps, fortunate, in the circumstances. Well, Sarah? Shall we be married, you and I? I am still awaiting your answer, you know.'

For any lady it was an offer not to be despised: for me, faced with choices which were by no means agreeable, this new prospect was quite dazzling. And if the gentleman I must take as my husband was, as he expressed it himself 'an ill-favoured cripple', he was intelligent, amiable, and had a shrewd wit.

Which was, upon giving the matter due consideration, more pleasing than the manners affected by other gentlemen of my acquaintance.

In the past, we had dealt well together: I thought we stood as great a chance of happiness as those who married for love.

Besides, I had no great opinion of marrying for love.

My sister professed to love Henry, a good man in his way, though he lacked humour and was too starched in his notions. Had I to choose between them, I would choose Mr Foster.

Mama had married for love and later found herself tied to a man just as crippled as Mr Foster, a man who was very dear to me, but he had no material advantages and he was by no means a gentleman. Mama had been distressed for money, dissatisfied with her circumstances and pulled about by child-bearing. Our household was crowded and disordered and she had grown impatient and ill-tempered. I could not feel love had survived.

13

'Sir, I—' I stopped. Family recollections had intruded into my vision of marital happiness and I said awkwardly, 'Sir, previously I had no reason to be wholly frank about my family, but now I fear I must be.'

Miserably, I went on to give him a full account of everything, and when I had finished, I said, 'We can scarce be called genteel! Before I came to Kilburn, Arabella had to teach me, even about finger bowls and napkins! I can easily comprehend you may wish to withdraw your offer, and no reproach to you. You cannot wish to connect yourself—'

'My dear, such evils are swiftly remedied! I presume we may find a larger house and good servants, even in Northampton?'

'Not if Mama's complaints are to be believed.'

He laughed and within minutes he made all dispositions for my family, suggesting a good-sized house, a sensible cook-house-keeper to have the ordering of things, enough housemaids, a scullery maid, and a generous quarterly allowance paid to Mama for the upkeep of her new establishment.

'What have I forgot? A tutor for the boys, or perhaps it would be better to send them to school? Yes? And a pony and trap to make excursions easy. When your mama is settled and less fretful, she will have time to teach your brothers and sisters all about finger bowls and napkins!'

Laughter had crept into his voice but I found I was weeping. 'You would do so much? How could I ever repay you?'

'All this can be done with very little inconvenience to myself, I assure you.'

'Your relations will not approve of the connection—'

'There are relations of mine who will trouble themselves over such matters,' he admitted. 'It will be enough for them to know you are niece to Sir Nicholas Kilburn! Now Sarah, will you have consideration for a suitor's very natural anxiety and answer me, yes or no? Are we to be married?'

'I cannot refuse you, sir.' I wiped my eyes. 'And th-thank you. Thank you very much for asking me.'

It remained to make my relations acquainted with our engagement. I could not suppose any would raise strong objections: with such promised benefit for herself, Mama certainly would not, and only her consent was needed.

My uncle was applied to for approval, which he was inclined to bestow. We settled upon three months of deep mourning for my aunt, after which our nuptials would take place.

Arabella did reproach me for choosing the mercenary motive, and her objections were not reduced when I explained how Mama would benefit.

'Mr Foster spoke as though he could effect a complete transformation, though I doubt he believes it, and I certainly do not! However, such measures must bring improvements.'

'Oh, but at what cost! Sarah, I implore you, do reconsider.'

'No; why should I? You know my situation, am I likely to receive a better offer?'

'Financially? I doubt it. But you are a beauty, Sarah, and I am certain there will be other gentlemen; you have only to wait. Why are you in such a hurry to sacrifice yourself?'

'Sacrifice? You speak too strongly, Sister. I do not consider it a sacrifice; in fact now I am accustomed to the prospect, I find it most pleasing.'

'If that is so, then I can only wish you joy.'

Arabella spoke doubtfully and my brother-in-law, when the news was made known to him, was also inclined to regard the matter with disapprobation.

'I cannot approve of it. Certainly you must pay attention to money, Sarah, but I do not recommend marriage where ambition is the sole object.'

'I do not deny that financial comfort is an object with me,' I said coolly, 'and though I had not expected such an advantageous offer, I see no reason to refuse it! I like Mr Foster and I believe we will be tolerably happy.'

There was more argument, but I remained firm and at last the situation was accepted. Practical matters were soon disposed of: I was to remain at the parsonage for the necessary three months, be married at Kilburn, and Henry would conduct the ceremony.

So all my relations were reconciled, as I thought, and I was startled and shocked when objections came from the one person I had expected to treat the matter with the utmost indifference.

My cousin Thomas received the news with a frightening display of anger and outrage.

Two

'Do not dare to tell me you wish it!' Thomas was red-faced and beside himself with fury. 'You cannot wish to tie yourself to an ungainly creature such as he! I will not believe you wish it! Why are you doing it, Sarah?'

He had interrupted us at breakfast. Having just learnt of my engagement he had come to remonstrate with me, and he had begun immediately, making no attempt to speak to me alone.

Now, three of us at table stared in astonishment as Thomas paced the room, too agitated to be still, protesting again and again against my engagement to Mr Foster.

I was silent, too amazed and shocked by his fury to answer, and Arabella could only produce a feeble, 'Now, Thomas—'

Henry also was cousin to Thomas and knew him well enough to be unsurprised by his temper, but the cause of this outburst occasioned some astonishment.

Too conscious of his dignity to bear such an ill-mannered intrusion, Henry spoke severely. 'Do you have any just cause for this objection, sir? For I have heard you speak none.'

'He is twisted, ungainly, wholly repugnant! He is a cripple!'

'For shame, sir!' Henry rose to Mr Foster's defence with all his authority as a clergyman. 'Such a misfortune can befall any man at any time if the Lord sees fit,' he pronounced. 'None of us are immune to accident. I think you have not heard any speak against his character, or his disposition, and if his disablement is the worst

17

you know of him, you have no reason for this complaint, no reason at all!'

My cousin was in too much of a passion to pay heed. 'I see what it is!' He turned to me. 'You meant to have him, right from the start! Well, I will tell you, you may have a husband with wealth at his disposal, but it will do you no good, no good at all, in polite society. You will be censured for a fortune hunter!'

I did not trouble to protest. Thomas knew very well that many ladies in my situation would do the same and I had heard enough of polite society to know how marriages were made up of schemes for advancement, not always by the couples themselves.

My silence raised a fresh indignation. 'Oh yes! Do not think I have forgotten the ball, and the way you engaged yourself to spend two dances sitting down with Foster!'

'Sarah, did you really? How profligate!' Arabella laughed, but Thomas was in no humour to see his absurdity.

'Giles Fortesque was not pleased by your refusal to dance! I see it all, now! You set your cap at Foster from the start.'

'Nonsense, I did no such thing.'

I was puzzled by this reference to the ball. It had taken place on my twentieth birthday, six months ago, before my aunt became ill. It had been by no means a grand occasion, just music and dancing for a dozen couples, but it so happened that Mr Foster was visiting and he had apologized and looked unhappy because he could not engage me to dance. I had said, quite truthfully, that I could spend time agreeably in conversation, sitting down with him, and I had given him permission to engage me for the duration of the third two dances.

'You are all kindness, madam.'

'Not at all,' I said. 'I hope you will exert yourself to restore my good humour, for certainly I shall be out of humour by that time. I am to dance the second two with Mr Harcourt.'

That had produced a salty chuckle, for Mr Harcourt was a tedious rattle who sought to entertain ladies with tales of his own sporting prowess.

I had danced with Mr Fortesque also. This gentleman had first approached when I was sitting with Mr Foster. I had explained, and saw no hint of the displeasure my cousin now spoke of: he had simply engaged me for the next two dances.

If Mr Fortesque had felt himself ill-used, it was the first I knew of it. I could not imagine why Thomas now chose to make much of such a trifling event.

Occupied with my thoughts, I had not troubled to listen to what Henry was saying to Thomas. It was, in any case, of a reproving and moralizing nature and it served only to increase my cousin's displeasure.

'If you cannot refrain from preaching, sir, I suggest you address your sermons to your sister-in-law, for she is more in need of them than I! She is a selfish, unfeeling girl who has used all her arts and allurements to captivate a man for whom she can feel nothing but repugnance!'

'Selfish and unfeeling?' That was Arabella, pink with indignation. 'I wonder you dare to speak so, sir, of the lady who so kindly and patiently attended your poor mama, day and night, throughout these last few months!'

Arabella would have launched upon a detailed exposition but I cut her short. 'It was little enough, after the kindness she showed me.' I turned to Thomas. 'You are presumptuous, sir, in your claim to know my feelings,' I said. 'I like Mr Foster very well and since he has offered for me, I shall marry him. And you may believe,' I added drily, 'I would rather marry him than your friend Mr Fortesque!'

'I do not wish you to marry Fortesque,' said Thomas impatiently. 'I wish you to marry me.'

Stunned by this announcement, I could not, for many minutes, collect my scattered wits. The others were equally dumbstruck.

Henry was the first to find his voice. 'If that is so, sir, then it is a pity you did not make your sentiments known to the lady before she became promised to another.'

'It is not past mending,' said Thomas. 'No announcement has

19

yet been made; your engagement is known only to the family. You could easily cry off, Sarah, and marry me, instead. Even Foster himself would not blame you!'

'No, I do not think he would,' I said slowly. 'I shall not do so, however.'

'You must, Sarah! Come now, I shall have fortune, too, you know, and the title, besides.' His voice took on a wheedling note. 'You would like to be Lady Kilburn, and be mistress of Kilburn Hall, would you not? And I am reckoned to be passably good-looking; you cannot deny I am an improvement on Foster!'

I could deny it, though Thomas would have been most offended had I done so. He was a handsome man of eight and twenty, but I had witnessed ill-humour and selfish behaviour, and heard many reports of his extravagance. I had no great liking for my cousin and I knew I would prefer to marry Mr Foster.

'I find this declaration quite astonishing,' I said, 'because for all the opportunities you have had to attach me, never have you shown any sign of particular regard until now, when I am become engaged elsewhere. How do you account for it?'

'I thought I had more time,' said Thomas sulkily. 'How was I to know you would engage yourself to such a one? And so soon after dear Mama had breathed her last! I could not declare myself at such a time, and I could not do so before, either, because she was ill, and you so busy attending her.'

For all these protestations I could not truly believe Thomas had any real regard for me. Hitherto, my impression had been that Thomas was in no hurry to marry at all and when he did he would choose a lady who brought with her some substantial fortune. I will swear I had never been of any consequence to him. I was merely a poor relation.

Now, I seized on our relationship as an objection to his proposal. 'I cannot feel Sir Nicholas would welcome such an alliance,' I said. 'I have, on occasion, heard him express uneasiness on the subject of marriage between cousins.'

Here, Thomas embarked on the most preposterous story yet.

He had, he said, loved me from the very beginning, but he knew Sir Nicholas held such views, and felt no straightforward representations would persuade his father to accept an alliance between us. Consequently, he had embarked on a series of wild escapades and extravagances, partly to relieve his own feelings but also, so he claimed, with purpose. For after such excesses, he thought his father would welcome his wish to settle down, and even the prospect of a cousin as his wife would be considered a lesser evil.

All that came to my mind were scathing retorts which were better left unspoken. A more seemly answer came from Arabella.

'Did you not think,' asked my sister unsteadily, 'that it would have been wiser to fix your interest with Sarah before you went ahead with such a scheme? There was no point in squandering your substance, you know, until you were certain of her sentiments.'

'Should I doubt that Sarah would marry me, situated as she is, with all I have to offer? She is willing to take Foster.'

This point of view was more in keeping with my opinion of Thomas than his declaration of love: it was also a fair statement, because I knew my acceptance of Mr Foster had been swayed by the promise of material comfort.

Now, I discovered peculiarity in myself: I could contemplate marriage to that ill-favoured cripple with equanimity, but even without that alternative, even with a bleaker prospect before me, nothing would persuade me to marry Thomas.

He was wheedling: no one would blame me if I broke my engagement; I would, I must, prefer to marry him.

'I am sorry, Thomas, but I have to refuse you.' To soften the blow, I added, 'I have no doubt there are many ladies who would be overjoyed to receive your proposals but, to me, you are a cousin and I cannot regard you in any other light.'

It was clear he was by no means willing to accept this, but before he could protest, my brother-in-law intervened. 'In any case, Cousin, you show a sad lack of propriety in the ill-mannered way you pay your addresses! I cannot approve of it.'

Thomas stared at me in astonishment. 'Does that offend you?' he demanded. 'You refuse me merely because you are troubled by notions of *propriety*?'

'No, but—'

'I see how it is! You see me as a cousin; you must become accustomed to the idea of me as your husband! It will take time, but I do not mind waiting. But you must cry off from this engagement to Foster. He is crippled and ungainly so you took him in compassion and I comprehend how you are reluctant to wound his feelings, but you know you do not wish to marry him. Well, you shall not! Leave it with me, Sarah. I will speak to my father; he will break it to Foster and you may be certain he will handle the matter with delicacy.'

He picked up his hat and cane as he spoke and was preparing for departure, his expression pleased and complacent. I said quickly, 'Thomas, I beg you, do not deceive yourself—'

He bowed. 'I shall leave you now. We will speak again when you are freed from this preposterous engagement.' And before anyone could stop him, he left the house.

'Sir!' I spoke to my brother-in-law. 'I beg you, go after him and undo, if you can, whatever mischief he may cause.'

Henry spoke rather heavily. 'Is it truly your wish that I should do so, Sarah? For Thomas seems to believe you refuse him merely to spare Foster's feelings!'

'I do not!' I was shaking with fury. 'Did I give him one word of encouragement? I did not! How dare he! How dare he be so presumptuous as to imagine he can overset my engagement, when I have refused him? You may believe,' I added drily, 'that I did not speak as plainly as I might, for it was *his* feelings I wished to spare! I do not want to marry him – I would *prefer* to marry Mr Foster.'

My brother-in-law seemed surprised, but when he was satisfied I meant it, he set off for the hall. Left alone, Arabella and I stared at each other until she succumbed to a fit of the giggles. 'My dear sister, I congratulate you! Two proposals in as many days! Pray how many more suitors do you have languishing after you?'

'None, as far as I know,' I said. 'Arabella, you have known Thomas longer than I, did you believe that faradiddle?'

Arabella was silent as she thought it over. 'There was truth, I think, mixed in with a lot of nonsense,' she said. 'You have become a beautiful woman, Sarah, and he could easily persuade himself he was in love.'

'Thomas could easily persuade himself to be in love,' I agreed. 'Were it to his advantage, he would do so with great determination. But he knows marriage to me would bring no advantage: it would be considered most imprudent.'

'Then perhaps he is truly in love with you?'

'No, I do not believe it. All this has come about because I accepted Mr Foster. I know my betrothed is no favourite with Thomas, though I confess I do not see why my engagement should so offend him. And to go so far as to offer for me himself. . . .'

'Thomas is a vain creature,' said Arabella dispassionately, 'vain enough to have persuaded himself you wished for him.'

'That much I can believe!'

'He might have been toying with the notion of marrying you,' said Arabella. 'You say there is no advantage, but there is advantage in appearance and the two of you would present a handsome couple to the world. Your engagement might well offend him! I comprehend his point of view, for a couple such as you and Mr Foster must present an odd appearance, you know.'

'If appearance is the only value—' I began indignantly.

'I said I could comprehend: I did not say I approved.'

Our conversation ended, for I had a visitor. Matilda Pringle had been maid to my aunt: upon learning of my engagement, she had hit upon the notion of seeking a new situation with me.

'Well, I confess I had not yet given thought to such matters, but I expect I will need a maid,' I said.

I thought I would like to have Matilda, for during my aunt's illness I had learnt how I could rely on her. So I promised to engage her provided Mr Foster made no objection, and on this under-standing we discussed the particulars.

Soon afterwards, a message came from Sir Nicholas summoning me to the hall. Upon arrival I was shown into the library, where I found my uncle looking perturbed and Henry red with exasperation. Thomas had an air of lofty arrogance, as though he considered himself above the proceedings.

Mr Foster sat in a winged armchair, his head leaning back, his face pale, his eyes closed, his knuckles white as he gripped at his crutch. He did not look at me.

'Sarah!' My uncle spoke sternly. 'It was most improper and, I may say, most unkind of you to promise yourself to Mr Foster with such a calculated design!'

'Calculated design, sir? I am at a loss to understand you.'

'It was done, was it not, with the purpose of bringing about a declaration from my son?'

'Indeed, it was not!'

My uncle seemed not to hear. 'Pray consider how intolerable his disappointment must be now, having believed he had won you, only to have the prize snatched from him! *He* has been everything that is noble and generous and is quite prepared to renounce his claim, but I cannot forbear to reprove you! It shows a want of conduct that is quite unbecoming!'

'Had I truly behaved in such a fashion, I would agree with you, sir,' I said.

It was clear Thomas had a complete disregard for truth, but it would not do to accuse my cousin of outright falsehood, so I spoke carefully. 'I am sorry, very sorry indeed, if any conduct of mine has led my cousin to this misapprehension, but it was quite unwitting on my part. Never had I any notion of marrying him, and never did I suspect his sentiments, which were made known to me only this morning.'

Here, Henry lent his support. 'I have been at pains to impress upon our uncle and upon Mr Foster, too, that you gave Thomas no reason to suppose his suit would be successful.'

'I am obliged to you, sir.' I returned my attention to my uncle. 'I have no wish to cause pain to Thomas,' I said, 'but I gave my word to Mr Foster, and I will hold to it.'

Confusion reigned for the next hour.

Thomas sought to strengthen his position by bringing up the past. He made much of small services which, as a poor relation, I had felt obliged to perform, but which he declared were positive evidence of my affection for him.

I apologized for causing such misapprehensions and said I had meant these services as an expression of gratitude for the kindness I had received.

My uncle, naturally concerned for his son, now pressed me to consider Thomas's declaration. 'I confess to some uneasiness in the matter of cousins marrying, but if you truly wish it, Sarah, I will not stand in your way.'

Mr Foster begged me not to be swayed by considerations of his feelings. 'I cannot hold you to our engagement,' he said distantly, 'should you find you had mistaken your heart.'

'I am doing my utmost to convince everyone I have not!' I said, only partly disguising my own asperity. I turned to my uncle. 'My cousin does me great honour with his proposals, but I feel there is a difference in our dispositions which would make us irksome, each to the other, should we marry.'

There were more protestations from Thomas: he repeated words I had spoken months ago and gave them a different tone and expression, changing the emphasis to imply that I had given him reason to hope.

I had to explain myself and repeat myself many times. At last, Sir Nicholas was convinced and forbade Thomas to continue on the subject.

Thomas flounced away: I sank into a chair, speechless.

Mr Foster had spoken only once throughout the argument. Even now he did not speak. At last, my uncle broke the silence, turning to him with apologies on behalf of his son.

He responded civilly and fell silent again, and it was Henry who, with a transparent attempt at tact, begged him to escort me to the parsonage. 'For I have some parish matters to discuss with Sir Nicholas and I may not return for some time.'

Mr Foster got to his feet and bowed. 'Then we will leave you,' he said. He turned and looked at me and I was startled by the expression in his eyes: they were as bleak and cold as an Arctic landscape.

Three

'I beg you will not look at me so,' I said, as soon as we were alone together. 'For this was none of my doing! I am sorry you have been subjected to such nonsense! I confess, my cousin has greatly taxed my forbearance. I know not what he is about.'

'To me it is evident what he is about,' said my betrothed coolly. 'He wishes you for himself.'

'Yes, but why?'

'I wonder!'

But as he looked at me, the anger left his eyes and he regarded me curiously. 'Are you so lacking in vanity?' he asked. 'Surely you understand the reason?'

'His proposal is no compliment to me. No, I do not understand the reason! I could not say so to Sir Nicholas, but I am persuaded my cousin likes me no more than I like him.'

That brought a smile, reluctant at first but in the end coming to cheerfulness. With self-deprecating humour, he described the scene when Thomas returned to the hall with the announcement that he, Mr Foster, might as well take himself home straight away because I was going to cry off from my engagement and marry him.

I was appalled. 'Sometimes I wonder if my cousin hears anything that is said to him,' I said. 'Had I suspected such incivility I would have been less courteous in my refusal. But I made myself plain; I could not have been plainer!'

'He said you had accepted me out of compassion. Is there truth in that, Sarah? Because I do not think—'

'Today we have learnt how my cousin will say anything!' I retorted. 'I am not so ignorant as to accept you out of compassion! I told you, Papa was disabled: I know how it is.'

It was true. Many can understand how disablement prevents energetic activities: compensation can be found in other pursuits, but not always consolation. Mr Foster could draw, he was an accomplished musician and he was adept at cards: he spoke little of those things he could not do, but I knew he would like to dance, and I thought he would like to join the other gentlemen at sport.

I did not speak of these matters.

'I know,' I said, 'I know of all the frustrations it imposes on daily life. I know how you have trouble with steps and stairs and doors, and picking up things you have dropped. I know you have difficulty manoeuvring your way around furniture. I know how you are limited to the use of one hand when the other is employed with your crutch. I know how much time is required for matters which others accomplish quickly, and I know how strongly you must exert yourself, simply to move around. Do not tell me you have invented your own way of dealing with these matters: I know that, also.'

He stopped short in his surprise.

'I have observed,' he said, 'how you have patience out of the ordinary: it is one of the reasons why I – I saw how my awkwardness did not appear to tax your forbearance. Until now, I had no knowledge of how far you understood.'

'I told you yesterday, I am accustomed to such. My cousin insults both of us by suggesting I would marry for compassion! I accepted your proposals because I felt we could deal well together and because you offered me a way out of many difficulties. I do not scruple to remind you, for you yourself pointed out the material advantages!'

'And now your cousin has made an advantageous offer, also,' he observed.

'How fortunate then, that you offered first, for Thomas would be a great deal more offended had I accepted you *after* refusing him. No. I kept my refusal civil, but I do not like my cousin and I could not marry him.'

'My dear Sarah,' he said drily, 'am I now to understand you remain with me out of preference?'

'Yes, why not? I would not accept any proposal in expectation of being miserable! You know I had no thought of marriage until yesterday, but I have since given thought to the matter. It has occurred to me there is no gentleman of my acquaintance whom I like better.'

He laughed, but I could see he was pleased. 'Have a care, my dear! I shall soon become quite puffed up in conceit.'

He returned to the scene at the hall. 'There was I, reeling from the blow Thomas had dealt me and your uncle demanding to know the particulars, when Henry arrived and gave flat denial to all. He said you sent him. Did you?'

'Yes.' I explained how Thomas refused to accept my decision. We discussed the matter, indignant with Thomas but making no sense of him.

The only profitable outcome of our discussion was a resolve to suspect Thomas in future and to consult with each other before we believed or acted on anything he said.

Arriving at the parsonage, we talked it over again with Arabella. When Henry returned, he expressed doubts as to whether Thomas would let the matter rest.

'Sorry I am to say it, but Thomas can be difficult. I fear he may importune you for some time to come, Sarah. I have been considering the matter and I think it best if you are removed from here.'

He rejected my suggestion of returning home to Northampton, saying Thomas would simply follow me. His idea was to send me to his sister's house in Melton.

'Have no fear, Sarah, you will be welcome and Mr Foster may visit you.'

I had met Mrs Taylor and her husband only twice, and though I found them agreeable, I was uncomfortable at this notion of foisting myself on them. But the idea found favour with my betrothed and Arabella persuaded me. 'They are my in-laws, you know, so you might almost call them relations.'

Matilda was explained to Mr Foster and we arranged for her to accompany me. So I went to Melton Mowbray and the Taylors welcomed me as warmly as Henry had promised. I was thankful to find there were ways in which Matilda and I could make ourselves useful.

My betrothed – I now called him James at his request – visited me occasionally, but he was also very much occupied with other business.

Our marriage settlements were drawn up and he also did all he promised for Mama, who wrote to me at greater length than usual, pleased she would have a new establishment, but surprised I had chosen Mr Foster in preference to Thomas.

Henry was right when he said Thomas would go to Northampton. He did, and attempted to persuade Mama into giving her support.

He was too late: she had given consent to Mr Foster. She told Thomas she was very sorry, I was the most perplexing of her daughters and she did not understand me, but she would not go against my wishes.

To Mama, Thomas made himself agreeable, although that might have had something to do with my brother Samuel who was home on furlough.

Samuel is the eldest of us, big enough to be intimidating when he so wished, a very useful lieutenant in Colonel March's regiment and more than a match for Thomas.

He is a man of action, this brother of mine, and rarely puts pen to paper, but he took the trouble to write to me because he was puzzled by something Thomas had said.

When Thomas took his leave of Mama, Samuel had walked with him to his hotel. Thomas, discontented, had spoken against

James and suggested he was not to be trusted. There was an odd moment when Thomas muttered that, 'Foster had got wind of Holroyd's scheme'.

Holroyd is our family name, but Samuel could not imagine what he meant and Thomas had refused to explain. My two younger brothers, Joseph and Edward, were children who could have no scheme to interest Thomas. Samuel had questioned the others, William and Robert, and they were equally mystified.

I also was mystified and perturbed. When I saw James, I showed him Samuel's letter and asked his opinion.

He read it, frowning and then asked, 'Is there another branch of your family? Uncles, cousins?'

'None bearing the name of Holroyd,' I said. 'Papa had only one brother and he was lost at sea many years ago.'

'What of your grandfather?'

'He, too, was an only surviving child. There may be other Holroyds, but any connection must go back several generations.'

James tapped Samuel's letter against his hand. 'Then I can only suppose this is an invention on your cousin's part, a ruse of some kind.'

I stared. 'For what purpose?'

'To cause mischief?' he suggested. 'To bring about suspicion of me, to create uneasiness, some perturbation of mind?'

'Suspicion of you he could not achieve,' I said warmly. 'But the rest, yes he has done that!'

I recalled the swift and easy way Thomas attributed all his previous wildness and excesses to his love for me. He could think quickly, my cousin, make up stories as he went along and, having been thwarted, he would like to sow seeds of doubt.

With little hope of success in his pursuit of me, a notion of starting uneasiness may have been in his mind even before calling on my family. He would know how one piece of nonsense, seeming accidental but uttered purposely, could bring about confusion.

'Yes,' I said. 'I do believe you are right! How foolish of me to trouble myself over his nonsense.'

31

I wrote to explain the matter to Samuel, then forgot about Thomas as I busied myself with making up my wedding clothes.

My uncle had given me money and I chose a blue-grey material which became me very well and which would also be suitable for travelling, for we were to travel to Derbyshire immediately after the ceremony.

Our wedding took place in Melton, and there was little to-do about it. Mama came and so did Samuel. My nuptials were conducted by my brother-in-law, I was attended by Arabella and given away by my uncle. The only other support for me was from the Taylors and two families of the Kilburn neighbours.

James was better supported and for his sake I was pleased. He had several cousins and a number of friends besides. They were introduced and all of them regarded me searchingly, well aware, I suppose, of my motive for marrying, not blaming, but not approving either.

The ceremony over, we left the church to good wishes from those who had been witness. In the carriage, James seated himself beside me, upright, and did not lean back until the business of leave-taking was over and we were in motion. Then, in a tone of quiet satisfaction, he said, 'It is done.'

I had nothing to say, but I felt some gesture was called for and I laid my hand over his. New gold glimmered on my finger. He regarded it for a moment, then raised my hand to his lips, and sighed, and was silent.

Studying him, I saw there were lines of strain in his face and a dark look in his eyes that spoke of deep exhaustion, and I knew, without knowing why, that he had not had proper rest for some time.

I said impulsively, 'You look tired, James. Do sleep, if you wish. Do not try to stay awake for my sake, I beg you.'

His carriage was far more comfortable than any post-chaise, well sprung, with deep seats. At present we were being jolted, but this would end when we came to good road, and he could take two hours of comfortable, undisturbed rest.

He protested, but I was not deceived. I fussed around him, persuaded him to put up his feet and indicated I would take the seat opposite and possibly sleep myself.

'You are my wife, Sarah, not my nurse.' But there was no reproof in his voice, rather a note of apology.

'We are to be together for the rest of our lives,' I said lightly. 'As well we should be easy with each other, right from the start.'

'From this day forth,' he murmured sleepily. 'Oh, Sarah!'

He mumbled something as he drifted into sleep. It sounded like 'seven shillings'.

I settled myself into a corner and watched the passing scene, sensible of peculiar feelings, a mixture of sorrow and contentment.

James woke when we arrived at the inn where we were to dine and change horses. He apologized for sleeping so long. 'What a poor bridegroom you must think me!'

'Even now, you have not slept long enough,' I said. 'James, how are you come to be so exhausted?'

'I have had a trying week,' he said, and would not elaborate when pressed. 'It is of no consequence. I feel better now.'

We resumed our journey: he refused to sleep again, pronouncing himself well rested. In July, the light remained long and though we were late in arriving at Foster Leigh House, I had a perfect view of it.

Windows flared golden reflections in the light of the westering sun, amber-coloured stone shimmered against a background of green lawns, and mature oaks and chestnut and beech gave to the place a timeless quality.

I stared as though in a dream. 'I am mistress of this place?' I felt a tremor of doubt. 'It is beyond anything I am used to,' I said. 'I hope I shall be equal to it.'

'Mrs Clegg will advise you.'

Mrs Clegg was housekeeper, and I knew she had been in command of all domestic arrangements since James's infancy, for his mother had died soon after his birth. James was confident of her goodwill but I was less sanguine on my own behalf, for it now occurred to me that she might resent my coming as an intrusion into her domain.

She looked to be a sensible woman, though her demeanour suggested I had much to do to win her approval. She had an army of servants lined up to greet us. I spoke to them, hoping I said everything that was proper.

I was relieved to see one familiar face: Matilda had preceded me to Foster Leigh, and if she was prepared to give me the same loyalty she had bestowed on my aunt, I would have a useful informant and ally among the servants.

I refused to inspect the house that evening. It was, in any case, so large it would take a long time.

'We are fatigued from the journey, and I can think of nothing either of us wish more at this present than some tea and bread and butter. Now James, where may we be comfortable?'

He took me into a panelled sitting-room, with mahogany furnishings, sofas and chairs with green and gold covers, a plain marble fireplace in the Rumford style, with windows looking westwards over the parkland, all gilded now with the last rays of the setting sun.

Tea came, candles were brought in, we ate and drank, talking little. James was tired and so was I, but I was self-conscious and a little hesitant about suggesting we should retire.

I was taken aback by the size of the bedchamber. My dressing-room, adjoining, was pleasingly furnished with a washstand, chests, screens, chairs and a dresser, but it had not prepared me for this opulence. An enormous bed, hung with blue and turquoise, rested on a thick carpet. Around the room were silk-covered chairs and ornately carved tables bearing ornaments and branches of candles, all of them lit.

Undressed, I sat on the edge of the bed waiting for him to join me. And when he came, he startled me for he stood directly before me, supported by his crutch, and with his free hand he pushed up my nightgown and thrust his hand against me.

I gasped, protesting against so intimate a touch straight away. He withdrew, but he laughed and there was a hint of mockery in his voice. 'What was sin yesterday becomes virtue today, my dear, for we have the benefit of clergy. Is it not strange we should need consent from Parson Henry?'

I said nothing, uncertain of his mood. He answered his own question. 'Well, there is purpose behind it.' He put his crutch on the floor, took my face between both hands and brushed his lips against mine, lightly at first, then claimed me in a firm and surprisingly sweet kiss. And when we drew apart, he pushed gently against my shoulder, indicating that I should get into bed and move across to leave room for him.

He followed me in a rather ungainly fashion, and there were kisses and caresses and his touches were gentle and pleasing. Then, as his breathing deepened, he murmured, 'Touch me! There! Like that!'

I think I was rather awkward in my attempts to please him. There was protest, a slight adjustment, a gasp of pleasure and his mouth was against my ear, murmuring affection.

Suddenly he stiffened and rolled away from me, muttering savage imprecations which I had better not repeat. I sat up, for fear I had made a false move. His back was arched and his crippled leg stretched out at an awkward angle.

'Cramp?' I asked, and he nodded, his lips pressed tightly together. I threw back the covers, saw his toes splayed out and scrambled to reach them. Pressing my hand against the ball of his foot I pushed hard against him.

'Dear God in Heaven, woman, do you think to – oh!' Anguish gave way to surprise as he was eased.

I continued to push with one hand as I felt the muscles of his calf with the other.

'I am better now, Sarah, I thank you.'

I said nothing, but I found a spot where the muscles were knotted and worked my fingertips around it, and pushed and kneaded, vigorous, until I felt an easing of the tendons, then massaged more gently, ignoring his protest that he was well until I myself was certain of it.

'Is this a regular occurrence?'

'Am I often seized with cramps when I am about to marry a wife? No, I cannot say it has happened before.'

'You know very well what I mean.'

'I have cramps occasionally,' he said in a bored voice. 'I forgot to take exercise, today. Foolish of me, was it not?'

'No doubt you were otherwise occupied?' I suggested and won a glimmer of a smile.

I shuffled back to my pillows and drew up the bed covers, tidying them. When I turned to him, he was looking a little sulky and he said, 'I might have guessed our wedding night would turn into a farce. You had better go to sleep, Sarah.'

For myself I wished nothing more and he was tired. But he was unhappy, also, and I thought we should not end this day on such a note. So I took the bold measure of kissing him and murmured 'Sleep can wait,' and he needed only a little persuasion.

Arabella had warned me that I might, at first, find my husband's attentions uncomfortable and I was prepared for that. But no one had warned me, and I was certainly not prepared for the searing, blistering agony of our first encounter.

I am not a lady who will scream with pain: for some reason, it is not in my nature. It is true I groaned with the first onslaught, whimpered as the agony continued and spent the rest of the time fighting back sobs and wishing for him to have done. And when he had done, after what seemed like a lifetime, I found he had completely mistook me and believed my pleasure had been equal to his.

I could not disillusion him. My pain was no fault of his, this was some difficulty of my own. So I kissed him and hugged him, glad I had pleased him, but wholly dismayed for myself.

He fell asleep, forgetting about the candles. I could, I suppose, have let them burn out but I was not accustomed to waste, and these were the expensive kind, made of paraffin wax.

So, gingerly, I rose from the bed and started a little as I saw how the sheets were stained with blood. I edged my way around the room putting out the lights, leaving the nearest one until last. Then I groped my way back to bed in darkness and felt him stir and heard him mutter in his sleep as I resumed my place beside him.

I lay awake for a long time, appalled to discover in myself such aversion to intimacy. I wondered how I was going to face a lifetime of such horror. Worse, how could I spend a lifetime deceiving my husband and concealing my own feelings?

Conceal them, I must. For now I knew the answer to a question I had never thought of asking: if my motive for marrying was suspect, his motive was quite pure and quite simple: this ungainly creature, this ill-favoured cripple, this dear, generous, little man was head over heels in love with me.

In his passion, he had whispered in my ear. 'Sarah! Oh, my love! How long have I loved you! So long! Loved you, wanted you, needed you! Can you love me, Sarah? Just a little? Love me Sarah, please, if you can!'

I could not. But I vowed then that never would I willingly do anything to hurt him.

Four

In the morning I opened my eyes to discover he had woken before me and had propped himself up on his elbow to watch me. When I stirred and blinked at him, I was astonished and touched to see his countenance become suffused by the deepest blush.

I made myself smile, touched his heated cheeks, running my thumb over his morning stubble. He caught my hand in his and brought it to his lips. 'Good morning, Mrs Foster. I trust you slept well?'

'Very well, I thank you.' I raised my face to his, inviting a kiss. 'What time is it?'

'Not yet six o'clock.' He snuggled down beside me, put his arm around me, smoothed my hair with his free hand and kissed me again, murmuring in my ear, 'We have plenty of time.'

Thankfully, I was looking over his shoulder and he did not see the expression of horror which must have crossed my countenance as I realized he meant to claim me again. Last night, I had lain awake steeling myself to bear the nights with fortitude. Never had it occurred to me that he might also wish for me on waking!

I determined I was not going to be a coward. So I caressed him and urged him to his pleasure and forced back my tears and let him think my stifled sobs were echoes of his own delight. I kissed him again when he had done and if my smile was one of relief because the agony had ended, he knew nothing of it.

Alone in my dressing-room I gave way to my true feelings, letting the tears pour down my cheeks in a way I had not done since I was a child. But I mopped up and inspected my face in the looking-glass before I rang for Matilda. My eyes were too bright, but there were no other signs of distress.

Matilda brought me some tea and a screen was put between me and the door. I heard a footman bring in a bath, which was followed by maids with cans of hot water.

Matilda seemed easy, but I confess to feeling embarrassment. Wishing to direct her thoughts, I began, 'Tell me, Matilda, what of the servants, here? How do you deal with them?'

'Oh, such an inquistion they put me through when I arrived! Wanting to know who you were, how pretty you were, whether you were agreeable, whether you would give yourself airs!'

I managed a smile. 'I hope you gave me a good character?'

'Indeed I did. I told them how patiently you had tended my poor lady. I told them. Certain they were your marriage was for gain and I said you had to have something to live on but you would not marry without liking too. I told them, told them straight, how you refused Mr Thomas, handsome as he is, with all his wealth and the title besides!'

'Oh Matilda, you should not have done that!'

'If Mr Thomas wants to make himself a laughing-stock, who am I to stop him? No, but they put you down as a fortune hunter, which you cannot wonder at, the master being as he is. I told them. "Handsome is as handsome does", that is what Miss Sarah says, I said. And that Mrs Clegg, she softened a bit and said the master was very handsome in his ways but not easily taken in, so they had better wait and see.'

So among the servants I was given the benefit of the doubt and I could hope to be accepted. I felt there was some irony in that Thomas had assisted me.

His behaviour had caused others to presume his addresses had been refused at some time previous to my acceptance of James.

Certainly, his outrage and anger could be explained more readily in such a case. Those who knew him would comprehend how his vanity had been wounded, particularly since, in preference to himself, I had chosen an 'ill-favoured cripple'.

Uneasiness stirred within me. Thomas would not be pleased, should he discover his folly had led to such assumptions. If he was now a laughing-stock, he had only himself to blame, but he would never see it in that light.

Matilda went on speaking of the servants until she had finished dressing my hair and when I was ready she bustled around, tidying up. I left her and went downstairs.

After breakfast, Mrs Clegg was summoned to show me around and I set about learning to be mistress of a great house. My time at Kilburn Hall proved useful, for I had the example of my aunt to guide me and I was accustomed to great rooms.

'The master,' said Mrs Clegg, 'does not make regular use of all the rooms. He prefers to have a few rooms close by each other for his own particular use.'

The great drawing-room was as large as an assembly room and the dining-room should, I felt, be called a banqueting hall.

'In a house such as this, that would seem a sensible arrangement,' I agreed. 'Excellent indeed for entertaining visitors, but too much for everyday life!'

After inspecting the many bedrooms we went to the top of the house: here were nurseries, crowded with rocking horses, hobby horses, story books and tops and toy soldiers. All had belonged to James, evidence of a rich, though somewhat lonely childhood.

'A house like this needs lots of children,' I said. 'It seems a pity that my husband was so alone.'

Mrs Clegg had been so far taciturn but this chance remark now had her talking, as we toured the schoolrooms and attics.

James could not be sent to school, he had a tutor at home, but there had been visiting children during the school holidays and she, Mrs Clegg, did not know which was worse, seeing the young master left out when they played their boisterous games of cricket and rounders or seeing him lonely with only his tutor for company, when they returned to school.

'Because he did like to have company to play the games he could enjoy: riddles and consequences and card games and such.'

She needed little encouragement to go on: I heard of the tortures devised by well-meaning adults in misguided attempts to correct his twisted leg.

Treatments had varied over the years and had, at different times, involved scorching him with hot poultices or surrounding him with mounds of ice.

Nor were these the only devices: 'Great lead weights strapped around him, mistress, hard enough for a strong leg to carry and him still a child. Oh, how the leather straps chafed his skin raw! Then there was a great iron brace he had to wear. And the contraption they rigged over his bed, all pulleys and weights tugging at him through the night! No doubt they thought they were helping him, but the only difference was to make him worse, if you ask me.' She sniffed. 'Doctors! Too many ideas and not enough sense!'

'They did little to strengthen his leg,' I spoke absently, 'but perhaps they brought out the strength in his character.'

James had no expectation that anything would improve his leg, but he explained to me that regular exercise was necessary to maintain the strength he had and also to avoid cramps.

He went for walks out of doors. Accustomed to going alone, he seemed a little nonplussed when I chose to accompany him.

'I pick my way carefully, you see,' he smiled, as he circled to avoid uneven ground, 'for it would be tiresome to sprain an ankle and be laid up for such carelessness. This is slow work for you, Sarah. I do not ask you to join every excursion.'

'When I have duties elsewhere, I shall not,' I said. 'But for now, we may be easy. There is much I need to learn, James. You must tell me who I will be expected to visit, and who will be our visitors, and what entertainments I must arrange.'

'I expect we must have dinner parties for our neighbours,' he said vaguely, 'but we shall not begin immediately. They will pay their bride visits and I have no doubt we shall be honoured with invitations. I thought,' he went on, 'to invite your mama and the children to visit at Christmas. Should you like that?'

I laughed. 'I have no doubt *they* will! But I confess to some trepidation, James. My younger brothers are noisy creatures, I fear.'

'We shall contrive.' Then he spoke in a teasing tone. 'They will teach me what to expect when I am a papa, myself.'

I blushed and he laughed and pinched my cheek and I think there was nothing in my expression to show the sudden lurch of fear I felt at the notion of bearing children. For how would I, who had recently discovered that intimacy brought with it such agony, how would I face the trials of giving birth?

I shook away my unease, determined I would not be a coward. Other ladies, less strong and healthy than myself, faced the same ordeal time after time. Arabella had suffered two miscarriages and Mama herself had born twelve children, nine of us living.

In that first week of my marriage, I privately christened our bedchamber the Torture Chamber, then threw the idea out of my mind lest I should speak it and cause pain. I did not shrink from my wifely duty, although I shed many tears in private.

When the thought of enduring a lifetime of such agony threatened to overset my courage, I told myself I suffered for a few minutes only and James himself had more to bear than I. I thought of other ladies who must undergo such torture with more courage and with less considerate husbands.

Never did I allow James to suspect my distress, for he was not rough or unkind and it was no fault of his. I wanted him to be happy, so I pretended to share his pleasure and I will hold that in such a case deception is no sin.

And I was rewarded: during the second week of our marriage, the pain became less severe, and later, to my great relief, it gave way to mere discomfort, which was something I could live with easily, if not quite happily.

We had been married a month when James was ill with some stomach disorder, suffering the kind of unpleasantness I do not wish to describe. For two days he could eat nothing, but he doctored himself with brandy in water and on the third day he could take some soup. Whatever ailed him must have been infectious, for, as he was mending, two of our servants were taken ill and so was I. By the time I felt better, the intimacy of our married life had been suspended for ten days.

It was a Sunday. In such circumstances, church could be missed, but whilst he was ill James had also suffered cramps, the consequence of neglecting exercise, and he determined to take a walk. I offered to accompany him. It was a dull day for August and quite cold, but this pleased me better than summer heat. I felt cool fresh air would be beneficial.

There was a strong gusting wind and rain threatened. I wore a pelisse and urged James to wear a greatcoat, saying I would carry it if his exertions made him too warm.

James liked to vary his walks, but for uncertain weather he had a route where shelter was never far away. It was fortunate, for the rain, when it came, was accompanied by such strong winds as to render my umbrella quite useless.

The nearest shelter was the hay barn of one of his tenants. 'I hoped to reach the Red Lion,' he said, 'for you would be be comfortable at the inn and there would be a fire and coffee, too. I fear you are cold, Sarah, dawdling along at my pace.'

'No, I am quite warm.' I stood in the doorway, watching as the wind forced the hedgerows to sway, and the driving rain bounced off the cobblestones. 'We may be obliged to wait here for some time, though.' I looked at him, seated on a narrow wooden bench, the wall behind hung with pitchforks and scythes. 'You look uncomfortable, James. Why should we not spread out your coat and make ourselves easy in the hay?'

He shot a quizzical glance at me and I blushed as I became aware there was an implication in my words which I had by no means intended. It may have been his look, or it may have been the wild weather, or the scent of new hay, or perhaps all these things working together. For I then felt a sudden heat, a delicious melting need such I had never before experienced. I passed my tongue over my lips. 'No one will come near in this rain, we are quite safe, quite alone.'

'Mrs Foster! Are you suggesting we should disport ourselves in the hay like a pair of common rustics?'

I had astonished myself and could not tell by voice or expression whether he was displeased or teasing. 'Should you dislike it, sir?'

His deep chuckle was answer enough. He set down his crutch and removed his hat and gloves and placed them carefully on the bench. I set down my umbrella and put my gloves and bonnet beside his. Intoxicated by the way we took our time, I took off my pelisse, he spread his greatcoat on the hay and we sat down, side by side, to remove our boots. Then we squirmed into a comfortable place and at last I sought the bliss of his arms.

All my previous pain and discomfort and fear was forgotten. I loosened his stock and fastened my lips in the hollow of his throat. Delighting in his gasps, in the things he said, I slid my hands under his shirt, spreading my palms against his back.

He unbuttoned my gown, and I pulled my arms out of the sleeves, thrusting aside the material so that he could reach my breasts. I sighed under his touch and felt long sweet tremors pass through me. I fumbled at his buttons, found him, exciting him with the touches he liked, and drew him towards me.

Urgent, gasping, muttering demands, every movement was a new sensation and though our clothes were in the way and we were hasty and clumsy, I experienced a most exquisite joy which I wanted never to end. And with the end came such a shock of delight that I lay shuddering for some time after we separated.

When I raised my head to look at him he was gasping still and he looked as though he had been stunned. And I, repenting all my former dismay and deceit, flung my arms around him and hugged him and burst into tears. 'Oh, James!' I sobbed. 'I am so glad I married you!'

I felt rather than heard the laughter in him. 'I am very happy to hear it,' he said. 'But why all these tears, Sarah?'

'I had no idea – I never felt so – oh, I cannot explain!' I checked myself on the point of blurting out how I had foreseen a lifetime of stoic endurance, gasped a little as I sought to account for myself. I blushed and said at last, 'Never before have I felt so wanton!'

He laughed again and kissed me. 'It is fortunate, then, that we are married,' he said. 'Well, we had a better sermon than the one being spoken in church, think not you?'

We laughed together and kissed again. I noticed the rain was beginning to slacken and we set about making ourselves presentable. As we examined each other and brushed away strands of hay, I confess to a little confusion and embarrassment.

Snatches of remembered conversation now had me in some perturbation of mind. For I had heard it said that a certain reluctance was becoming, and that ladies who displayed their eagerness were disgusting to gentlemen.

James did not look disgusted: in fact, he was looking very pleased with life and when I held out his greatcoat he said mockplaintively, 'You promised you would carry it if my exertions made me too warm!'

His words were accompanied by a sideways look: there was no mistaking his meaning and my expression made him laugh. As we resumed our walk he took to calling me 'Mrs Foster' with a certain relish, bringing me to determine that the talk I heard could not apply to every gentleman. Certainly, it did not apply to him. I felt I was fortunate to have married such a man.

In the following days, we grew bolder, discovering new delights and I was happier than I had thought possible. Moreover, we enjoyed each other's company. I congratulated myself in being wiser than I knew in marrying him, for we were easy together, there was none of that awkwardness which, from what I had heard, made being in love so very uncomfortable.

When we were alone together, James's talk would occasionally border on the indelicate: having been raised with five brothers, this discomposed me very little, a circumstance which delighted him and my only reproof was a mild request that he would not engage in such discourse in the presence of others.

He laughed, but he behaved seemly when our neighbours paid their calls and seemed pleased to accept invitations.

The ladies welcomed me to the neighbourhood with civility, displaying a little reserve, but no more than is proper at the beginning of a new acquaintance. We talked of Derbyshire, of fashion, I heard something of their relations and answered their delicate enquiries about my own family with composure. I spoke no falsehood, but I saw no reason to be wholly frank.

There was one lady who did not please me. Her name was Mrs Blundell and she was too friendly, too soon. Half an hour of her company convinced me she was nothing but a featherbrained chatterbox.

Her manner vexed me, for upon discovering I had five brothers and three sisters, she was quick to deduce that none of us could have expectation of a large portion, which led her to assumptions about my marriage.

'You must not blame your mama, my dear,' she said. 'For your marriage must be advantageous to your sisters and I have no doubt she wished the best for you.'

'Madam, I assure you. . . .'

'I am more fortunate than most, for never was there any question of compelling me to marry against my wishes. Though Mr Blundell did say he would have married me without a portion, for we were taken with each other right from the start. We met at Almacks, you know, during the London season, and I was wearing a most exquisite gown of blue satin and we were both dancing with other partners, but our eyes met, and nothing would do for him but to seek an introduction straight away!'

She told me of other meetings and how she was dressed, and how she was dressed when he came to pay his addresses and how she was dressed for her wedding, but she had not forgotten her conviction that I had been sold to the highest bidder.

'Yes,' she sighed. 'I have been fortunate indeed! I am very sensible of it. Though I do believe,' she added kindly, 'that Mr Foster is an amiable gentleman.'

'I am very sensible of it,' I said.

I said no more, for she was a lady who would be talking rather than listening and though her chatter did not entertain me, my curiosity was aroused: I looked more closely at Mr Blundell to discover what inspired her attachment.

To me, it was by no means apparent. He was a stocky young man with sandy-coloured hair which was already beginning to recede and he walked with an affected mincing gait which I found quite ridiculous. His manners were, admittedly, unexceptionable, but he did not strike me as intelligent.

I preferred my husband.

Mr Cross and Mr Dutton were elderly and I did not subject them to the same scrutiny, but I looked at the others, not liking the pompous manners of Colonel Flint, or the prominent teeth of Mr Lockheart, detesting the spotty complexion of Mr Woodward, despising the high-pitched giggle of Mr Parker, pitying the nervous manner of Mr Bell and impatient with the fussy Reverend Tomlinson. Mr Truman, the only one I might have considered handsome, was far too familiar with all the ladies.

My own ill-favoured cripple was, in my opinion, far superior to any other gentleman in this neighbourhood.

One evening, towards the end of October, we were in our carriage on the way home from a neighbourly party and James drew me close in the darkness, kissing me and murmuring in my ear all the very interesting ideas he had for our mutual entertainment later on.

By the time we reached home, we were impatient for each other and we were not happy to learn that our plans had to be postponed.

A visitor had arrived whilst we were out: he had told our servants who he was, requested stabling for his horse and said he expected to stay the night. And, even though I had cause to be grateful to him, I was not best pleased to receive him.

'Why, Henry!' I exclaimed, putting the best possible face on it. 'This is an unexpected pleasure. I am so sorry we were not here to welcome you. Why did you send no word . . . Henry? Henry, whatever is the matter?'

Henry looked pale and tired and had completely lost his authoritative manner. It was clear he brought dire news and my first alarm was because I feared for Arabella.

'No, no, I assure you, she is perfectly well, though very shocked of course, as we all are.'

And he went on to tell us that Kilburn Hall had been utterly destroyed by fire.

Five

*F*rightened and shocked, our first insistent questions gave Henry no opportunity to relieve our fears.

'Sir Nicholas is safe, I assure you,' he said at last. 'We have been fortunate indeed, for there was no loss of life.'

Injuries had occurred. A footman burnt his hands in the initial attempts to beat out the fire, and in the confusion another footman sprained an ankle, a housemaid injured her shoulder and a groom had a broken leg.

There had been some tapestry wall-hangings in the library at Kilburn Hall. Of Flemish origin, dating back to the sixteenth century, they were tinder dry and brittle and heavy with dust; it had taken only an accidental touch with a candle-flame to set a blaze which had flared instantly. Flames had climbed upwards, beyond the reach of a man and, as it spread, sparks were thrown everywhere.

The other tapestries had caught and soon burning fragments drifted around the room setting light to my uncle's papers, his books and the rugs and carpet. All the servants came to assist, but even as one fire was extinguished, another was begun. At last, driven back by heat and smoke, they knew the library was past saving.

Windowpanes were broken in the heat, great gusts of air fuelled the flames and moved the fire relentlessly onward: upper rooms took light, then the attics and then the roof and Sir Nicholas, wise enough to foresee the outcome, ordered the servants to cease their attempts to fight the fire, to salvage as much as possible, but take no risks with their lives.

'Indeed, I believe it was the safest and best of all possible measures,' said Henry. 'No lives lost, which must be our first cause for thanksgiving, and many valuable items removed, which would have been destroyed, you know, had all exertions been directed towards extinguishing the blaze. Yes, I call it a very prudent measure. Even some furniture and carpets were saved.'

'That is well, but what of our uncle?' I demanded. 'Where is he? And – and *how* is he? How does he fare, after such a blow? First my aunt's death, now this! How can he bear it?'

'To own the truth, he seems utterly bewildered,' said Henry. 'At first, all he could think, all he could say, was that your aunt never liked those tapestries.'

He had been persuaded to take refuge at the parsonage and was being comforted by Arabella and attended by Wilson, his valet. And before we heard any other thing of consequence, we were obliged to listen to Henry's account of how this man had, in the middle of all the commotion, with the fire raging below, taken care of his master's clothing and personal items, packing everything neatly into portmanteaux, which he then dropped through the window into the shrubbery before making his escape.

'That sounds like Wilson,' I said, amused. 'Come hell or high water, Sir Nicholas must be properly attired: Wilson's pride depends upon it.'

'I call it foolhardy!' said Henry austerely. For an instant, my brother-in-law was himself again. 'I cannot approve of it! He caused such anxiety to Sir Nicholas and all his friends, risking his life merely for the sake of a few shirts! He would have done better to save items of greater value.'

'What of Kilburn Hall?' I asked. 'Can it be repaired?'

Henry shook his head. 'I have no knowledge of these matters. The masonry remains, but the plaster, the timbers, the roofs, the windows, all are gone.'

'No doubt Sir Nicholas will engage a master-builder to examine the ruin,' said James, 'it might be rebuilt, but it would be a prodigious task.' He turned to Henry. 'Has he made any determinations on the matter?'

'At present, he is uncertain. We have advised him, Arabella and I, to take no hasty decision.'

'Something must be done,' said James. 'He has estates, the farms, his tenants, he has duty there he should not neglect.'

'He will not,' I said. 'But I confess I have misgivings for the future: in fact, I had misgiving for the future of Kilburn even before this event, for Thomas will inherit and I cannot place reliance on him to serve Kilburn's interest.' I turned to Henry. 'What does my cousin himself have to say on the subject?'

'He is in Brighton,' said Henry. 'As yet, he knows nothing. I offered to go, but Sir Nicholas felt it wiser to send his steward, for he knows I am no favourite with Thomas.'

My husband had that vacant look which I had learnt to be deceptive: his mind was at its busiest. 'Tell me, sir, how may we be of assistance? Does Sir Nicholas desire our presence at Kilburn? We would go, gladly, if we can be of service, but there could be awkwardness, for I am no favourite with Thomas either. You may depend upon it, he will resent any meddling of mine.'

'We do not ask it,' said Henry. 'Indeed, we are quite unable to offer hospitality. I fear the parsonage is crowded.'

Arabella had taken in my uncle, and also those servants who were injured, and two others to assist the care of them.

'No,' continued Henry. 'Sir Nicholas wishes to be at Kilburn when Thomas returns. He values your opinions, sir, and believes he would be served by them, for he declares his own wits are quite addled. He begs you to advise what *might* be done, so that he may better determine what *should* be done.'

'Then he has not altogether lost his wits!' I said. 'To consult a sensible man at such a time, that is wisdom indeed.'

'I must pray my endeavours will justify his faith in me,' said James. 'There is much in what you say about the disposition of your cousin, Sarah. If the estate is not entailed it might be best to give it up and live retired. These days, there are those got rich from trade who would become gentry; he could sell, and leave new owners to rebuild the hall.'

'Oh, James, no!' I protested. 'Kilburn has been his home all his life, it would break his heart to leave.'

'To leave the future in better hands than your cousin's? Your uncle will speak no ill of Thomas, yet I doubt he is deceived. Well, it is but one measure: there are others.'

The gentlemen became immersed in discussion. I listened for a while, but I was too shocked, my mind too occupied, to pay proper attention.

I gazed into the fire, watching little tongues of flame licking at the coal. Fire! Here it was contained, caged behind bars. It looked tame, a lazy contented creature, but I shuddered with imaginings of a raging, roaring beast set free to destroy, and I wept for my uncle's house, that gracious mansion where I had been welcomed and taught and regarded, all gone now, fallen prey to a monster.

We pressed Henry to remain with us, but he would stay no longer than one night, for he had parish duties to attend to. He set off the next day, carrying with him a letter from my husband for Sir Nicholas and one from me to Arabella.

Matilda also was greatly distressed by the fate of Kilburn Hall, and it was she who put into my mind how it would be wise to take precautions against the like happening at Foster Leigh.

Mrs Clegg was pleased to be consulted. 'From what I have heard, mistress,' she said, 'I cannot but feel the tragedy would have been prevented had there been water to hand, only a pitcher of water, to throw over the blaze at the onset.'

This observation had me grieving again for Kilburn Hall, and how easily it might have been saved! We devised a scheme for all our rooms to be furnished with ornamental pitchers, discreetly placed, water to hand in case of need.

James laughed when I told him, and made a most indelicate suggestion which I shall not repeat.

'Undoubtedly,' I said, 'it might serve, but nobody thinks of that when faced with an emergency! Now, James, I beg you, be serious! I confess, this occurrence has made me uneasy: better to take precaution than be wise too late! Have I your permission, sir, to purchase such vessels?'

Satisfied when our house was in order, I waited to learn from Arabella what was going forward at Kilburn. News was not long arriving: Thomas had returned, insisting that Kilburn Hall should be rebuilt and my uncle also wished it. There were savage disagreements, nevertheless.

My uncle had other property, including a house in town. For many years it had been let, since my aunt had not liked London and suffered sickness when travelling. She had preferred to remain at home, happier to entertain than visit. When business took my uncle to town, he stayed at an hotel.

Striving to assist my uncle with such ideas as he had, James brought the town house into the reckoning. 'The sale of that property would assist the cost of rebuilding,' he said.

Sir Nicholas looked carefully at my husband's proposals and consulted his man of business, who agreed that selling the town house would raise sufficient funds to rebuild.

His idea was to build a new hall, smaller than the original, but so designed as to allow extensions to be added by future generations. Thomas wished to keep the town house, but his ambition of rebuilding was to erect a lavish mansion in the style of an Italian palace.

'Common sense does not appear to be your cousin's strong point,' observed James, when he saw me giggling over Arabella's letter. 'It is fortunate your uncle has the final word.'

'Indeed it is, though Thomas can be wearisome with his importunings. Arabella says whenever anyone tries to impress upon him that funds will not meet his proposals, he hints he will soon increase his fortune, but he does not say how.'

'Then I expect he has now determined to marry where there is substance,' said James. 'Has he a particular lady in sight, I wonder, or is he merely looking about for a wealthy bride?'

'Should I know? Ladies of fortune, as I understand, are usually encumbered with guardians and trustees. Thomas may find his ambition thwarted yet again.'

'He is handsome enough to please some ladies less discerning than yourself,' James said with a faint smile. 'Do not forget, the title will be his; there are those who would pay for such a connection. I do not despair of his success.'

No further light was shed on whatever scheme Thomas had in mind, but when I next heard from Arabella, I learnt my uncle had become tired of argument and ended it by expressing an inclination to sell the Kilburn estate and live retired in Bath.

He allowed himself to be talked out of this, but not until Thomas accepted the first proposal. Sir Nicholas had his way.

He left the parsonage and hired a house in Leicester: from there he conducted his business whilst rebuilding was underway.

Thomas remained long enough to demand alterations to the design until at last, still dissatisfied, he announced he had business of his own to attend to and took himself off.

At Foster Leigh, I was happy in my daily life, though sometimes distressed because certain pleasures, such as dancing, were denied to my husband.

Neighbourly dinner parties occasionally resulted in an impromptu ball. James was always willing to provide music and he would not hear of me refusing to dance with other gentlemen.

'I know you enjoy dancing, Sarah; should my infirmity deprive you of your pleasures? Go, dance; it pleases me to watch you.'

At one of these parties, I was told how we were situated near Dovedale, which I had not realized. When I exclaimed how very much I should like to visit that famous beauty spot, James promised to take me there on the first fine day.

It was early in November; no summer visitors disturbed the peace; on this bright autumn day we had the dale to ourselves. The air was still and cool and scented with a hint of woodsmoke. Rosehips, red and amber, hung amid dark leaves, dewy cobwebs stretched across the bushes, glistening in the light. Trees had turned to russet and gold, and only an occasional leaf fell, a golden fragment here and there, spiralling lazily into the river.

Pebbles shone like jewels beneath the gentle waters of the Dove, a family of ducks squabbled noisily, some water creature splashed, leaving a V-shaped wake as it swam upstream.

Unable to use the stepping stones, James waded the river, but soon after we passed Thorpe Cloud the path became too rugged for him to continue. He knew it would, and had made dispositions. Two footmen were to escort me further, and they now spread a rug on the grassy river-bank. He settled himself on it, declaring that he was happy to sit and watch the ducks.

Perhaps he was, but I was less happy at the thought of him waiting alone whilst I indulged in scenery. I went on because he insisted, but I turned after twenty minutes, reflecting it would take another twenty minutes to walk back.

I wished I had turned back sooner, because when I reached him he was in agony with cramp. I snapped at the footmen, 'Remove his boot! Be quick!'

The operation caused him fresh anguish, and it took some time for my probing fingers to undo the knotted muscles of his calf and ease his pain. At last, I could give way to gentle massage, and he sighed, 'I am better now, Sarah, I thank you. Come now, my dear, this is nothing to weep for!'

'Had I known this would happen I would not have left you! How is it now? Is it truly better?'

He said it was and blamed his own folly for sitting long enough for the earth to strike cold into his bones. He replaced his boot and got to his feet and when we had crossed the river we sent the footmen ahead to have our carriage ready.

'Now there is no one in sight,' said James happily, 'and that is well, because I want to kiss you!' He drew me close, traced a finger down my cheek and smiled into my eyes before claiming my mouth with his own. 'Lovely, lovely wife,' he murmured. 'What have I done to deserve you?'

What had he done to deserve his cramps? What had he done to deserve his lameness and his banishment from pleasures which others took for granted? What had he done to deserve contempt and ridicule from such creatures as my cousin Thomas? But I smiled at him and said nothing, because my distress could make nothing easier.

I had some perception of what it was like for him because of my own inadequacy at the pianoforte. In my early life, I had been accustomed only to such music as one heard at church and dancing classes. At Kilburn, an instrument was kept for visitors who could play and there had been parties where musical entertainment was offered, but it was James who brought me the pleasure of hearing music whenever I wished and now, besides all the popular songs and country airs, I was listening to Bach and Handel and Mozart and Beethoven and learning to appreciate the subtleties of tone and composition.

'Such a gift you have, James,' I said enviously. 'How I wish I could play as you do!'

'If you truly wish it, Sarah, you could learn,' he said. 'I would be happy to teach you.'

'Could you?' I asked doubtfully. 'I always supposed one had to begin as a child?'

'Much would depend on your natural aptitude,' he said. 'You may learn to play a few airs. With diligent practice you could become accomplished.'

He had looked out his old primers, teaching me as though I were a child. 'Every Good Boy Deserves Favour', he said, and I laughed, but it was a mnemonic, by which to remember the notes, E, G, B, D, F, and he gave me exercises, beginning with breves.

Bar by bar, I struggled and stumbled, wincing at the discord of wrong notes. At last I mastered two simple tunes, childish and laughable in comparison with his rich music.

I watched his fingers rippling effortlessly across the keys. At the instrument, he was the one who danced, I the cripple.

I pressed on, practising scales, adding a few more airs to my repertoire and he was pleased with me and remarked how I would surprise Mama when she visited at Christmas.

They were to come on Christmas Eve, Mama, two sisters, Harriet and Emily, and two brothers, Joseph and Edward. James sent his own carriage to make their journey comfortable and he improved on the scheme by inviting Arabella and Henry, also.

I was looking forward to my visitors, for it was nearly four years now since I had seen the children. I was particularly eager to see Mama and to learn how well she liked the new establishment which James had so generously provided.

My disappointment was bitter indeed: despite the great improvement my marriage had brought to her own situation, it seemed to me that Mama came to Foster Leigh that Christmas with a savage determination of making herself thoroughly unpleasant.

Six

*H*er pelisse looked new and so did her boots and she carried a fur-lined muff, which was a luxury unheard of in former times.

In the flurry of greetings, with the boys jumping around and demanding our attention, I believe I was the only one who noticed how Mama's gaze travelled around the courtyard and took in the size of our house. Through an archway, she could see the stables and she had also caught sight of formal gardens.

It seemed to displease her: she stiffened and compressed her lips, quite beside herself with anger.

Had not my husband been present, she might have given free expression to her temper, but he was there. He greeted her and enquired after her journey and she was obliged to swallow her vexation and make a civil answer.

My sisters thanked James for sending our coach, and said how comfortable it was; they had scarce felt any draught thanks to the sheepskin lining. They claimed my attention; they admired Foster Leigh; they liked my gown and wished to know how I liked their attire. I answered them as best I could, for I saw all Mama's dark looks and I was occupied with wondering why she was so displeased.

I had no opportunity to discover the reason: supplied with tea and bread and butter, she admonished Edward not to stuff his mouth so full and told Emily to sit up straight – 'you are not at home, now, you know' – and looked around the green saloon. She remarked on the furnishings and enquired of the neighbour-hood. All the time she spoke pleasantly to James, but cold looks were cast in my direction.

The others had changed in the four years since I had seen them. Edward had been only six years old: now he was ten, a foot taller, talking very noisily and, when not talking, whistling through a gap in his front teeth. Joseph, two years older, was no more subdued than his brother in his constant demands to see our horses.

Emily was now fourteen and awkward as I was at her age, with fine brown hair which she had not yet learnt to manage. But it was Harriet who held my attention. She was seventeen; not a regular beauty, for she had a snub nose and her figure was sturdy rather than elegant, but she was pleasing, for all that. She had taken Papa's looks, so her hair, unlike mine, was very dark with a nat-ural curl and it contrasted well with her fair complexion. Her eyes were enormous, dark brown, and surmounted by a pair of straight dark brows. When she saw me studying her they lit up with a con-spiratorial merriment, as though she and I shared a secret known to none of the others.

'Do not look so severely, Sarah,' she said. 'I assure you, I have kept my promise of tending Papa's grave.'

'I am very happy to hear it,' I said. Once, I had that duty and I charged her with it when I left. 'Did I look severe? I did not mean to. I was thinking how long since I last saw you. You are quite a stranger, now.'

She said, 'I fear I have not written as often as I should, though I do think of you. And our sister Arabella is expected, as I under-stand? With her I have such scant acquaintance that I scarce dare claim her for a sister! As for her husband, I have never met him! What is he like?'

'Oh, Henry is a good sort of man,' I said, smiling. 'Though he has some very starched notions, I fear.'

'Then he will not approve of me!' She gave a little gurgle of laughter and turned to speak to Emily and I had leisure to pursue the thought that Harriet had begun.

Until I went to Kilburn, I had but little acquaintance with Arabella, either. Yet there was no great distance between, nothing to prevent occasional visits. I could comprehend why my aunt never came to us, for travelling even a short distance had made her ill and besides, we in Northampton had not the means of providing lavish hospitality.

It seemed strange, however, that my family had never been invited to visit at Kilburn. Mama had not been present at Arabella's wedding, even; neither had she attended the funeral of her own sister. It had never been suggested that she might.

'Edward, do not you dare!' Emily's voice interrupted my musings: my brother had taken a penknife from his pocket and was about to carve his initials in the wainscot.

James laughed, though I doubt he would have been so diverted had Edward caused damage to the fine linenfold panelling. To my astonishment, Mama did not reprove my brother.

My eager expectation of their visit gave way to despondency: I was thankful to hear the arrival of the post-chaise which brought Henry and Arabella.

I rang for more tea and there was a confusion of greetings and everybody talking. Presently Mama said she would like to rest. James promised the boys that he and Henry would take them to inspect our stables. I left Arabella to get acquainted with our sisters whilst I conducted Mama to her bedchamber.

Her cold displeasure towards me had never been absent. All the time, there had been a tightening of her lips when she glanced in my direction, and so far, she had barely spoken to me. I searched my conscience, and found nothing to reproach myself for: now I began to feel vexation on my own account.

I disguised it. As I led the way, I remarked how all were grown and enquired after my older brothers, Samuel, William and Robert and said it was a pity they could not be with us.

'They have their duties,' said Mama repressively. 'They are not gentlemen of leisure.'

They were army officers; Samuel in the regulars and the others in the militia. They would have leisure over Christmas, though insufficient to allow for a journey.

I led Mama into her bedchamber, thankful to see there was a good fire and a plentiful supply of candles. 'Here is your room, Mama. I think you will find it comfortable.'

I hesitated; I wished to make my escape but felt something more was required. 'Do my brothers write to you? And they are all in good health? Then we have much to be thankful for.'

'*You* certainly have,' said Mama with bitter emphasis. 'So fine you are become!' In a high, mocking falsetto, she went on, 'Quite the lady of consequence!' Then her voice dropped and I was taken aback at the savagery of her attack. 'You do not deserve to be mistress of a house such as this.'

'Perhaps not,' I said. I wondered how one was supposed to deserve it, and in my astonishment I could only add, 'But I am mistress, nevertheless.'

'Well, a brick is still a brick, no matter how often it is whitewashed, so do not come playing off your airs and graces with me, my girl, for I am better born than you!'

I gasped at the absurdity of hearing this from my own mother. She went on triumphantly, '*My* father was a gentleman born, and a colonel of the regiment! Yours was merely a gamekeeper's son, who owed his commission to his master's favour! And he was only a captain, for all that.'

I laughed and dropped a mock curtsy. 'I am suitably chastened, Mama.'

My humour was ill-judged. 'That is quite enough of your insolence!' she snapped. 'I know you too well, my girl, and you will do well to remember that, for I can tell some stories about you, if I so choose!'

I stared, feeling that some grievance from the past was in her mind, though I could not imagine what.

As I searched my memory, what came into my own mind was how, when I was barely eleven years old, I had assisted her to give birth to Edward, for he came without warning. There was no other person nearby and no time to run for help; no time, even, to help her upstairs to bed.

It was distressing, at that age, to have such responsibility so thrust upon me, yet I received no thanks. She said only that Edward must indeed be a lusty infant to have survived my clumsiness at his birthing.

I had said nothing then and I said nothing now, but I felt tears prickle behind my eyes. With an adult understanding, I could recall her acid remark with more resentment than I felt at the time. Always, I had tried to be a dutiful daughter and always, it seemed, I had fallen short of pleasing.

I had been so looking forward to her visit, eager to learn how she liked the new establishment James had provided, and I truly believed she would be delighted to have a daughter settled and happy and in a position to assist the other girls.

Instead, I found myself reviled as a pretentious upstart.

Indignation swelled in my breast, but I bit back my angry retorts, reflecting that an open quarrel would cause discomfort to everyone. I urged her to rest, saying she must be tired after her journey, and left her alone.

I had never been a favourite with Mama, but acrimony such as this had not been visited upon me before. Too shocked and hurt to disguise my distress, I did not return to my sisters.

Instead, I sought the solitude of my dressing-room, angry with her for spoiling all my pleasure.

'You do not deserve to be mistress of a house such as this!'

Neither had I deserved such an ill-natured attack. I could not hold back the tears and, as I recalled her words, I was filled with a burning sense of injustice.

Though I had, in the last few minutes, regretted taking certain advice from Mrs Clegg, I now reversed that regret and began to consider the matter with determined cheerfulness.

The dining-room was so grand that I had privately renamed it the banqueting hall. Only when we had company did we use it, for James and I preferred the breakfast-room as being altogether more comfortable. This room could seat twelve: the addition of my family made up a party of only nine, and I thought they also would prefer to dine in comfort rather than in grandeur.

Mrs Clegg now had my interest at heart (I suspect it had been Matilda's doing) and often ventured a little advice. She had tactfully suggested it would be a proper compliment to Mama to dine in the grand manner.

Now I thought it would merely confirm Mama's opinion of my upstart pretensions. Yet, had I made the alternative choice, she might again revile me for considering her and the family of too little consequence to entertain properly.

Feeling unable to please her, I determined to please myself. I would become grand and pretentious enough to justify all her accusations!

I had a gown of bronze silk, severely cut but elaborately embroidered with gold thread. James had insisted I should have it, though I had been appalled at the cost. Now I determined I would wear it at dinner and I would abandon the rose-point cap in favour of a jewelled and feathered headdress.

So I washed away my tears, fixed a smile on my face and went to join my sisters. James and Henry were there also and James told me, with a rueful smile, he had recollected how there were many things in the nurseries which might amuse my brothers and he had sent them upstairs, consigned to the care of a footman.

Harriet laughed. 'It is to be hoped he has his wits about him!' she said. 'They can be such rascals!'

Henry was intent on informing my husband of all the proposals for Kilburn Hall and Arabella was talking to Emily, but I was not displeased to be left with Harriet, who opened the conversation by enquiring whether she would meet any rich and handsome young men in this neighbourhood.

'There are some young men amongst our neighbours, but none

who answer all your requirements,' I said, smiling, 'though some of them have Christmas visitors, who may. On Boxing Day we are to hold a ball. Then we shall see.'

'I insist upon rich,' said Harriet, though her tone was humorous. 'And I would prefer him handsome and young, also.' Then she gave me a saucy look. 'I declare it is too bad of you, Sarah, not to have invited Sir Nicholas and our cousin Thomas here this Christmas. Why deny your sister such an opportunity? I believe I should like to be the next Lady Kilburn!'

I stared at her. 'Can you be serious?'

She flushed and glanced at James. Her expression showed what she thought, but she only said, 'You may not have wished for Thomas, but he has attributes which I, for one, do not despise. I believe I could console him admirably! His circumstances may be reduced, at present, by the cost of rebuilding Kilburn Hall but he is not wholly without substance and he is handsome and he will have the title. Do not forget the title!'

'No, indeed,' I said drily. 'Much can be forgiven, if a gentleman is handsome, especially when he has a title.'

'Ah, we understand each other!' she said brightly. 'I shall forgive him for loving you first, for at that time he did not know me! Well, I concede it might have been a little awkward to invite him to Foster Leigh after refusing his proposals so I will forgive your neglect, in the circumstance. I wonder if our sister Arabella might be prevailed upon to invite me to visit at the parsonage?'

Clearly, Harriet believed this would bring her into proximity with Thomas and I did not inform her of her mistake. Until the hall was rebuilt, Thomas could not offer his friends hospitality as he was used to, so he was unlikely to go there, even less likely to visit the parsonage.

I could not tell how far Harriet was serious. There was a bright merriment about her, but I suspected this disguised a deep sense of purpose.

Now, I could not forbear from saying, 'Harriet, I beg you, have no serious design on our cousin, for I doubt he would make you happy. There is something about Thomas that I cannot like.'

'Indeed? Well, Sister, I cannot imagine what it can be. I find him perfectly charming!'

'You cannot have seen him often: how then, can you judge?'

'He has visited us in Northampton. Since we moved into our new establishment, Mama has taken to holding little card parties, and Thomas has been present at several of them.'

I was all astonishment. Thomas? At Mama's card parties? And often enough, it would seem, to give Harriet notions of captivating him.

I had no time to pursue any enquiry, for my brothers burst in upon us: they were hungry and demanding dinner.

I conducted my guests to their rooms, and again sought solitude in my dressing-room, my reflections confused and uneasy.

I knew I should warn Mama against allowing Harriet to set her cap at Thomas, yet I could not feel any hint of mine would be heeded. Indeed, in her present vexation, Mama might even become contrary and encourage what she ought to stop.

I toyed with the idea of asking Arabella to try her influence with Mama, and knew this also was unlikely to produce a satisfactory result. Mama, by her threat of revealing past events, had raised some memories of my own: the nature of them was such that I was, reluctantly, forced to acknowledge that she could not always be relied upon to do what was right.

Harriet's own proposal of securing an invitation to the Kilburn parsonage might, in fact, be the best solution. Should Thomas have serious design on Harriet, moving her to Kilburn would not keep him from her. But I could warn Arabella and she and her husband would advise and protect our sister.

Having determined to arrange this, I prepared myself for dinner, although I was in no happy frame of mind, for I had not forgotten Mama's acrimony. I kept to my design of dressing in my finest, and I was glad I had, because when James came in, the appreciation in his eyes made it all worthwhile.

He was in good spirits: he found my brothers diverting and believed I was pleased to have my family about me. But although I tried to disguise my perturbation, he noticed I had cares.

'What is the matter, Sarah?'

'I hardly know.' I hesitated over repeating all Mama's bitter words, and in the end I only said, 'Mama seems displeased, although I cannot imagine what offends her.'

'I observed some ill-humour,' he said, 'but I cannot think there any cause other than weariness, after all. She has been travelling with your brothers, cooped up in a coach with them. I can easily comprehend that is enough to try the sweetest disposition! Come, Sarah, I am persuaded you are mistaken.'

I shook my head. 'I think not.'

'Did you say anything to offend?'

'No, I merely asked after my older brothers, had they written, how were they faring, and so on. She said they were well, but she was curt in her answers.'

I might have said more, but this sent his thoughts in another direction entirely. 'Ah, yes, your brothers!' he exclaimed. 'You remind me, I have been meaning to speak of them. I believe it is time I did something to procure their advancement, do not you?'

'Oh, James! Already, you have done so much for my family, I scarce feel comfortable asking for more.'

He laughed. 'My dear, never do I recall your asking! This is my own idea. Samuel, at least, ought to be made up to captain.'

'Well, I cannot refuse,' I said, smiling. 'I know how much he would like it.'

'Then I shall write to his colonel very soon,' he promised. 'And do not fret over your mama, my dear. It is natural you are disappointed by her ill-humour, for I know how you were eager to see her. She was a little thoughtless, to be sure, but I am persuaded she will be in better humour, directly.'

'Indeed, I hope you are right. But James—' I hesitated, then said, 'I believe your scheme of advancing my brothers would please her. I may seem contrary, but I would not have her know of it, not immediately, not today. I am averse to goodwill by purchase. May I beg you not to mention it?'

I secured his agreement and we went downstairs together to find the rest of our company already assembled: our footmen had conducted them into the great drawing-room, a room grand enough for entertaining the Regent himself; quite enough to displease Mama, since she disapproved of my upstart pretensions.

Here, the furniture was ornately carved and richly gilded, the chairs upholstered with gold silk. The walls were covered with damasks and Genoese velvets. The decorative plaster-work of the ceiling was gilded and two great chandeliers were fully furnished with candles, all of them lit. Numerous branches of candles were set about the room also, so we stopped on the threshold, blinking in the sudden blaze of light.

Pride stiffened my backbone, and I stifled my nervous qualms. I was mistress of this house and all should know it, including Mama! So I sailed forward, graciously regal and told her she had found her room comfortable and I was certain she felt better after her rest.

'You were tired, I know, and surely it is not to be wondered at after your journey. Do take a little wine, Mama. It is really quite excellent and sure to improve your spirits.'

I heard her swift intake of breath: she had taken my meaning, though how far she would acquiesce, I had no means of telling. She said nothing then, for the others were talking, with Harriet openly envious of my gown, and Arabella and Henry asking James about the fireplace. 'It is really quite magnificent. Was it designed by Grinling Gibbons?'

Emily gave quiet instruction to my brothers. 'When I am uncertain I shall watch Sarah and Arabella and do as they do, and I advise you to do the same.'

I felt a rush of sympathy for this sister, nervous, watchful of my brothers and concerned to do right. I went to talk to her. 'Do you like the new house in Northampton?'

She said it was comfortable and she liked it very well, and she thanked me for some money I had sent on her birthday.

She looked ill at ease. I abandoned my regal manner, flickered a wink at her and kept up inconsequential chatter and she was easier by the time we went into the dining-room.

'Oh, famous!' This exclamation came from Joseph and had more to do with the selection of meats on the table than any interest in the grandeur of the dining-room. My brothers cared nothing for the painted scenes from ancient mythology depicted on the ceiling, nor for the gilded wall-brackets, or the Chippendale mirrors, or fine porcelain or the colourful twisted ornament decorating the stems of wine-glasses. The liveried footmen who waited to attend us did merit a second glance, but their main interest was in food. 'We are ravenous!'

Henry said grace and we settled down to eat. I was pleased to see that someone had taught the children all about finger bowls and napkins. The boys were too intent on satisfying their hunger to be noisy, so I was able to converse with Henry and Arabella, who were seated on either side of me.

Separated from James by the length of the table, I could not see him when he was seated, because three branches of candles hid him from view. I could see Mama talking to him and occasionally directing a remark at Harriet, but not until James stood to carve the haunch of venison, and the others fell silent could I hear what she said, and then it was wholly upsetting.

'Well, sir, I hope you have persuaded Sarah against befriending all the riff-raff of the neighbourhood! I fear I never could impress upon her how unbecoming is such conduct. But of course, I am only her mama, she does not have to listen to me! Such creatures she would take up! I cannot forget how her dear papa was scarce cold in his grave before she gave away his clothes to a nasty, smelly, dirty old tramp!'

James cast a startled look at me, then concentrated his attention on his carving, and I could not read his expression.

Indignation rose in my breast, because all I had done on that occasion was to assist, in some small way, someone who was far more unfortunate than ourselves and who had kept his religion and shown me kindness, in spite of his own poverty.

Mama twisted the occurrence, implying the acquaintance was something less wholesome.

I felt compelled to defend myself. 'Tramp he certainly was, Mama, but Mr Benjamin was not nasty, or smelly, or dirty; in fact, he took great pains to keep himself clean, which could not have been easy in his situation. And I gave only Papa's coat and boots which, as you very well know, were not of a size to be useful to us any longer.'

'Useful enough to sell and bring a shilling!' she retorted. 'We were not so well-to-do that we could afford to throw money away. Charity begins at home, that is what I always say!'

'Indeed, ma'am, I have often heard that said,' said Henry in non-committal tones, which Mama chose to take as agreement.

'It is so like Sarah, she can be generous to every one except her own family!'

I could have said I had, at that time, very little to be generous with, and Papa's coat would find no eager purchaser, for though of good quality, it looked odd.

Like James, Papa had been obliged to support himself with a crutch and this exposes the underarm part of clothing to excessive wear. James could afford to replace his coats, but Papa could not: he had repaired his coat with leather patches.

These retorts were not spoken, for at the time I was too shocked to think quickly. Indeed, her influence upon me was such as to make me feel uncomfortable, as though I had indeed been unforgivably thoughtless.

'Nothing will do for Sarah but to be showing off, acting Lady Bountiful!' said Mama peevishly.

I looked at James, still silent, attending to the carving, and I cringed: I could tell what he was thinking. 'Her own mother will say so? Then it must be true.'

I lost all appetite: I experienced a sick, hollow feeling inside, as Mama, triumphant, knowing her power, continued to bring up past events. She placed black constructions on well-intentioned acts of mine and she maligned my character to all, including my husband, the one person in the world whose good opinion I valued.

Seven

Mama, I now realized, was my worst enemy.

At table, all were silenced as she went on enumerating my sins. Always, in her view, I was grievously at fault in everything I did. When I had run errands it was to avoid less agreeable tasks; when I took pains I was too finicky by far; when I worked quickly I was slapdash and slipshod. There was such a thing as a happy medium, or so she said, but I went from one extreme to the other.

Arabella, pink with indignation, muttered something and was about to get to her feet, but I stopped her. 'Bella, no!' I whispered. She stared at me incredulously, but I shook my head: it would do no good for Arabella to offend Mama.

Henry signalled agreement with me by nodding to Arabella: with some reluctance, she subsided.

Her support soothed me, but it could not console me because I could see how Mama was delighted with the effect she had on James. Determined to ruin my happiness, she was intent on destroying his good opinion of me.

She implied how all my motives were suspect: I had no design of pleasing, but rather a selfish expectation of admiration or reward. My character was exposed as shallow, thoughtless, lazy, unkind, greedy, calculating, conceited, and vain. James was seated again, my view of him obstructed by candles, but I could guess how he was taking it.

Our servants, also, were influenced. I had seen a shocked expression on the face of a footman, and I knew everything would be repeated in the servant's hall. I forced down a sob: after this, I would never regain goodwill.

I stared miserably at my plate, unable to eat for the constriction in my throat. I was too upset, too angry, to defend myself without a sacrifice of all propriety, which would only strengthen her cause.

'Mistress!' A footman was by my side, but so distressed was I that he had to speak twice to gain my attention. 'Mistress, the master appears to be in pain.'

Mama was instantly forgotten. I was on my feet, seeing the familar grimaces and the stiffening of his posture. I threw down my napkin and went to his side, but when I knelt and felt for the knotted muscles, I discovered to my astonishment that his calf was perfectly relaxed.

A hand touched my head, a thumb briefly stroked my forehead and when I looked up at him, wondering, he smiled and said, 'I am easy now, Sarah, I thank you.' Puzzled, I stood up and he took my hands into his own. He turned to the others and explained about his cramps.

'I am fortunate indeed to have such a wife,' he went on, and his smile told me Mama might have saved all her breath, for he would not heed a word. 'Sarah knows how to give me ease.'

He stood and kissed each of my hands in turn, and when he turned his head to look at Mama his expression changed to one which was cold and stern and forbidding.

Now I understood. He had feigned a cramp with the design of reproving Mama. And I, who truly believed she had given him a disgust of me, was filled with an overwhelming rush of relief and gratitude and joy. And, I confess, I was mean enough to enjoy a sense of triumph as I watched her comprehend she had done herself no service.

When the time came for we ladies to withdraw from the dining-room, I led the way with all my dignity restored, and lines from the Twenty-third Psalm playing over in my head.

They seemed appropriate.

> *My table thou hast furnished*
> *In presence of my foes.*
> *My head thou doth with oil annoint*
> *And my cup overflows!*

Not the solemn music which I heard accompanying these words in church: it was a jaunty little air which I had heard only once, but now, because of the memories Mama had raised, I could not get it out of my head. For I had learnt it from the tramp she had so disdained, Mr Benjamin.

There was awkwardness in the drawing-room. Emily looked miserable, Harriet was fidgety, and Arabella had taken on something of her husband's disapproving air. Mama seated herself rigidly, her lips compressed.

My brothers had remained in the dining-room but conversation between James and Henry soon bored them and their early return to the drawing-room was welcome indeed. They were insensible of Mama's ill-humour, loudly appreciative of the dinner, and eager for fresh entertainment. Emily proposed a game of hunt-the-thimble and with four of them thus engaged, I drew Arabella aside, under the pretence of asking advice about my embroidery.

Out of Mama's hearing, Arabella could not be restrained from delivering an opinion of her conduct, which I shall not repeat.

'Do not imagine yourself at fault, Sarah,' she said at last. 'Mama was equally disagreeable to Aunt Kilburn, you know. One can only suppose it to be jealousy. Considering the difference in their situations, one cannot wonder at it, though she did herself no service by showing it so clearly.'

'That explains why she was not invited to visit Kilburn,' I said. 'I confess, I never wondered until today.'

'She was invited,' said Arabella. 'She would not accept. I believe Aunt Kilburn was distressed by her coldness, though Sir Nicholas once said it was easier to be charitable from a distance. I was not intended to hear that.' Her colour rose. 'But really, Sarah, after all that has been done, she owes you some civility! Should she make more ill-natured attacks, I shall speak my mind, whether you wish it or no.'

'I think she will not, for my husband was quick to make clear where his loyalties lay. Arabella, I beg you, do nothing to offend Mama for we have Harriet to consider.'

Arabella looked astonished. 'How so?'

I told her what I had heard from our younger sister, and Arabella forgot the rest, her perturbation equal to my own.

'You tell me Thomas is in Northampton? I thought he was in London! What is he about? I find it hard to believe he has serious design on Harriet, he knows she has no fortune.'

'He had serious design on me,' I reminded her. 'I had no fortune, either! He has spoken of a scheme for increase, but we may be wrong to suppose he means to profit by marriage! He may have some other scheme in mind.'

'Such as?'

'Can I say? I merely point out we cannot know his intentions. Now, Harriet hopes to captivate him. She is not in love with him, but she has a fancy to be Lady Kilburn.'

'But does Thomas have a fancy to make her Lady Kiburn?'

'If he has not, why then have Northampton card-parties become a favourite means of recreation?'

'Perhaps he knows some other lady in Northampton?' said Arabella doubtfully. 'A lady with fortune at her disposal?'

'That is possible, I suppose, but I do not depend upon it.'

'So you wish me to wheedle Mama into permitting Harriet to visit with us, at Kilburn?'

'If Henry does not object. You will judge if Thomas has designs, and she will be safer with you than with Mama.'

'If he does not follow her? He may continue to take in Mama's parties. What then?'

The idea seemed a little preposterous, but I could not rule it out. I said, 'If Harriet is not his object, then he has some other design,

74

though I cannot imagine what it might be!'

Neither could Arabella. She was quiet, her thoughts busy and at last she confessed to a notion which she felt was not quite proper. 'Henry will not like it,' she admitted, 'though I do feel there is necessity.'

Her idea was to take Emily into our confidence and ask her to write to us on whatever Thomas was about in Northampton.

'Young as she is, I believe Emily knows Mama cannot be relied upon to do what is right.'

Later that evening, when the boys had been sent to bed and the rest of the company had had enough of cards, James opened the pianoforte. After he had played for a while, he demanded that I should demonstrate my own recently acquired skill. I protested and the others laughed, but he was insistent. 'Come, Sarah, there is no need to be shy, not with your family!'

With a repertoire of only five simple pieces, my performance did not take long, and I was embarrassed by an undue amount of praise from Arabella and Henry. Mama, of course, refused to be impressed. 'Well, it is hardly anything to write home about, is it? Is that the best you can do?'

James answered, rather coolly. 'For someone who has only lately begun to learn music, madam, Sarah's progress is quite outstanding! She has genuine musical ability and it is a great pity she had no opportunity to learn during her early years.'

Mama coloured at the implied reproach and I, fearing an open quarrel, hastily began to play again.

I did not play any of the music I had so painstakingly learnt; this seemed to come from another part of my mind. I might almost say I was dreaming the music, and I will swear that if I had been trying I could not have done it. I believe I astonished myself more than anyone else.

I was playing that jaunty little tune which had been going around in my head ever since dinner, a tune I had heard only once, accompanying the Twenty-third Psalm, sung by the tramp, Mr Benjamin.

James wanted to know how I had learnt it, and my explanation was confused and incoherent. 'I know not. I did not know I could play it, it just happened.'

'Then you have more talent than we suspected, if learning a little music has brought out an ability to play by ear.'

The others now wished me to attempt more pieces. I could not play them, and unaccountably I became cross and tearful.

James closed up the pianoforte. 'Enough,' he said gently. 'It is a gift which may be cultivated but not forced.'

Later, having retired for the night, James confessed himself impatient with Mama and he recalled my first unease and understood there had been an earlier ill-natured attack.

He was half shocked, half diverted when, at his persuasion, I disclosed the whole of it. 'And James, I cannot tell you what it meant to me, when you took my part,' I added gratefully. 'I quite thought she had given you a disgust of me.'

'Indeed? And how did I go on before I had her to determine my opinions?' he asked indignantly; then he laughed. 'She is spiteful, but she can do you no harm with me, Sarah.'

'I think she does me harm with myself,' I said. 'At dinner, I really believed I was as thoughtless and selfish as she implied. I declare, I was ready to sink!'

He laughed and kissed me and talked me into more agreeable feelings and I forgot Mama in the interlude that followed.

We settled down to sleep, but my indignation surfaced again and I was restless. At last, James sat up and rekindled a candle. 'It is of no consequence,' he said, when I apologized for disturbing him. 'Do not make yourself uneasy, Sarah. Should your mama continue with her spite, she may find herself back in Northampton sooner than she expects! Come now, she is not worth all your pain. Let us think of something more agreeable.' He slipped a comforting arm round my shoulder and said, 'Suppose you tell me about your friend Mr Benjamin?'

I hesitated, uncertain how to begin, and with Mama's words ringing in my ears I might even have felt a little ashamed, for I said,

'James, please believe I do not make a habit of taking up with tramps, whatever Mama says. Most tramps frighten me, they seem so violently angry. Mr Benjamin was different.'

James was prepared to accept this. 'How did you meet him?'

I was fifteen when I met Mr Benjamin, and it was September, not long after Papa died. I was taking a roundabout route to the churchyard, crossing some meadows so that I might gather a nosegay of wild flowers to place on the grave, and I came upon him at a place where I had to cross a stream.

He was seated on a boulder, a cracked mirror in one hand, a pair of scissors in the other, and beside him his sack was open and some items were spread out on the turf: a sliver of soap, a ragged towel, a broken comb and a razor.

He saw me hesitate and got to his feet, favouring me with a bow. 'I beg you will forgive me,' he said, 'for I was about my toilette and not expecting a visitor! How may I be of service?'

I blinked, surprised but not displeased by his politeness. I said awkwardly, 'I would not wish to disturb you.'

'See how I have trimmed my beard,' he said, and indeed, it looked very neat. 'I am now engaged in barbering my head, and making sad work of it, I fear. I would do better had I another pair of hands. Fair maiden, may I beg you to assist me in this most important matter? Would you be so good as to hold the mirror? With both hands free I might work more deftly.'

'If you will trust me with the scissors, sir, I can do the cutting,' I said. 'I am accustomed to cutting gentlemen's hair, always I do – did – Papa's and I do my brothers', also.'

Even as I spoke I regretted it, for I had belated notions of head-lice. Yet having made the offer, I would not withdraw.

'Truly an angel!' he said warmly. 'I thank you most profusely, O blessed one!'

He passed me the scissors and comb, seated himself so I could work, and took up the mirror, holding it at arm's length. He seemed to be enjoying himself immensely.

I need not have troubled about headlice. He was clean and

though his clothes were distressingly shabby and worn, patched beyond patching, with holes and tears beyond mending, he behaved in a rather lordly way, and dismissed his present situation as ill-fortune, from which he knew he would very soon be rescued.

'I have not always been a tramp,' he told me. 'Once upon a time I was very well-to-do, quite the man about town, in fact. Soon, the day will come when I am rich again!'

'Since once you were rich, sir, one might suppose your present poverty to be the result of carelessness. Mama would say so, at all events.'

He laughed and shook his head. 'No carelessness, Sarey my dear! But I will not burden you with my tale of woe! You have your own sorrow, I think?'

I was taken aback by his perception and the gentleness of his voice. 'I have, sir, and I confess I find it hard to bear, but it is a natural one, for all that.'

He got out of me the circumstances of Papa's death, condoled with me, comforted me by saying I was living proof that Papa was a fine man, and I was a credit to his memory. When he learnt I was on my way to attend the grave, he declared he would accompany me and pay his own respects to the man who had fathered his barbering angel.

On the way he cut a shoot from an ash plant and twisted it into a circle, and with twine and greenery and columbine flowers he fashioned a very pretty wreath.

'Weeds,' he said, 'but we do the best we can and the flowers are much like lilies in their appearance, do you not agree?'

We came to the churchyard and at the graveside he handed me the wreath to lay against the headstone. Then, without any embarrassment at all, he began to sing.

He attracted attention from passers-by, for though he sang well, this was not considered seemly behaviour. It was, however, a religious psalm, and none had courage to venture reproof.

He made a production of the final 'Amen' then he turned, smiling. 'Think you your papa is turning in his grave?'

'I believe your singing would please him, but I am unfamiliar with that tune. Are you a dissenter, sir? An evangelist?'

'I? No indeed! One needs learned arguments to support such a cause, and I have discovered, Sarey my dear, that it is possible to become very confused in matters of religion! I do not think Our Father in Heaven wishes His children to stumble so. I keep a simple faith and leave argument to others.'

I saw Mr Benjamin several times over the next few weeks; he offered me a kindly friendship; he encouraged me to tell him of my family and all our doings and he listened patiently, concerned with my feelings, and did much to help me come to terms with losing Papa.

Always, I took him something: bread and butter, a few cakes or a piece of cheese and these were treats for him, but food was not his most pressing need for he had ways, unlawful ways I fear, of finding food for himself.

He attached importance to keeping clean. He had a tinder-box, he could make fire and could get warm water thereby, and though he never asked for anything, I saw what he needed. I found him some soap, a good towel and a brush and comb. He took these presents with surprise and gratitude, but for me it was not enough.

I worried how he would fare thoughout the approaching winter. I wanted to give a blanket but we had none to spare. Then I realized he was much the same size as Papa: I could give him a warm coat and a pair of strong boots.

'Take them, sir, do,' I urged, for he seemed hesitant. 'They are not of a size to be serviceable to us and you will put them to better use than the moth.' And even though I had doubts as to the truth of it, I went on, 'I believe my papa would wish you to have them.'

So he tried them on and then began to parade around with a mincing walk, acting the dandy to make me laugh.

Still acting, he halted in his walk, examined the sleeve and, with an extravagant gesture, he brushed away an imaginary speck of dust. And my laughter died, for I was then overcome by the most extraordinary feeling of recognition, as though all this had happened before, in a dream, exactly as it was occurring now.

I am told this is a common feeling and known as *déjà vu*. Never have I met anyone who could explain it and never have I met anyone who thought it signified anything particular. Yet to me, as I sat on the wall watching Mr Benjamin's clowning, with the autumnal sun on my back and the trees already taking on their rich seasonal colours, it seemed as though the moment had been charged with mystery and grave importance.

I did not mention my encounters with Mr Benjamin to Mama. I was not silent with any design of deceiving, but because she had been abstracted since Papa died. I knew she had cares and felt she would have no interest in my doings, neither would she wish to trouble herself over Mr Benjamin's plight.

When she found out, I was shocked by her fury. She was not, at the time, aggrieved because I had given away Papa's clothes, her annoyance was because I had taken up with a tramp.

To her he was suspect and she would not believe anything I said. She screamed, called me a fool, even a doxy! 'Have you no pride, have you no regard for your own credit? How often have you been seen with him? How much gossip is there already? Do you not know what people will say?'

I was forbidden to meet him again. I thought he would be hurt and think ill of me if I did not at least explain how it was, but when I said so, she struck me across the face and screamed at me and refused to allow me out of the house.

I fretted. Two days later, she was angry again, this time with my brothers. When a friend called asking me to accompany her walk, Mama forgot her displeasure with me and let me go.

Three years older than myself, my friend had an assignation with a young man. For once, I was not displeased to be made her accomplice, for it gave me opportunity. I was careful to let no one see me as I sought out Mr Benjamin and blurted out my story.

There was something cold and disdainful in his manner as he listened, but his face softened when he looked at me.

'Well, I am sorry I got you trouble with Mama, Sarey my dear, but she is concerned about you, and rightly so! Do not fret over me, for I am smart and I shall do very well.'

He took my hand and raised it to his lips. 'Go home now then, quickly! I shall not forget you, and one day, you may depend upon it, we will meet again.'

I had sobbed and flung an arm round his neck and planted an awkward kiss on his cheek before rushing away in tears.

'And that,' I told James, 'was that. We never did meet again, of course. Often I have wondered what became of him.'

'Well, Sarey, my dear' – James smiled as he used Mr Benjamin's endearment – 'it is indeed a curious story. A clean, good-humoured, kindly, religious tramp! And one with a decided taste for theatricals, I think! I confess, I have never come across the like. Where did he come from, do you know?'

I shook my head. 'He told very little of himself, though I did ask. He said he had been in foreign parts and I think that was true, for he had that fading bronze colour, from sunburn acquired in a hotter climate.'

James thought he might have returned from Australia after serving a term as a convict, a notion which upset me though I could not deny it was possible.

'Most do not return,' said James, 'but he could have found a ship and worked his passage. Well, this is conjecture only: we have no means of truly knowing what he was or what he is now.'

James reached to put out the candle and in the darkness he caressed my cheek. 'I am glad he was kind to you. Should you happen upon him again, I will see what might be done for him.'

'I am unlikely to meet him now,' I said sadly.

James admitted it. 'He is a wanderer. I think. But, who knows, we may encounter him on his travels. Stranger things have happened, Sarey my dear, so remember what I have said.'

I smiled as I settled down, much taken with a pleasing idea of

Mr Benjamin comfortably established in one of our own cottages. As I drifted towards sleep, the music of the Twenty-third Psalm was going round in my head.

Eight

On Boxing Day, we held a ball. James had insisted upon it, but always, since my marriage, such affairs were a mixture of pleasure and pain, for dancing was a delight he could not share. He wanted me to accept other partners, saying he liked to watch and indeed, he spent more time in the ballroom than in the card-room. I took care to spend time sitting with him.

My brothers were sent upstairs with supper on a tray. Emily also should have been confined to the schoolroom, but we relaxed the rules and gave her permission to attend.

Among the company were some unknown to me, for since our neighbours had their own Christmas visitors, we extended all our invitations to include them. As I sat down with James, I observed how Harriet seemed particularly taken with one rather exquisite young man. He had been introduced as Mr Lyndhurst: now, I ventured an enquiry about him.

'He is handsome, is he not?' said James coolly. 'So elegant and such polished manners! You must dance with him, my dear, he is certain to do you credit. The Honourable Frederick Lyndhurst is a fashionable young man about town with excellent address. Nor is that all he has to recommend him. He is heir to a barony.'

'Ah, now I understand!' I laughed. 'I wondered why Harriet was looking so pleased with him! Well, he is an improvement on Thomas, at all events. Though I cannot admire his waistcoat. Is that up-to-the-minute fashion?'

'Since we see it adorning the person of Freddy Lyndhurst, my dear, we may depend upon it.'

I thought I had been hasty in assuming Harriet had serious design on Thomas, and I said so to Arabella. 'Perhaps she is getting a notion she might do equally well, elsewhere.'

'Perhaps,' said Arabella. 'Though I am uneasy. Harriet speaks of ambition and though she does so light-heartedly, I cannot disbelieve her when she says she would be Lady Someone Rich. We know she cannot marry without paying attention to money, but I told her she should also take account of the man.'

'And what did she say to that?'

Arabella blushed. 'She was very pert. If you must know, she asked if I had given you the same advice! With your example before her, she is not amenable to counsel. She does not admire your husband and she cannot believe you have a particle of regard for him.'

'Indeed?' I said coldly. 'Well, she is mistaken.'

'I know! Indeed, I do know! I told her you held him in great esteem, which is important. I doubt she heeded me. Harriet does not have your strong common sense, Sarah. Only marriage to a man she loves will induce her to settle, but she means to marry for advancement, and we cannot rule Thomas out of the reckoning. I confess, I fear for her.'

I was then claimed by a partner and for the rest of the evening I had opportunity to do no more than observe Harriet. She was animated, but kept her behaviour in check. Several gentleman paid attentions and she clearly enjoyed her power.

Arabella had not yet issued an invitation, feeling she should first become better acquainted with Harriet, but all her attempts to speak seriously to our sister were foiled by careless, light-hearted responses.

I talked it over with James when we retired for the night. 'I confess, I am perturbed,' I said. 'We have no means of knowing how far Harriet means anything she says.'

'Emily will have better knowledge of Harriet,' he suggested.

'You might do well to ask her opinion.'

'Oh, James, I never thought of that! Such a sensible idea.'

Emily knew Thomas had attended Mama's parties, but she was considered too young for company and had not observed his attentions to her sister.

'Harriet likes to boast,' she said disapprovingly. 'She says he paid her particular attention, but she would make much of any attention, however slight. Had his manner been pointed towards her I think Mrs Preece would have remarked upon it, for such matters do not escape her notice.'

I knew Mrs Preece, a friend of Mama's, and I had suffered from her, many times. It was her insinuations which put an end to my friendship with Mr Benjamin. Had she any suspicion that Thomas was taken with Harriet, there would have been many sly, impertinent and spiteful allusions.

Easier, but not yet satisfied, I continued, 'I wonder at Thomas attending Mama's card parties,' I said. 'I cannot believe he finds sport in playing whist for sixpences!'

'But Mama's invitations were so very pressing,' said Emily showing a touch of humour. 'For she has discovered how the relationship increases her own consequence and widens her circle of acquaintance.'

'Does it?' I confess I was surprised.

'Indeed it does. In Northampton, our cousin makes himself agreeable to all. He is esteemed as a pleasing young man and so handsome! Many find it remarkable that you married Mr Foster, when offered such an alternative.'

'I dare say,' I said drily. 'Yet my husband is a man of principle, and Thomas is careless of such matters. What is more, James is thoughtful, attentive and kind and he has a great deal of humour. These are qualities which Thomas lacks. I prefer my husband.'

'If you are happy, I am very pleased for you,' said Emily.

'Well I am, but we were speaking of Thomas,' I said. 'You say Harriet merely supposes he has interest in her. Yet if it is no more than her vanity, if he has no interest, I cannot imagine why he is cultivating Mama's acquaintance. So let us pay attention to all his doings. Tell me what you know, Emily, even though it may seem trifling.'

I discovered Thomas had attended only three parties, less than I had supposed. His visits occurred when he was in Leicestershire, quarrelling with his father about rebuilding Kilburn Hall.

'Is that all? He has not been since?'

'Well, no. He has returned now to London.'

So we had been mistaken, Arabella and I, in supposing he was in Northampton. I breathed a sigh of relief. Harriet had made something out of nothing.

Now I understood Thomas. Angry and frustrated because he was not getting his own way, he would, whilst he was in Leicestershire, determine to take off in search of diversion elsewhere. If he found nothing better to do, he might seek to improve acquaintance with his relations in Northampton. Some twenty-five miles was an excessive distance to travel to a card party, but it was in keeping with what I knew of Thomas.

No sooner had I persuaded myself that all my fears were groundless and he had gone to the parties merely out of boredom, when my alarm was raised again by Emily's intelligence that he had struck up a correspondence with Mama.

His first letter was to cry off from the next party for he was returning to London. He pleased Mama by assuring her that he found the occasions most agreeable and he hoped he would be welcome to call when next in the neighbourhood.

A second letter came from London: a trifling account of his own doings, and flattering remarks about his pleasure in their society. He begged Mama to write and tell him how they went on.

Knowing how infrequently he had written to his owm mama, I was perturbed and bewildered. Certain I was that Thomas had some purpose, yet it seemed as though he wished to please Mama rather than my sister.

He might have begun a correspondence to ensure receiving news of Harriet.

'Does Mama wish Thomas for Harriet?' I asked.

'I cannot think she would,' said Emily. 'For certainly she did not wish him for you. She said it had been intolerable to have her sister as Lady Kilburn, giving herself airs and showing off her wealth and consequence, and it would be even more insufferable coming from you!'

'Upon my soul!' I blinked at this insight into Mama. 'But she was pleased to consent to my marriage with James!'

'She was by no means averse to having you comfortably established, and she was pleased to accept assistance for herself, but she did not wish you the future Lady Kilburn.'

'Now she has seen Foster Leigh House and feels she has been abominably deceived,' I said drily. 'Well, that accounts for her present behaviour!'

Yet my marriage had improved her situation. Now she had a spacious home with good servants and this had opened up the opportunity of entertaining and receiving invitations. I felt aggrieved. Common gratitude should have governed her behaviour.

Mama had notions as to what was due to her consequence: I could not wonder she was offended by her sister's good fortune, when her own circumstances were so different. Yet she placed herself in those circumstances when she married Papa, for the modest income from her fortune would have provided a single woman more comfortably than it kept a large family.

From a material point of view, she had no need to marry, so what had induced her to marry so far beneath her?

She must have been very much in love, I supposed. Papa had been handsome in his regimentals. A captain, an officer, his birth obscured by his rank, she had perhaps determined he was acceptable. Others, with like beginnings, had fared well.

Mama must have begun with notions of advancement for him, not considering the hazards of a military profession and no thought of a life encumbered with nine children and a crippled husband. Small wonder she had grown complaining and bitter when all her expectations went awry.

87

Feeling sorry for her, I resolved to be more patient.

On the fourth day of Christmas we awoke to discover there had been a heavy snowfall during the night. The roads were blocked, and all our planned excursions were cancelled as were the neighbourly parties. We were obliged to spend all our time at Foster Leigh and entertain ourselves as best we could.

Being snowed in was disagreeable to Harriet. She had met young men at our ball, but all hope of improving her acquaintance with them was at an end. She had, however, received and accepted Arabella's invitation to Kilburn.

'Though how I shall prevent myself falling into disagreement with Parson "I-cannot-approve-of-it" Henry, is more than I can say,' she confided. 'How does our sister bear with him?'

'Henry has many good qualities,' I said repressively. 'If you are bored, my dear sister, you may divert yourself by attempting to discover them.'

'When I am as bored as that,' retorted Harriet, 'I shall know it is time for me to put an end to my existence. Do you wish to keep these fashion journals, Sarah, or may I take them? I have seen a gown I would like to copy.'

I began to feel an irritation of the nerves. Harriet, in her boredom, now directed her charms at my husband. It was done in a spirit of pure vanity, for she did not admire James and desired only that he should admire her.

James countered this by paying attention to Emily. I watched Harriet and enjoyed her vexation. Later, he said, 'Removing Harriet to Kilburn may bring benefits to Emily.' He laughed. 'She is a minx, is she not, your sister?'

'She is indeed.' I sighed. 'I have been separated from my family so long, I had forgotten how tiresome they could be. I confess, I long for them to be gone! Thank heaven the thaw has begun. Will the snow melt in time, do you think? How I look forward to being quiet again, and comfortable together.'

They were to leave on Twelfth Night, and by that time most of the snow was gone and news had reached us that the weather was less severe to the south, so they were assured of a safe journey. Nothing was to prevent their departure.

I was subjected to another attack from Mama before they left. I had invited both Harriet and Emily to choose one of my gowns, which Matilda had altered to fit.

Mama was annoyed. 'Giving the girls your cast-offs,' she sniffed. 'That is all very well, madam, but what of your brothers? For them, you do nothing at all!'

'I cannot feel that Joseph and Edward would wish for my gowns, Mama, and we are not sending them away empty-handed, for James has said they may have the toy soldiers.'

'I meant the real soldiers,' she snapped. 'You know your husband is in a position to secure their promotion, but have you spoken to him? Oh no! Never given them a thought, I dare say, for all your pretence at concern for their welfare.'

Was this why we had suffered twelve days of ill-humour? All my good intentions of remaining patient and kind dissolved and I said coldly, 'Had you wished favours from my husband, madam, you would have done better to be conciliating, rather than make your request in such a way as to imply that I am neglectful!'

She gasped and drew in her breath in preparation for a bitter denunciation, but I was too angry to give her chance.

'It so happens,' I went on, 'that I discussed this matter with Mr Foster and he was quite willing to advance my brothers until your own manner towards me brought him to second thoughts! He feels that if I am so little regarded, then none can complain of being disregarded.'

James had no intention of retracting his promise, of course. This was my own blending of truth and falsehood and it astonished me. I had not known myself to be capable of such.

I felt Mama had deserved it and struggled against my feelings of compunction when I saw a stricken look on her face.

'Well,' I said, unable to prevent myself softening a little, 'I shall persevere, for I see no reason why my brothers should suffer for your ill-conduct.'

'Sarah—'

'Do not imagine, madam, that I have any intention of teasing my husband. I shall speak my opinion. Should he disagree, you will have only yourself to blame.'

I left her then and took care not to be alone with her again. At last James and I saw them off, and not until we went indoors together did I mention my last altercation with Mama.

'I should not have spoken so, I know,' I said.

'Do not reproach yourself, Sarah,' he said. 'If your reproofs overstepped the mark of propriety, they were well deserved for all that!'

Despite his displeasure with Mama, James went ahead and made the necessary dispositions for advancing my brothers.

Everything settled into a regular train at Foster Leigh. Our neighbours visited and we returned the calls; we took pleasure in parties and gatherings, but most of all James and I found pleasure and contentment in our own society.

The next letter from Arabella informed me she was with child. Having so far experienced two miscarriages she was now uncertain whether it was better to rest or keep busy.

She had little to say of Harriet except Sir Nicholas was taken with her and that she was a favourite with the young men of the neighbourhood. Thomas remained in London and Arabella doubted whether he knew Harriet was at Kilburn.

If Thomas took the trouble to read Mama's letters, then certainly he knew. I had asked Emily to keep me informed and her letter told me Mama had written to Thomas.

She received a reply. This appeared to be a short missive, and Emily had not been privileged to read the content.

She had, however, heard Mama boasting to Mrs Preece. Thomas had so many engagements in town that he could not say when he would be returning. He had described all the entertainments in London, and said he often thought how pleasing it would be to show Mama and his young cousins around the capital.

The first part sounded much like Thomas. The rest so unlike

him, that I could not help wondering how far Mama had embroidered his short missive when boasting to Mrs Preece.

James laughed when I said as much. 'My dear Sarah, that is the most cynical speech I have ever heard you utter. Such a way to speak of your own mama! Now, would she do such a thing?'

'You know very well she would. Well, they go on. Mama writes to Thomas, encouraged by her recent discovery that such a nephew increases her consequence in Northampton society. So far, I can easily comprehend. But I cannot comprehend why Thomas takes the trouble. I had thought he wished intelligence of Harriet: it makes sense if he is pursuing his interest with her, yet it begins to look otherwise.'

'He wishes intelligence of some kind. Has it occurred to you, my dear, that he may wish to be informed about you?'

'Heavens, why should he? He cannot hope to marry me now!'

'He may hope for your sudden widowhood,' said James coolly. 'Though I believe he will be disappointed. I cannot pretend to be sound in wind *and* limb, but my internal organs are in good order and I mean to preserve my life as long as possible.'

'So I should hope! I would not marry Thomas, in any event. I would not marry him to preserve my own life!'

'Indeed?' His tone was cool as he went on, 'Yet he is a handsome young man. Together you would make a striking couple.'

'Well, I do not like him,' I said. 'What is the matter, James? Surely, you do not imagine I regret marrying you?'

I got up and went to stand behind his chair, leaning over to murmur in his ear, 'I like being married to you and if you have not yet learnt that, sir, then I shall have to spend all morning teaching you.'

I felt him relax, his hands covered mine and he twisted in his chair to raise his face for my kiss.

'Pay no heed to me, Sarah, for I know jealousy is a failing of mine. Well, I am foolish. I cannot help but notice the way people look at us, sometimes: the knowing smirks, the whispered asides. I am a poor deluded fool and you – heaven knows what they say about you!'

'I know of one who believes I was sold against my will to the highest bidder! Does it matter what the gossips say?'

'For myself, I care not. But it pains me to feel there is gossip about you.'

'We cannot prevent. Always there are those who pretend to be wiser than they are. We may confound them by being happy.'

My cousin was forgotten in our subsequent conversation, but James remained perturbed by his own proposal that Thomas wrote to Mama with the design of gaining information about me. The next day he returned to the subject.

It was one of those most precious evenings when we had no engagements and no company. On such occasions I would take off my cap and let down my hair because he liked it and we would sit together at our own fireside, lazy and happy. I did not wish to think about Thomas at such a time and I said so.

'Sarah, I believe we must,' he insisted, and when I looked my surprise, he went on, 'your mama may pass on information and see no evil.'

'What can she say to interest him? That we are married and living at Foster Leigh he might deduce for himself, without recourse to Mama.'

'At this present, that is so,' he admitted. 'But Thomas goes to great lengths to achieve his ends, whatever they might be. There is something you do not know, Sarah. I said nothing, for I have only recently come to wonder if it was more than it seemed. I think I should tell you.'

He was uneasy and I prompted, 'Something to do with Thomas?'

'I cannot say, for certain, but something happened to me.'

Again he hesitated, and I said, 'I know you would scruple to betray my cousin's mischief, but James—'

'I scruple lest I falsely accuse him,' said James. 'For I have only my own conjectures to offer. But I suspect he made an attempt to prevent our marriage taking place.'

To my utter consternation I now learnt James had been set

upon. He had been blindfolded and robbed, bound and gagged and shut in an empty warehouse, left alone to struggle with his bonds.

The event had occurred only two days before our wedding.

Nine

'Calm yourself, my dear,' he said. 'I am here, I am well, as you perceive.'

'Yes, but – oh dear! Never have I been more shocked! How can you—?' I paused in my agitated pacing about the room. 'You seem to take it very calmly, James.'

'At the time I did not,' he admitted. 'I confess, I despaired of our wedding!'

Occupied with disquieting fancies, I continued to pace the room, wretched and anguished, exclaiming all my horror. James gazed at me steadily, smiled and held out his hand. 'I would not have you distressed,' he said. 'It is over and no harm done, after all. Come, sit by me.'

I settled myself on a footstool and laid my arms across the arm of his chair, still uneasy, but calm enough now to listen to his account.

'Despite my struggles,' he said, 'I was tied up for more than twenty-four hours: I doubt I would have freed myself, so tightly was I bound. By the greatest good fortune, I was found by a group of ragamuffin children, playing where they ought not. They set me free.' His smile was self-derisory. 'Know what I am worth, Sarah. My freedom cost me seven shillings!'

Seven children, one shilling each, he explained. 'My money had been taken but I had funds at the inn. Would those beggars let me

94

out of their sight before they had their reward?' He laughed. 'They found me a stick, for my crutch was lost, and followed me through all the streets of Northampton.'

'Northampton?' I blinked. 'You were in Northampton?'

'Signing papers, putting the finishing touches to the arrangements I made for your mama,' he said. 'The attack occurred soon after I left the attorney's office and do not ask me to recall how it happened, because I cannot! I suffered a blow to the head and knew nothing more until I awoke to find myself alone, bound, gagged and blindfolded! The blindfold,' he added, 'I worked loose but the rest proved too much.'

'Thank heaven for those children! Oh James!' I shuddered. 'You might have lain there for weeks, you might have died!'

'As to that, I doubt it. I do have a manservant, you know. When I had not returned to the inn by nightfall, Francis became anxious and reported my disappearance to the constabulary. It might have taken several days to find me, though I was searched for. Those infants should have driven a harder bargain,' he admitted, 'for I was deuced uncomfortable.'

Uncomfortable! I winced. He said nothing about the violent headache which must have followed a blow to the head; he said nothing about his cramps; he said nothing of hunger and thirst, or of fear and confusion, but I knew all his suffering. I went to the sideboard to pour out brandy for him.

'Now I recall how you were so exhausted on our wedding day, and I am sure it is no wonder!'

'I had freedom, but too much time had passed,' he told me. 'I knew I must make all haste. First, I had to get word to Francis who was out searching for me; I had to procure another crutch, and I was devilish hungry. I had to dine before I could undertake the travelling to Melton! And Sarah, I know Henry meant well when he moved you there from Kilburn, but I cursed him! It added thirty miles to my journey. On the way, one of the carriage horses went lame, and more time was wasted. I arrived with scarce an hour to make myself presentable! You never knew, my dear,' he added wryly, 'how nearly you were jilted at the altar.'

'I am obliged to you,' I said politely, 'for taking such pains to spare me that unpleasantness.'

'Such a stupid bridegroom I must have seemed! And not one word of complaint.' He caught my hand and kissed it. 'I said nothing,' he went on, 'for I held my misfortune accountable to common thieves. But other thoughts have intruded and they will persist, despite all my attempts to dismiss them. I wish your opinion, Sarah. Suppose Thomas sought to prevent our wedding?'

'Would he go to such lengths?' I asked doubtfully. 'To take measures such as that would seem a little excessive. He is selfish and ill-humoured when he cannot get his own way, but I do not think him criminal! If you were robbed, then surely it must have been the work of footpads?'

'Money was taken,' he said. 'My pocket watch was not, neither was my ring. I have come to doubt robbery was the real motive.'

'Could it be. . . ?' My words died away. If the attack was not for robbery, there must be another motive. James was right: we had to suspect an attempt to prevent our wedding.

'Consider this, Sarah! Footpads would knock me down and take my belongings, but would they convey me across town and leave me bound and helpless in a lonely spot? I think not.'

'Were you conveyed across the town? How do you know? You said you suffered a blow to the head, you were insensible.'

'Indeed, I was. When I was released and escorted by my rescuers back to the inn, I discovered I was in quite another part of town from where the attack occurred.'

I felt a sudden lurch of fear. 'That would imply,' I said, 'that someone lay in wait for you, that you were kidnapped and taken to a hiding-place which had been previously determined.'

'Yes, I believe I was,' said James. 'From a public thoroughfare, in broad daylight, and not as difficult to accomplish as one might suppose. It takes but an instant to deliver a blow, it might be done without being observed.'

'Surely not,' I protested.

'I can recall nothing, Sarah, but I have my conjectures to show how it was. I think I was caught as I fell: to passers-by I would appear to be taken ill. Who would think it strange when he assisted me into a carriage? To be bound and gagged and blindfolded, I would have to be hidden from view. What more likely than I was put inside a carriage?'

The scene he described was all too credible to be denied. 'It could not be done in the street,' I admitted. 'It must have been done that way. Oh, but can you be certain it was Thomas? Might there be some other explanation? Could it be that someone thought to hold you for ransom?'

'None came to extract ransom and who could be approached other than myself? No, I believe we must discard that notion. Do not forget, my dear, this affair might have prevented our wedding.'

'It might have delayed,' I said, 'it could not prevent.'

'What?' He stared at me, his brows raised in surprise. 'You would marry me still, after being jilted at the altar?'

'Should I refuse to wed another day, for what was no fault of yours? Some unpleasantness I might have suffered, but I would not believe a desire to cry off, not in such an unseemly way as that! I would not believe you less than a gentleman. Even Thomas must know that!'

'I think Thomas does not know that,' he said gently. 'Your cousin may cling to the belief that you would prefer him.'

'How can he?'

'Others besides Thomas think your choice an oddity,' he reminded me. 'His fortune does not quite compare with mine: nevertheless it is not to be despised, and he has attributes which I have not.'

'Yes, indeed, I know all about them,' I said drily. 'He is able-bodied, he is handsome and he will have a title!'

'The world considers such trifles important. So does Thomas. Perhaps he thought you rejected him out of compassion for me, or perhaps he thought you reluctant to break your promise. He cannot bring himself to believe you chose me out of preference, therefore he must find another explanation, one to assist his self-regard.'

'He is conceited enough, I grant you.'

'Perhaps—' James smiled mirthlessly. 'Perhaps he thought you would be relieved to find yourself abandoned, so you could turn to him with a clear conscience.'

I was so indignant with Thomas that I got up and began to pace the floor again. 'That a relation of mine could use you in such a way!' I said, forgetting, for a moment, this was no more than conjecture. I stopped and turned back to James. 'You cannot be certain it was Thomas?'

'Not beyond doubt. Indeed, it is only these last few days I have wondered, only since we learnt how he was taking such pains to preserve his acquaintance with your mama. How long has he been paying her particular attention? We heard of November card parties, but he may have begun earlier than we supposed.'

'What?' I was aghast. 'Do you accuse Mama of involving herself with this? No, James, she can be unkind, but never would she do any such thing!'

'I had no thought of it,' he assured me. 'But she may, in all innocence, have talked of her new establishment, describing the arrangements, and perhaps mentioning when I would be visiting Mr Scofield's office to sign papers.'

I was silent, reflecting how easily, with information such as that, Thomas could make his plans and lie in wait for James.

'It is a possibility,' I said slowly. 'I do not admit a certainty. I wish I had questioned Emily more closely. I asked about card parties, never did it occur to me there might have been earlier visits. Well, I might yet discover that much.'

Upon consideration, I determined I would not approach Emily in case Mama took it into her head to read my letter. 'For she may do so, you know. No. I shall ask Arabella to enquire of Harriet. That may done without seeming pointed.'

'Such stratagems!' teased James. 'How can it matter now? We are married and Thomas has nothing to hope for. It is over.'

'James, if you are trying to rid my mind of uneasiness, you will not succeed. It is not over. You know it is not! Thomas is importuning Mama and he has some design, we both know it! You have told me this story because you felt there was cause for perturbation.'

We talked over the whole matter again, seeking other explanations, finding none, and my apprehension increased.

'How I wish we could be certain!' I said. 'Suspecting but not knowing is the worst aspect of the whole case. But I fear for you, James, and I wish you to promise me you will have a care for yourself, especially when you go out for exercise. If I am unable to accompany you, do take a footman with you.'

'I will do no such thing!' he exclaimed. 'A sudden freak like that will have me the butt of the neighbourhood.'

'Well, then, take the dogs. Thomas dislikes dogs, as I recall, and Bundle and Clincher are well trained; they will protect you.' I saw he was looking displeased and said gently, 'I would be easier in my mind, James. Since we suspect ill-will, let us take such precautions as we may.'

'As you wish.' He spoke curtly, and I knew he felt his own disadvantages. But even a strong man may be taken by surprise and I said so. 'All of us are vulnerable to those who wish us ill.'

James wished to keep suspicions between ourselves, and I saw the sense in this, so when I wrote to Arabella I said only that we had reason to suppose Thomas had become friendly with Mama earlier than we thought and I wondered if Harriet had said anything about it.

Arabella's reply brought the information I wanted: Thomas had, whilst staying in Northampton, once invited Mama, Samuel and Harriet to dine in his hotel, but she, Arabella, could not be certain when this occurred.

Samuel had rejoined his regiment directly after our wedding, so it must have occurred before my marriage. It was indeed possible, if not certain, that Thomas knew enough to plan an attack.

Arabella's letter informed me there had been some trouble,

unintentionally caused by Sir Nicholas, who had made a proposal of taking Harriet to London, with Arabella as her chaperon, to enjoy some of the amusements.

Henry scotched this idea because Arabella was with child and feeling the discomforts of her condition: it would not be sensible; he could not approve of it.

In this, I was much in sympathy with Henry. Arabella herself, though unwilling to disappoint Sir Nicholas, was also in accord with her husband.

Harriet was not. Deprived of her enjoyment and her hopes of meeting other young men, she was very much annoyed. What she had to say on the matter was not disclosed, but it was enough to bring Arabella to consider sending her home to Northampton.

'Oh really, I have no patience with Harriet!' I exclaimed. 'How can she be so selfish? As though her paltry amusements were more important than her sister's health!'

'Do not be so severe on your sister, Sarah. Harriet is young and lively and so far she has enjoyed little in the way of amusement. One cannot wonder at her disappointment.'

'I do not wonder at it. I am merely displeased that she has caused distress to Arabella. Indeed, I feel that Sir Nicholas should have known better than to suggest such a thing.'

'Does Harriet yet entertain hopes of Thomas?'

'He has not been to Kilburn these two months she has been there, so such hopes as she had must be reduced. Thankfully, she has the sense to be silent on the matter, for it would not do to let such ambition be known in the Kilburn neighbourhood.'

We heard no more and in the days that followed we went about our usual pursuits.

Often during the winter, James had been obliged to take his exercise indoors, trudging patiently along corridors, complaining only of monotony. I had taken to sharing this penance, sometimes talking, sometimes reading poetry to him, anything to make the business less tiresome. We were pleased when the weather improved and we could walk out of doors.

In March, the light remained longer and some days were mild and bright, with promise of spring. Crocuses carpeted the lawns in a drift of yellow and white and purple, daffodils were thrusting up spears, catkins appeared, and the bare trees were just beginning to take on buds.

One day he said, 'We could take the carriage and go further afield. A walk along the Manifold Valley would be pleasant if the weather remains fine. Would you like that?'

'The Manifold Valley,' I said, savouring the name of the place. 'It sounds pretty. But James, is it easy for you? I will not leave you alone, not as I did at Dovedale.'

There was a path by the River Manifold, he said, which he had walked before and though it was not as pretty as Dovedale, it was pleasing.

It was dry, but the sun did not shine, that day. The grass was long and lank and wet and dead rushes hung over the river, but a few primroses showed, birds were gathering nesting materials and I could easily imagine it in sunshine and clothed in summer greenery.

Most pleasing was the path, which ran straight and true and James managed easily. We were alone, no need for decorous behaviour, so I laughed and danced beside him, holding his free hand and swinging his arm as though we were children and, in a sudden spirit of gaiety, James began to sing.

Where hast t'been since I saw thee?
On Ilkley Moor bar t'at

'Good heavens!' I exclaimed laughing. 'What on earth is that?'

'I wish I could claim it for Derbyshire,' said James, 'but it belongs to Yorkshire, where Ilkley Moor is situated. "Bar t'at" means without thy hat.'

'Does it?' I blinked at this oddity of language, but I had heard stranger phrases since coming to Derbyshire. I pressed James to sing the whole, and laughed a great deal and joined in the repetitions and afterwards said ruefully, 'Had I known it went on as long as that, I would not have made such a request! Well, how delightfully vulgar it is, to be sure.'

He looked at me oddly. 'But you have heard it before, surely?'

'Would I forget it? No, no, I am quite sure I have not.'

'How, then, could you play the tune on the pianoforte?'

'What?'

'You did, Sarah. You played by ear. On Christmas Eve. . . .'

'You are right!' I exclaimed in astonishment. 'It is the same tune! But James, that was because I had been reminded of Mr Benjamin, and I heard very different words!'

I sang: *'The Lord's my shepherd I'll not want. . . .'*
James sang: *'On Ilkley Moor bar t'at!'*

'Oh, James, you should not!' I gasped, unable to control my laughter. 'I declare, you are teaching me to be quite irreligious.'

'What would Henry say?' he asked, and in unison we chorused, 'I cannot approve of it!' and laughed again.

Such nonsenses could be indulged only when we were alone together, but they intensified our happiness. This particular nonsense had reminded us of Mr Benjamin and when we were on our way home, James said, 'There are caves, you know, here in Derbyshire, and some of them maintain a constant temperature. A little too cold for real comfort, but certainly warmer than freezing weather, and some such as he come to winter there. I sent some comforts with the hope we might gain intelligence of him, but I fear it has come to nothing.'

'Well, you tried. Few gentlemen would do as much.'

'It is difficult to get word of one who would be elusive, for he would suspect the worst, should he learn of a gentleman who is searching for him. There is so little one can do.'

I was touched that he had done so much, and I said, 'He may have established himself, by now. I told you, he is clever.'

Other concerns were revived the next morning, for whilst we were at breakfast, the post arrived bringing with it four letters for me. I recognized the hands. One was from Mama and the others from each of my three sisters.

'Something has set the family in a flutter,' I observed. 'Four letters at once! What has occurred, I wonder?'

All contained the same information. It transpired that Sir Nicholas, unhappy because Harriet had been disappointed in her hope of a visit to London, now had the idea of inviting Mama, instead of Arabella, to be Harriet's chaperon.

They were to go. Mama's letter informed me of the arrangements. My younger brothers would remain at home in the care of the housekeeper. Emily was to be escorted by Mama to Kilburn parsonage, and stay with Arabella. From there, Mama and Harriet would set off for London with Sir Nicholas.

Harriet had much to say of the purchases they must make and the delights in store for them. She added how she meant to give Thomas a severe scolding, for all his neglect of them.

James laughed. 'That *will* teach him a lesson!'

Emily felt uncomfortable because she had been foisted on Henry and Arabella. She hoped they would not feel it too much of an imposition, because she had intention of being useful.

For Arabella, the exchange was welcome. She felt some consternation, however, about what Harriet would be doing in London with none but Mama and Sir Nicholas to restrain her.

I also felt some consternation. Harriet would escape the guardians I had chosen for her and venture upon London society with Mama, who would scold but give no good advice, and Sir Nicholas, who was too much inclined to be indulgent. I could not feel it was a happy circumstance.

'And do not forget Thomas is in London,' I said to James. 'Whatever his feelings on the matter, I would not be surprised if Harriet still has notions of captivating him.'

James was not the kind of husband to insist on reading my letters, but I had passed them to him. Now he folded them and his countenance wore the vacant look, which I had learnt was deceptive. His mind was at its busiest.

At last, he said, 'There are pitfalls enough in London society, and I think your sister should have others to guard her. It would be well for us to go to town, Sarah, where we may keep an eye on what transpires.'

'Go to town?' I said in dismay. 'Oh, but I had been so looking forward to spring at Foster Leigh.'

'It is a pity, but there will be other springs, after all. Here, we can no longer learn what is going forward, for Arabella and Emily remain at Kilburn with no more intelligence than ourselves. I do think we should go, Sarah.'

I knew James had a house in Mount Street, though I had never seen it. 'Do you wish them to stay with us?'

Sir Nicholas had sold his own house in town to assist the cost of rebuilding at Kilburn. For this excursion, he meant to hire a house.

I thought we could spare him the necessity, but James said, 'Certainly not! I draw the line at having your relations to stay in our house after the way your Mama upset you at Christmas. But we shall see them often and if there is mischief, we shall hear of it!'

'Will they not suspect our reason for going?'

'Why should they? I have relations too, you know, and what could be more natural than I should wish they and my beautiful young bride to become better acquainted? And they, my dear' – his eyes sparkled with sudden mischief – 'they move only in the best circles and you will receive invitations to the most fashionable parties and balls! Mama and Sister Harriet will be quite green with envy! Now then, I command you to visit all the fashionable dress-makers and be vastly extravagant in the matter of your apparel! Yes! And I shall be vastly extravagant in the matter of your jewels! You go to outshine your sister!'

I could not help laughing, but I said, 'I should like to see London, for I have never been, you know. But I fear I am not well acquainted with up-to-the-minute fashion. I could easily be deceived into purchasing and wearing something quite unsuitable!'

'Should you feel in need of advice, my cousin Gideon, Lord Pangbourn, has a wife who likes nothing better than purchasing fine apparel. She will be delighted to assist you.'

It was settled, we were to go. James sent servants to open up the house in Mount Street and three days later we set off for London.

Ten

'My cousin Gideon,' said James, 'is a most remarkable creature.' He was referring to Lord Pangbourn, who we were
on our way to visit at his house in Grosvenor Square. 'He has one
head, two arms and two legs.'

'Ah, but does he have a nose on his face?' I enquired.

'Only one,' he assured me. 'But he has a pair of eyes: they
match! And he is quite famous for his eyebrows.'

These pleasantries were begun because I had asked him to pre-
pare me for his cousin by telling of his disposition. The gentleman
and his lady had been in church at our wedding and I had been
introduced and exchanged greetings, but so I had with his other
relations. All the encounters had been brief and now I could not
recall them with any degree of certainty.

I knew the Pangbourns had influence and James had explained
his hope that Helen, Lady Pangbourn, would advise me on fashion, procure a voucher for me to Almacks and launch me in
London society. This visit was important, yet I had a suspicion that
James did not look forward to it with pleasure. Though he said he
was fortunate to have such a cousin, I had the impression that
Lord Pangbourn was no favourite with James.

He would not tell me what to expect. He said it pleased him better I should form my own opinion.

This was our second day in London. We had arrived late on

Saturday and I had spent yesterday, Sunday, indoors, at his insistence, to rest and recover from the journey. I had felt queasy whilst travelling and since I do not suffer from travelling sickness as a rule, I had to suppose I was taken with some other disorder. A day of rest had set me to rights.

James had told me I must purchase a good deal of fashionable apparel. I, in my innocence, thought myself already well provided, but I discovered I was mistaken.

Matilda had gone out purposely to look at fashions and determine which of my garments would serve for the present. 'The bronze silk will do very well, even in London,' she said. 'Other items are out-moded: well enough for the country, but they will not do here.' She saw my grimace and added severely, 'Much importance is attached to fashion, mistress, and you cannot ignore it. You must be well turned out, for it would reflect on the master if you were not.'

Matilda knew her business. For years, her situation had kept her in the country and though she had been happy enough, she had been trained up to serve a lady of fashion. Now, having observed the apparel of ladies in the park, she trimmed one of my bonnets with curled feathers, declared my braided blue pelisse was the only thing that was fit to wear and quite despaired of all my morning gowns until she had the notion of attaching a quantity of lace to my turquoise crepe.

Not wishing my appearance to reflect on the master, I allowed Matilda to dictate what I should wear in a way I never would at home and I was startled, though not displeased, by the elegant creature who stared from the looking-glass.

I was stylish enough, at all events, to be greeted by Lord Pangbourn without occasioning that gentleman to raise his famous eyebrows. He was tall, elegant in a rather intimidating way and he moved with graceful ease, in sharp and painful contrast to my husband's ungainly progress.

He was civil and we exchanged some commonplace conversation. Towards James, he was friendly, though there was something superior and patronizing in his air, which I found irksome. My attempts to form an opinion of him were overset by the assessing look I observed in his cool eyes. Lord Pangbourn was at present occupied in making up his mind about me.

Reserving judgement on Lord Pangbourn, I turned my attention to his wife. Lady Pangbourn was a sandy-haired woman of more style than beauty. Her large blue eyes were a little too prominent and her chin showed a tendency to recede.

She was good-natured and remarked on my beauty without the least appearance of envy. She called me a 'ravishing creature' and promised to send an invitation to her dress party for the following week, declaring, with some satisfaction, that I would take London by storm.

She talked about fashion and at first I thought the subject had been raised because it provided a convenient topic of conversation with a stranger, but I soon discovered it was her most passionate interest. James took the opportunity to ask her which dressmakers I should patronize and, upon learning I needed to be brought up to the minute, she said she would accompany me to her own dressmaker straight away. It was agreed, and arranged that her carriage would afterwards convey me home to Mount Street.

So James left me in Grosvenor Square: Her Ladyship ordered her carriage and went upstairs to put on her outdoor clothes. I expected Lord Pangbourn to excuse himself and leave me alone for the few minutes I must wait for his lady, but he did not. Instead, he seated himself on a sofa on the opposite side of the fireplace, crossed one shapely leg over the other and took a pinch of snuff from an elegant enamelled box.

I watched him warily. He had purpose and there was a curl to his mouth which I did not like. I remained silent, unwilling to betray my uneasiness by rushing into speech.

'I do not care,' he said lazily, 'what designing arts and allurements you used to captivate my cousin. Indeed, I perfectly comprehend how a damsel in circumstances such as yours must exert herself to marry as profitably as she can. I congratulate you on your success.'

I bit back my denials, knowing very well they would not be believed. I said stiffly, 'That is very obliging of you, sir.'

'I do not even care,' he went on, 'if you make James unhappy. He deserves to be unhappy for so far forgetting what is due to himself and his family as to form such an alliance. I have been investigating your antecedents, madam. Does James know your grandfather was a blacksmith?'

'You have been misinformed, sir.' I said coolly. 'My grandfather was a gamekeeper.'

'That is hardly an improvement. Too ramshackle by half!'

'My grandfather,' I said, 'was a very good gamekeeper!'

'Do not trifle with me, madam, for you know very well what I mean. He was by no means a gentleman.'

'He was not,' I admitted. 'But he was a courteous man, by all accounts.' I had not intended this as reproof, so I was surprised to see a hint of colour in His Lordship's complexion.

'I am aware my marriage is a trifle irregular,' I went on, 'but James knows of my family and if he does not object I cannot see why you should think it matters.'

'Had you been content to remain countrified, I should not be in the least perturbed,' he said coolly. 'However, I thought it would not be long before you teased James into bringing you to town and foisting you on polite society. Since he is my cousin I am obliged to receive you, though I do not do so willingly. Your marriage and your relationship to me will give you some standing: do not abuse it, madam, for I give you fair warning, cousin or not, these doors will be closed to you should you conduct yourself in any way to occasion the censure of society.'

He paused, whilst I regarded him without enthusiasm. I said, 'You appear to expect a reply, sir, but the words that spring to my mind are, perhaps, better left unspoken.'

I was not in charity with him but there was, I was forced to admit, something attractive about him when he laughed, and he did laugh, then. 'Aye, you are clever enough to be discreet. But you have connections, madam, which could prove an embarrassment.'

I longed to retort, with one particular emphasis, that so did my husband. But I was a guest, although by this time an unwilling guest, and I would not insult the gentleman in his own house.

Instead, I contented myself by saying, 'I have some genteel connections also, and those whom Your Lordship might consider an embarrassment, my grandfather and my papa, are unlikely to trouble you, since they are now deceased.'

'But what of your uncle, madam? He is upon the town, is he not? What of him?'

'My uncle?' I was all astonishment. 'He is here? I had thought some time yet before he arrived. Well, sir, I see no reason why you should despise that connection. James certainly does not. He has been friend to Sir Nicholas for many years.'

A shadow of annoyance crossed his features, but whatever he might have replied was lost for his lady entered the room, resplendent in blue velvet and chinchilla, having much to say about a lost glove. I scarce had time to make a civil leave-taking before I was swept away in a stylish barouche.

I was in some perturbation of mind. I could not imagine why His Lordship disapproved of Sir Nicholas who was a gentleman born, and always conducted himself impeccably. I could only conjecture: Lord Pangbourn might have learnt enough of my cousin Thomas to think the connection a disgrace. He might even, I thought uneasily, have met Mama and Harriet, and found something there to offend his fastidious notions.

Lady Pangbourn gave me no time to ponder. She kept up a flow of animated but inconsequential chatter. I quickly discovered I was not required to respond in any intelligent way and the occasional interpolation of 'indeed', or 'quite so ma'am', was enough to set her tongue wagging again.

She was kind, but a short time in her society was enough to convince me she was also trifling and foolish and knew nothing of what was in her husband's mind. Lord Pangbourn, possibly with discretion, did not confide his opinions to her.

I might have wondered why he married her had not his own discourse taught me the reason. She had, no doubt, connections and possibly fortune enough to accord with his notions of what was due to his consequence. I was persuaded he could feel for her no more than tolerance: it was a marriage with little affection and no companionship.

I felt my own blessings more keenly than ever before.

Her Ladyship's carriage drew up outside an establishment which looked modest, from the outside. Inside, however, we were ushered into a long saloon with chandeliers, fine carpets, gilt and brocade chairs and a good many tall mirrors.

The proprietor appeared, all smiles and curtsies, and Lady Pangbourn informed her she was to have the privilege of supplying me with a number of garments. Two girls scurried back and forth with a bewildering variety of gowns, braided, embroidered, flounced, decorated with ribbons or fringes or lace or beads.

I found myself standing before a mirror, first in an elegant walking dress of dark-blue crepe, then in dresses in calico and muslin, then an evening gown, layers of olive-green gauze over an underdress of gold silk, next in a ball gown of lace over oyster-coloured satin with a velvet pelerine over my shoulders.

Lady Pangbourn rejected the pinks, the yellows, the reds, without ceremony. 'Not with your fair colouring, Sarah dearest. It is a pity, because that red evening cloak is quite beautiful, but it will not do for you. However, I have no doubt Madame could supply one in – let me see – dark-green velvet, I think, with a lining of gold silk.'

Madame agreed that such would look ravishing on me and she could supply it within two days. And although I was delighted with all the garments, and quite giddy at the thought of possessing so many new gowns all at once, I was in some apprehension as to the cost.

Her Ladyship began to talk of pelisses and bonnets and shawls and gloves. Only Matilda's admonishments about being well turned out for the master's sake kept me meek and acquiescent.

James had said the expense should not be charged to my allowance: he would pay the bills. That evening, as we waited for dinner, I warned him I had been a little extravagant.

He laughed and settled himself on the sofa, lifting his lame leg on to a footstool. 'Only a little?'

'Well then,' I amended, 'I suspect I have been very extravagant indeed, but I did not dare mention anything so ungenteel as prices! That dressmaker – I beg your pardon – that modiste, must have the most expensive establishment in town. It did occur to me,' I went on, 'that I could buy material and copy the fashions, but I thought you would not wish me to suggest that to Lady Pangbourn.'

'Indeed, no! It would completely do for you, in her estimation.'

'That is what I thought.'

'Besides, there is not the least necessity. I am not a pauper, my dear.'

'You might be, when Madame sends her bill.'

'Well then,' he said lightly, 'I shall be obliged to recoup my losses by selling your emeralds.'

'An excellent scheme,' I approved, 'had I emeralds to sell, which I have not.'

Under my fascinated gaze he withdrew a jewellers' box from his pocket. 'You have now.'

I beheld a triangle of flashing green fire. String upon string of emeralds set in gold, and a larger emerald, the size of a walnut, dangling as a pendant from the centre.

He wanted me to try the necklace on, took it from the box, and bade me sit beside him, and I did so, speechlessly, and remained speechless as he lifted it to my throat and fastened the clasp.

I was silent as I regarded myself in the looking-glass, and when I turned to James to speak I could find no words, only an exhalation of breath, a spread of the hands and a bemused shake of the head.

'Do you not like it?'

'Not like it? Dear heaven, how could anyone not like it?'

'I fear the gown you are wearing does not show it to the best advantage, but I dare say there is something amongst your recent purchases which will set it off admirably.'

'I – oh James! What can I say? You are far too generous!'

He shook his head and smiled and told me how well emeralds became me and teased me about my notion of making up clothes to wear with them and I laughed a little and wept a little, and took a last peep in the looking-glass before returning the necklace to its box.

'You shall wear it,' he promised me, 'at the Pangbourns' dress party, next week.'

'Do we go?'

'Helen promised an invitation, she will not forget. Certainly, we go. It will be a dreadful crush, I have no doubt, but one does not refuse an invitation from the Pangbourns, my dear. Now why are you looking at me like that? Surely you are not afraid of them?'

'I am, a little,' I confessed. 'Oh, not Lady Pangbourn, she is most agreeable, but your cousin is my enemy. Well, no, not precisely that,' I amended, 'but certainly no friend.'

I had, at first, determined to keep the substance of Lord Pangbourn's discourse to myself, but later reflection had led me to the uneasy conclusion that I must inform James of it.

I did so and watched his mouth tighten. 'This is insufferable! I will have something to say to my cousin when next I see him.'

'No, James, I beg you will not quarrel with him. I know very well such views are widely held in polite society.'

'It is very impolite society, in my view.'

I giggled. 'I knew you would say something like that! Well, a shaft of mine hit its mark!' I repeated what I had said of my grandfather's disposition. 'Never did it occur to me that your cousin would take it as reproof, but he did.'

'I am very happy to hear it.'

'Well, it will do me no service to have you quarrel with him, and

I beg you will not. I shall not seek to ingratiate myself, but neither shall I do anything to give him a disgust of me, and I dare say we shall come to tolerate each other. And if we do not,' I added thoughtfully, 'I shall lose very little, for I have a notion that you have no great opinion of your cousin, am I right?' His expression answered for him and I asked, 'Is that why you would not tell me what to expect?'

'I – oh, hang it all, Sarah! How could I express my opinion of Gideon when I half-suspect I am soured by jealousy? Him so tall, so handsome, so strong, whilst I' – he gestured at his crippled leg – 'I am like this. I confess, I feel it!'

I caught his hand, held it between my own and raised it against my cheek. 'You have the better nature,' I said warmly, and I told him what I had thought of his cousin's marriage. 'Lady Pangbourn's affections are easily bestowed, she may be content with such a husband, but I am far happier to be Mrs Foster, indeed I am!'

'Are you, Sarah? Truly?'

'How can you doubt it?' I kissed him, and Lord Pangbourn was forgotten then, and not until we were at dinner did I recollect what His Lordship had said about my uncle. After dinner, away from the servants, I raised the subject again.

'Were it merely his opinion of myself, I would not mention it. No, what troubles me, James, is how he spoke of my uncle. I cannot imagine why he should feel Sir Nicholas is an undesirable connection.'

James was frowning, attentive and grim, but he only said, 'Nor I.'

'I did suspect, at first, that he might have a disgust of Thomas, or even of Mama and Harriet, if he has chanced upon them. But I cannot feel that is the case, for why then would he say "your uncle" instead of saying "your cousin" or "your mama and sister"? It makes no sense at all.'

'He said they were here, in town?'

'He said my uncle was, so I have to suppose it.'

'It appears my cousin knows more than we,' said James. 'Were we not told they would arrive next week? Some alteration of their plans must account for it. Tomorrow, we must visit them.'

Their delay was because my uncle had proposed his scheme rather late for the hiring of a suitable house: he had, in the end, been obliged to take one in Harley Street, which, James told me, was not a genteel address, being in general the residence of people such as bankers or merchants or nabobs.

'Nabobs?' I exclaimed. 'That sounds dreadfully vulgar. What on earth are nabobs?'

'Those got rich from trade in India, by fair means or foul,' he said. 'They have influence; they flaunt their wealth and their vulgar manners are annoying to polite society.'

I laughed. 'Such a pity there are no nabobs among my relations! That would give Lord Pangbourn a seizure! Could it be my uncle's direction has brought your cousin to his disapprobation? Do you think it might?'

'I doubt it. He knows who your uncle is, and the two of them have met.' He saw my look of enquiry and reminded me that both gentlemen had been present at our wedding.

'Oh, yes, of course. Well, they may have taken each other in dislike,' I said. 'Certainly, Sir Nicholas does not condemn me on account of Papa's family. Indeed, I think he would scorn to do so. Well, James, however your cousin objects, I hope you will not wish me to renounce my uncle. A paltry trick, that would be, after all his kindness to me.'

'You know very well I would not ask it.'

'Thomas,' I pursued, 'is one relation I could do without, but he is my cousin for all that. I would not deny it, even if His Lordship's doors were closed to me.'

James wanted me to wear some of my new finery when we paid our visit to Harley Street and I was not averse to the idea for I smarted, still, whenever I thought of Mama's unpleasantness at Christmas. Like a nabob, I would flaunt my fashion and Mama would be obliged to swallow her vexation.

So I wore a dark-brown pelisse and a hat with gold feathers and smiled at the appreciation in my husband's eyes and looked forward to seeing my uncle.

It was a fine day and we drove in an open carriage. I remained seated when we arrived at the house in Harley Street. James alighted and set the doorbell ringing.

The door was opened by a janitor: James was told the Kilburn servants were expected but not yet arrived, and we learnt that my uncle was to come on Wednesday week, as we had previously supposed.

'Curious,' remarked James as he clambered back into the carriage. 'Gideon must have been mistaken, after all. Why, Sarah, you are blushing! What is the matter?'

'I appear to be the object of some attention. Do you see that gentleman in the blue coat with silver buttons? He has been staring at me for some time. I declare, it puts me quite out of countenance!'

James laughed. 'You must accustom yourself to such, my dear! You are a beautiful woman, dressed in the best of fashion. You are bound to attract attention, you know.'

'I think it is not that. Do we know him, James? I cannot help feeling I have seen him before, though it puzzles me to know where.'

James turned his head to scrutinize the stranger, who had been standing quite still with both hands folded over the knob of his cane. Now, meeting my husband's gaze, the gentleman smiled, touched his hat and turned and walked away.

'I have never seen him before,' said James. 'He does not seem ill-disposed, however. How old would you say he was? Fifty? Sixty?'

'Somewhere between, I fancy.'

'And he is handsome for a man of his age; he has the kind of face that is not easily forgot. Had you met him before, Sarah, surely you would know him.' He laughed. 'Depend upon it, my dear, he is a connoisseur of beauty, who was spellbound by the vision of your loveliness.'

I made no attempt to quarrel with this explanation, for there had been visitors at Kilburn Hall who affected to be entranced and I had fully expected to meet their like in town. Neither had I opportunity to chase the will o' the wisp in my memory, for James had returned his thoughts to that other teasing matter: how Lord Pangbourn had come to suppose Sir Nicholas was in town and what had brought about his disapproval of the connection.

We talked it over without reaching any sensible conclusion, agreeing only that it would be foolish and theatrical for James to visit his cousin demanding an explanation.

'I think we should go about,' said James. 'We will pay some calls on my other relations, mention how your uncle is expected, learn what they know.' He gave directions to the coachman and sat back. 'I hope we may find the Merediths at home. You will like Emma, I think. She is the best and dearest of my cousins.'

With his affection for the lady so clearly stated, I hoped I could like her, too. She was, in fact, a second cousin, six years older than myself, and her relationship to James was not, as the Pangbourns was, through his mother, but his father.

She was good-looking, not quite as tall as I, and in spite of her relationship to James being a distant one, there was something of my husband in the calm brown eyes and the humorous curl of the mouth. Her husband was fair-haired, with an agreeable countenance and equally agreeable manners.

'So,' she said, after we had exchanged civilities and sat down, 'you are the fair beauty who used arts and allurements to entrap James into marriage?'

'Emma!' protested her husband, but she was laughing and so was James. 'Madam, I beg you will paid no heed to my wife. She is joking you.'

'My dear Charles, Sarah had my measure the moment she set eyes on me and she knows perfectly well I am joking,' she said. 'Is that not so, Sarah?'

'I saw your design,' I said, 'though I must disclaim your opinion of my shrewdness. I do not pretend to have your measure entirely.'

'Another half-hour should do it,' said James. Then, to our hostess, 'Already, Sarah knows Gideon for a cold fish.'

'I knew we should deal famously together!' exclaimed Emma in delight, whilst I blushed and protested to my husband that never had I said any such thing.

James did not disclose what His Lordship had said to me, though in talk of the Pangbourns the others were more outspoken than myself. Presently, James turned the talk to the expected arrival of my uncle, with Mama and Harriet.

The others expressed only the polite interest of strangers. 'We have never met Sir Nicholas,' said Emma, 'although James has mentioned him from time to time. I look forward to making his acquaintance.'

'Would he be related to Thomas Kilburn?' asked her husband.

'Sir Nicholas is his father.'

'Ah!' Mr Meredith coughed and looked a little confused and embarrassed, for we had deduced there was some meaning in his exclamation, but he quickly began to talk of something else.

'It was because he felt he could not speak openly with ladies present,' James explained after we left. 'Which leaves me to deduce that Thomas is behaving in his usual shameless fashion. I shall draw Meredith aside tonight, and hope to learn the particulars. That is why I invited them to share our box at the theatre. I trust you do not object?'

'No, not at all. I find them most agreeable. I own, I am excited. My first visit to the theatre!'

'I hope it meets your expectations.'

We spent an evening enjoying pleasurable entertainment, though I could not help feeling a little anxiety: my husband had taken Mr Meredith for an airing in the corridor during the first interval, and returned with a very grave expression. He saw my anxious look and smiled and shook his head, meaning he could not discuss it until later.

When we were home and retired for the night I heard what he

had learnt. What had taken Mr Meredith a long time to tell was expressed to me very quickly.

'Thomas is gambling heavily, losing too much and, Meredith suspects, but says he cannot be certain, that he is borrowing from the money-lenders.'

'Oh, no!' I exclaimed in dismay. 'And my poor uncle will be obliged to pay his debts, when he has all the expense of rebuilding Kilburn Hall. How can Thomas be so thoughtless?'

'As yet I am persuaded Sir Nicholas has no knowledge of it. Much as I detest the notion of tale-bearing, I fear I must tell him. It would do him no service to conceal this intelligence.'

'Must you?'

'I must; but though I would trust Meredith's word, I cannot speak to Sir Nicholas on the strength of hearsay alone. I must observe for myself what Thomas is about. Which means,' he grimaced, 'that I must frequent a few gaming houses!'

'James, I mislike this notion!' I spoke in quick alarm. 'Do not forget, we have reason to believe Thomas wishes you ill. You must be careful, you must take someone with you!'

'My dear, do not make yourself uneasy! There will be company within, he will not attack me! And when I leave I shall send a porter to find a sedan chair. With my infirmity,' he smiled, 'that will occasion no surprise, even though most gentlemen choose to walk. Have no fear, Sarah, I shall take no risks. But it troubles me that I shall be obliged to leave you alone.'

'Sir! Do you not know it is most unfashionable for married couples to spend all their time together?'

'So it is,' he said, reaching for me. 'Except when their name is Foster.'

I sighed and forgot our troubles in the delight of our coupling and afterwards, drowsy, we settled down to sleep. And in that semi-conscious state between sleep and waking, of all the events of this day, the memory that came into my floating mind was of a gentleman in a blue coat with silver buttons, and at the same time came words from a song:

119

Where hast t'been since I saw thee?

Instantly, I was wide awake and sitting bolt upright. 'James!' I gasped. 'James, I know who it was!'

'Huh? What? Who?'

'The man who was watching me in Harley Street, this morning. James, it was Mr Benjamin!'

Eleven

James yawned, but he got up and rekindled a candle from the dying embers of the fire and, when the room was lit, he turned to me with a frown.

'How can you be so certain?' he asked. 'This morning you had no notion.'

'James, it is more than six years since I saw him! He was bearded then, and shabbily dressed, and how should I be expected to recognize him straight away, him being clean shaven and looking so fine? I think he was uncertain of me, too, because I look very different from the way I looked at fifteen. I am taller now, and no longer fat and spotty, as I was then.'

James found that diverting. 'Were you fat and spotty?'

'Indeed I was! I cannot tell you how it pained me!'

'Well, yours has been a natural improvement,' he observed, 'but I find it hard to believe a man could rise from vagrant to Harley Street beau. His coat was made by no mean tailor, as I judge, and the buttons were silver. He was altogether attired in costly fashion. Can you account for such change in his fortunes?'

'I cannot, but I do not find it impossible. How can we tell? Much may happen in six years. Mr Benjamin must have made himself useful to someone and thus procured advancement.'

'Honest advancement?' asked James sceptically.

'I cannot feel he would do otherwise.'

James was clearly doubtful. 'You may be right,' he said at last. 'I hope you are, because for your sake I feel goodwill towards Mr Benjamin, and it is pleasing to think he has means at his disposal.' He yawned again. 'Sarah, I am tired, my thoughts are in a muddle, I make no sense of them. We can talk in the morning, but now I must sleep.'

I had woken him on the verge of sleep and now I felt some compunction for having disturbed him so. He put out the candle, and was asleep within seconds.

I lay beside him, tired myself, but restless also, fretting a little because I had not instantly recognized Mr Benjamin and taken the opportunity to speak with him. And now, in the dark, as I tried to compose myself, my certainty wavered and I could no longer know whether he was indeed Mr Benjamin.

'The case is confusing,' said James, when I made this rather shame-faced confession the next morning. 'We cannot be certain. But he was staring at you, Sarah, and you were puzzled by a sense of something familiar: to me, it appears that each of you half-recognized the other, so for the moment we may suppose it was he. We may chance upon the gentleman again, for we will be visiting in Harley Street. Should we encounter him we may have speech with him and settle the matter.'

That day, James had business matters to attend to, so he had urged me to engage myself with Emma who invited me to a morning ball, explaining that such gatherings were for those who wished to practise or learn new dances. I went, and was introduced to new acquaintances and found myself an object of admiration to a certain gentleman.

'I cannot imagine why Mr Roxwell troubles to pay me so much attention,' I said, flushed and displeased by that gentleman's fulsome compliments. 'He knows I am a married woman. What does he mean by it?'

'It is precisely because you *are* married,' Emma explained. 'He is too careful to pay marked attentions to unmarried ladies. I would not be at all surprised should you gather about you a court of such gallants. Have no fear: he will not step beyond what is pleasing.'

'I do not find it pleasing to have poetry misquoted at me.'

Emma giggled. 'Did you tell him so? I meant he would not act with any want of propriety.' She paused a little thoughtfully, then added, 'Some there are, who might. Sarah; you will not take it amiss should I venture a little advice?'

'Concerning those who would step beyond the bounds of propriety? Madam, I assure you. . . .'

'You may be tempted,' said Emma. 'You must know that in our society, affairs are tolerated, providing one is discreet. With beauty such as yours, and a husband who is by no means a fine example of manhood, there will be—'

'I mislike the way you speak of my husband, madam,' I said stiffly. 'His infirmity is no fault of his own and he bears what he has to bear with dignity and grace. I would not have him otherwise.'

She stared at me in astonishment and I stared back, angry how so many considered James a lesser man by reason of his lameness. I had looked at her husband, handsome and amiable, certainly, but I thought James had more strength of character.

Emma's astonishment gave way to giggles, which disconcerted me and when she recovered, she said, 'I fear I did not make myself clear, Sarah. There are many gentlemen who will interpret your situation in a way that suits them: more than most ladies, I think, you may be troubled by those who believe they have only to cast out lures.'

'Any such will quickly discover his mistake,' I said drily.

During the next few days I spent more time with Emma than with my husband. She introduced me to two other ladies, her particular friends, and I found myself popular with them. Four of us together, we visited exhibitions, took airings in the park, and I listened to their confidences, ventured a few opinions and heard more gossip than I wished, a circumstance which made me wary of betraying confidences of my own.

James was following his self-imposed task of discovering how far Thomas was taking his excesses, a task which had him out until dawn and sleeping until noon. All he had so far learnt was that my cousin did not frequent any of the more genteel gaming houses.

'Why are you looking at me like that, Sarah?' he said. 'Do you fear I shall be ruined? No, no, my dear! To own the truth,' he said smiling, 'I have to employ all my skill to be certain of not winning too often, for it is not my design to make myself unpopular. I go to hear the gossip, I sit quietly, I watch the play and when I play myself I win first and then take care to lose my winnings. Except,' he added mischievously, 'when I played piquet with Gideon. I betrayed no knowledge of what he said to you, but I had my revenge in another way.'

I laughed, but said, 'I had no fear of your being ruined.'

He had skill, acquired in boyhood. Often suffering acute discomfort when subjected to the latest notion of a remedy for his lameness, James had found distraction by playing card games against himself, studying several hands at once with fierce concentration.

'By the way,' he said, 'someone has been asking after you: the Honourable Frederick Lyndhurst, no less. He asked if he might wait upon you, one morning.'

'Frederick Lyndhurst?' I frowned. 'That name I have heard before, but I cannot remember where. Who is he, James?'

'He attended our Boxing Day ball. You remarked him particularly, as I recollect.'

'Did I? Ah, yes, now I have it. He was the young man who made himself agreeable to Harriet. Perhaps I shall contrive to renew her acquaintance with him, and hope he will take her mind off Thomas. Which reminds me, James,' I said anxiously, 'have you any intelligence of Thomas?'

'I have heard where he goes, no more. I fear it is not a genteel establishment: the stakes are high and I am told the play is suspect. I would not visit by choice, and I hope once will be enough.'

He went that evening and returned earlier than usual. Thomas had been there, he said, but he had taken exception to James's presence, flushing and demanding to know what he was doing there, angry, and accusing James of spying on him.

'Which is true, I suppose,' admitted James ruefully. 'Though I did not say so. I merely asked him why he thought I should wish to, which did not improve his temper. He was obliging enough to tell me my society was abhorrent to him and he would not stay to endure it. So he left and I had no opportunity to observe what he was about.'

'So all has been for nothing!' I exclaimed.

'Not quite: some little I heard, for his behaviour caused embarrassment and then talk, enough to confirm what I learnt from Meredith. I shall advise Sir Nicholas what is said, and he may take action as he chooses. I can do no more.'

'Then you may begin to keep regular hours again,' I said, regarding him critically. 'All this dissipation does not agree with you, James, I declare you are looking quite pale. Well, tomorrow is Sunday and you, sir, shall pay heed to your wife. We may take a stroll in the park after service, and spend the rest of the day quietly together.'

'How agreeable that will be.'

I was as thankful as James to take the opportunity to rest, for I felt London did not agree with me. My constitution is generally robust, but during these last few days I had been overtaken sometimes by feelings of lassitude, which I attributed to the smoke and noise and bustle in town.

'I shall become accustomed, I dare say,' I told James. 'I have been spoilt these last few years, by remaining in the country. But should you wish a return to Foster Leigh, James, it will be no hardship for me to give up London.'

On the following day we gave a small dinner party, inviting the Merediths and those other ladies with whom I had become acquainted, with their husbands. I had been introduced to these two gentlemen and we had exchanged civilities, but so far I had no opportunity to become acquainted.

That evening, I understood why those two ladies so often

sought feminine company. Their husbands were handsome, impeccable in their attire and they could talk with great animation of sporting matters. We heard a great deal about field sports, prize fights and horse races, but when the conversation turned to other topics, they had nothing to say.

'Indeed, I wonder how it came about they could refrain from their sporting interests long enough to attach their wives,' I said to James, after they had left. 'I feel I should apologize for inviting them, but truly, I had no notion how it would be.'

The Honourable Frederick Lyndhurst called the next morning and he brought with him his sister. The reason was quickly explained: Miss Lyndhurst was nineteen years old, and engaged to be married to Sir Martin Colworth, a gentleman not yet known to me, but who had recently inherited his title and an estate in Derbyshire, not far from Foster Leigh. When Miss Lyndhurst became Lady Colworth, she would be our neighbour.

I regarded the lady with some interest. She was no beauty, but pleasing for all that, with straight brown hair and hazel eyes. She was reserved, but no more than is proper upon a first acquaintance, and I thought she was intelligent. She would be a welcome addition to our neighbourhood.

'A pleasing lady,' said James later. 'She will be an agreeable neighbour. What of Lyndhurst, Sarah? There are many ladies who would like to attach him; he is considered a matrimonial prize, you know. I fear you will be disappointed if you hope to match him with Harriet.'

'Do not make yourself uneasy,' I said. 'I assure you I have no such ambition.' Then, with a surge of ill-humour which is unlike me, I went on pettishly, 'After all, he could hardly wish to connect himself with *my* family, could he? A gamekeeper's granddaughter? As I have so recently been reminded, we are too ramshackle by half!'

'I do not venture to speak for Lyndhurst's views on that subject,' said James coolly. 'I merely point out that he is accustomed to having ladies set their caps at him.'

'Well, I shall throw him together with Harriet, if I can, because if she cannot attach him, she is vain enough to imagine she may and that, I hope, will deter her from setting her cap at Thomas!'

'Some ladies,' observed James, 'are perfectly capable of setting their caps at half-a-dozen gentlemen, all at once.'

'That sounds like Harriet!' I admitted. I apologized for my ill-humour, attributing it to nervous qualms at the prospect of spending the evening under the cold scrutiny of Lord Pangbourn.

I took great care when preparing myself for that evening. Lord Pangbourn would not say my appearance did no credit to James, even though he deplored my upstart pretensions.

When shopping with Lady Pangbourn I had purchased an olive-green gauze over an under-dress of gold silk, which was perfect to wear with my emeralds. Matilda had taken up my hair in a plain, severe style in contrast to the prevailing fashion, but she said it would lend distinction to my appearance and I was by no means averse to that.

Upon arriving at the house in Grosvenor Square, we were greeted by His Lordship with urbane civility and by his lady with that affection which she bestowed on all her acquaintance.

Lord and Lady Lyndhurst were among the many new acquaintance presented to us that evening. Miss Lyndhurst and her brother were with them and all four showed a flattering preference for our society, a circumstance which did me no harm at all with the other guests. We sat with them, and Miss Lyndhurst requested me to tell her a little about Derbyshire.

Dancing began and I did not lack partners. I spent intervals with James, but he was well acquainted with many of the guests and had company when I left his side.

Since the Lyndhursts had been so obliging as to favour us with their notice, I felt less dismayed by James's lordly cousin. Nevertheless, I allowed myself to hope the evening would pass without any further ado with Lord Pangbourn.

It was a forlorn hope: for the first time since we arrived, James and I were enjoying a few quiet minutes together when His Lordship approached. He addressed himself chiefly to James, but he was civil enough to include me in the conversation and when the set began to form for the next dances he enquired of me who was my partner.

'It is my intention to sit with my husband, sir,' I said.

'Oh, come! James may claim your company whenever he wishes it, he may spare you for one half-hour, is that not so, Cousin? Madam, I beg you will honour me with this dance.'

James smiled at me and flickered an eyelid and I, not very willingly, said, 'Very well, sir, if you insist.'

He danced well, this cousin-by-marriage, and though it was churlish of me to hold it against him, I did. I was reminded of James's shame-faced admission of jealousy and I resented, on his behalf, the fates which had supplied this less-deserving gentleman with an ease of movement denied to my husband.

'I am sorry,' he said with a curl of his lips, 'to have dragged you away from your husband's side. Such a wrench it must be for you!'

My irritation mounted, but I only said, 'It is of no consequence: however one feels, it is necessary, sometimes, to give way to the demands of society. As you so penetratingly observed, a husband and wife have many opportunities for spending time together.'

'More, perhaps, than one might wish for?'

'Do you speak of your own experience, sir, or do you presume to speak of mine?'

I was passing under his arm as I spoke and I heard his sharp intake of breath. 'Upon my soul, you are uncommonly pert for a gamekeeper's granddaughter!'

I smiled, pleased because I had nettled him.

His Lordship continued to make his cynical observations. I countered them as best I could, but I was thankful when the dance ended and I could return to James.

'I beg you will not oblige me to accept another partner,' I said. 'I really must sit for a while!'

'Has Gideon upset you again?'

He had not. I did not like him well enough to care for anything he might think.

'No, but my slippers are pinching. They grow ever more uncomfortable, and I fancy my feet are swollen.'

This was enough to have James making polite excuses for me, but it was only part of my trouble: several times that evening I had been overtaken by a now familiar feeling of lassitude and with it came a slight queasiness. They were trivial complaints, and I made no mention of them, but I wished an end to the party.

My wish was granted within the hour and I sank thankfully into the velvet squabs in our carriage. As we set off, James said, 'Did Gideon make any further mention of your uncle?'

'He did not, and I had no thought of asking, for he was making himself disagreeable in quite another way. Does it matter?'

'I cannot imagine how he thought Sir Nicholas was in town last week, when he does not arrive until tomorrow.'

'Perhaps he mistook someone who resembled my uncle.'

Not wishing to appear inattentive, we paid a visit to the house in Harley Street the day after my relations arrived. It was raining that day, and we had the hood drawn over the carriage and though I looked about me, I saw no sign of the silver-buttoned gentleman.

Arriving, we were shown into their morning-room and I was shocked to see Mama pale and drawn, propped up by cushions, with a heavily bandaged ankle resting on a footstool.

'A most unfortunate accident,' said Sir Nicholas. 'Your mama stumbled as she alighted from the carriage. We feared her ankle was broken, but the surgeon says it is only a sprain. But she must not attempt to walk for a week, at least.'

'That surgeon is a fool,' sniffed Mama. 'Samuel says a pad soaked in cold water and pressed against the affected part is the best way to relieve a sprain. But would he hear of it? Oh no! What can a military man know of injuries? More than most, I told him, but nothing would do for him but to apply hot poultices and now I am blistered, besides hurting abominably!'

'Do you have some laudanum, Mama?' I asked. 'Shall I procure some for you? It would give you respite from the pain.'

'I have some, but I do not hold with frequent doses. Laudanum is an opium drug, it can induce dependency.'

James ventured the opinion that Samuel's remedy could do no harm, so we tried it and sent out a servant to purchase a soothing lotion for her blisters and when we had fussed around her for a while she became easier, still refusing laudanum but promising to take a few drops before retiring for the night.

'The difficulty now,' said Sir Nicholas, 'is that until your mama recovers, Harriet is without a chaperon.' He brightened as he looked at me. 'Unless, Sarah, you would be so very obliging as to take on that duty?'

Twelve

James would not allow my uncle to impose Harriet on me.

'I fear there will be times when it is not possible for Sarah to chaperon her sister,' he said. 'We will do what we may, of course, but we have our own engagements.'

I had a notion by which I might procure introductions for her and I said, 'I am going to Hookam's library, this morning. You may accompany me, Harriet, and choose some books for Mama.'

'A capital notion!' said Sir Nicholas. 'Your mama will be pleased to have some reading to while away the hours.'

James suggested we should take our carriage and he would wait for our return. Our eyes met and he nodded: I knew he would take the opportunity to consult with Sir Nicholas about Thomas.

Thomas was the first person Harriet asked about as soon as we were on our way. She wanted to know if I had seen him since coming to town.

'I have not,' I said. 'James had a chance encounter with him, but he was abominably rude, so to own the truth I would rather not see him. Why do you ask?'

I thought I knew why she asked, but she surprised me by saying, 'Sir Nicholas is in some perturbation of mind. He has heard nothing from Thomas for some time, but when I quizzed him he laughed and said Thomas was not one who was forever writing letters. That was a few weeks ago and he was not concerned, not then. But I think he has since become uneasy: he has a notion of something amiss. I wondered what you knew.'

It came as a relief to learn that Sir Nicholas was prepared, in some part, for what James had to say, but I felt I was not at liberty to disclose information to Harriet. I said only, 'I believe Thomas is in good health, but more than that I cannot tell you.'

Some days ago, I had voiced my concerns to James. 'Clearly, Thomas cannot continue in this fashion. I confess, I am at a loss: short of placing him under lock and key, so little can be done to restrain him.'

'He could find himself under lock and key, in a debtor's prison,' said James drily. 'Oh, do not look at me like that, Sarah, your uncle will not permit it. But if Thomas has debts to be paid, it will be possible to make conditions. I think he should be compelled to take up a commission in the army. I mean to suggest as much. Your cousin would benefit from regimental discipline.'

'I believe my uncle once held that same opinion,' I said. 'But nothing was done because my aunt shrank from the notion. Thomas was her only child, she would not have him exposed to the dangers of a military career.'

Had my cousin shown an interest in the management of the Kilburn estates, the scruple might be honoured, but he had not, and neither had he displayed interest in any other worthwhile occupation. As far as we could ascertain, Thomas spent his days in idleness and dissipation. If he was not to ruin himself and Kilburn, something would have to be done. James's proposal made sense.

The idea pleased me also, because it would get Thomas out of my sister's way. Harriet's discourse suggested she had abandoned her ambition to attach Thomas, but given the least encouragement it could be revived. Harriet was one who would perceive and welcome opportunity, and shrug and look elsewhere if opportunity was not forthcoming. With Thomas in the army she would have to look elsewhere.

Harriet's present thoughts were turning another way: she said,

'Sir Nicholas thinks Thomas is quite unable to overcome his disappointment over your refusal to marry him.' Her tone was altered now, and spiced with amusement. 'Were you very cruel to him, Sarah?'

'Cruel? No, of course not, how absurd you are!' I said crossly. 'Short of accepting his proposals, I was as civil and forbearing as may be.'

'At Kilburn, they are saying Thomas would have borne it had you preferred any other gentleman, but he feels it the more because you chose to marry Mr Foster.'

'Then I have wounded his vanity,' I said, 'not his heart.'

Harriet shrugged. 'Perhaps you have wounded both.'

I was spared from answering, for our carriage had turned into Bond Street, drawing up outside the library, and within, as I had hoped, I encountered some of my acquaintance and introduced Harriet.

Among our encounters was the lady who was to be our hostess that evening, and she was obliging enough to beg Harriet to join us. My sister accepted the invitation prettily enough, but when we were alone, she was inclined to be scornful.

'Such dissipation! A card party! Even in Northampton we can do better. I own, I hoped for dancing, at least.'

'You should not despise any opportunity to widen your circle of acquaintance,' I said. 'Do not forget, one introduction may lead to others. Well, I may take you there, Harriet, but do not accept invitations for tomorrow evening, for I cannot escort you. James and I have a dinner engagement.'

We had, that morning, received a note from Lady Lyndhurst, inviting us to dine with the family. Sir Martin Colworth, the gentleman who was betrothed to Miss Lyndhurst, had returned to town and Lady Lyndhurst wished the opportunity to make us acquainted with our future neighbour.

I was about to tell Harriet all about it by way of reminding her of Mr Lyndhurst, but she was looking in a shop window, admiring a bonnet. I purchased it for her and an Indian silk shawl for Mama.

Harriet then expressed a wish to visit a linen-draper.

'My uncle has given me some money for clothes and you may depend upon it, I mean to be in fashion!'

Whilst she was deliberating over muslins and ribbons and gloves, Arabella's words came back to me:

'I cannot disbelieve her when she says she would be Lady Someone Rich.'

I gave up the idea of telling her about Mr Lyndurst, for fear of starting her ambitions. It would be more appropriate, at this present, to issue a warning, so when we returned to our carriage, I told her of Lord Pangbourn.

'I will not repeat everything he said,' I went on, 'but he made it clear he thought James had married beneath him. A gamekeeper's granddaughter! Too ramshackle by half, that is what he thinks.'

'Then you must persuade him to hush it up!' said Harriet. She was laughing, not taking my meaning at all.

'He will not broadcast the fact. He merely let me know my birth is a matter for disapprobation. And the fact is, my dear, his views are shared by many in polite society. There are some,' I went on, 'who would overcome their scruples in the matter of a lady's birth, had she fortune to recommend her. But with neither birth nor fortune, even your undoubted charms may not avail you. I do advise you, Harriet, to moderate your ambition. Avoid becoming a subject of gossip and, more importantly, avoid disappointment.'

'I doubt I can moderate my ambition,' said Harriet, but she was laughing again. 'Have no fear, Sister. I know how to moderate my conduct.'

With that, I was obliged to be satisfied. I returned her to Harley Street and found James sitting with Mama, Sir Nicholas having straight away determined to call on Thomas in his lodgings.

Mama said her ankle was easier, liked her shawl, admired Harriet's purchases and approved our choice of books. Never had I seen her in such good humour and I discovered James had not only promised to take her in our carriage for an airing in the park as soon as the weather permitted, he had also hinted at a box at the theatre.

'And I declare it is no hardship for me to sit with my feet up today, indeed it is a most unaccustomed luxury and the weather does not tempt one to be out of doors! I shall indulge myself with tea and toast and if you can find my spectacles, Harriet, I shall be happy to read as long as there is daylight. *Evelina*! How delightful. Yes, I read it once before but that was many years ago. I shall enjoy renewing my acquaintance with Lord Orville.'

We left after fifteen minutes. James asked if I would care to visit an exhibition, but I was again feeling that lassitude from being in town. 'Can we not go home? To own the truth, I wish nothing so much as to rest. How tired I am of being tired! I declare, I am quite out of patience with myself.'

'Sarah, do you think you should see a physician?'

'Goodness, no! I am not ill, just tired. Did you speak to Sir Nicholas? Harriet said he was already in some perturbation of mind about Thomas.'

'Yes, I told him, and you are right, he had received a hint from another friend, so he was not wholly surprised. I offered to assist, should he have need of money. A gift he will not accept, but a loan without interest will ease his difficulty.'

'Oh James, how thoughtful and generous you are!'

By the time we reached home the sky was darkening for another downpour and we were happy to settle ourselves by the fire in our sitting-room. It was wholly delicious to be sitting comfortably indoors, drinking tea and listening to the wind and rain and hail outside.

We took Harriet to the card party that evening and she behaved very prettily, just as a young lady ought, conversing easily, not at all abashed at being quizzed by the older ladies, but revealing no more than was proper.

At supper, conversation turned to a balloon ascent which was to take place in Hyde Park on Saturday. Emma and Charles

Meredith had the notion of getting up a party of friends to witness the event.

'I have a matter of business that cannot be delayed,' said James regretfully, when we were invited to join them. He had promised to meet with Sir Nicholas to learn what he had set in motion with Thomas and to make whatever dispositions he could to assist. 'But my business need not prevent you going, Sarah, if you would like to.'

The Merediths offered to take Harriet and me. Others expressed an interest in joining us, the matter of carriages was decided, and in the end we had a party of fifteen.

'Such an event must attract a considerable crowd,' said Harriet, as we conveyed her home. 'I may hope to widen my circle of acquaintance even more. How fortunate I can speak of my uncle, Sir Nicholas; it is most influential. By the way, Sarah, did you hear what Mrs Stanway had to say about Thomas?'

'I did not,' I said, startled. 'Is he causing gossip?'

'Not precisely, no. She says he has formed an attachment for Earl Cardew's daughter, Lady Julia.' There was amusement in her voice and a hint of malice directed at me. 'Our cousin grows ambitious! Will she have him, do you think?'

Why such intelligence should make me uneasy, I know not, but it did. I only said, 'Not being acquainted with the lady, I cannot say.'

'It would be quite advantageous, would it not, to be related to an earl's daughter?'

By no means mortified at the notion of Thomas marrying another, Harriet was now considering how it might open up her own prospects in society. She became quite animated on the subject.

I said nothing. When we had taken Harriet home, I turned to James. 'I fear this will lead to trouble. Did you know of it?'

'I did not, and neither do I share your perturbation. Lady Julia is blessed with a large fortune, Sarah, any number of gentlemen have tried to fix their interest with her.'

'Are you acquainted with the lady?'

'Not well enough to judge how far she will favour your cousin. She may do so, but I doubt her father will allow her to bestow her hand and fortune on Thomas. Cardew is shrewd enough, you may depend upon it, he will have Thomas's measure.'

'Perhaps that is why I am uneasy!' I shook my head in perplexity. 'You would think if Thomas has ambition there, he would seek to recommend himself to her family! Yet he does nothing of the sort. Instead, he keeps low company, he gambles recklessly, he squanders his substance and he must know his doings will be noticed. Has he no sense at all?'

'I am not in his confidence,' said James. 'I suspect he seeks to increase his fortune and is not particular whether he gains it at play or by marriage.'

I forgot Thomas then, because I heard in his voice a tightening of the vowels, a sure sign he was in pain, and my attention was called to easing his cramps.

It rained again the next day, but James's cramps were a consequence of neglecting exercise and I was determined he should not suffer so again. We took our carriage to the park, waiting within until the downpour ceased, then set off, walking comfortably side by side, with me carrying an umbrella in case the rain returned.

On such a day, few had ventured out of doors: we had a wide area of the park to ourselves and we began our nonsenses again, making ourselves laugh. And once again, I reflected how fortunate I was to be married to James.

He was generous with money, but he could afford to be, and though his gifts pleased me, I was better pleased by his thoughtfulness and his manner towards me. Admittedly, there were times when I had to coax him into better humour, but these were short in duration and I did not begrudge it because I knew he had much to bear.

Our intimate life was a constant source of delight. Since overcoming my initial difficulty, I had discovered in myself a strong and passionate nature: I was easily aroused and soon discovered that far from disgusting him, as I had once feared it might, it was a joy to him.

At other times he was a good companion, even willing to talk over matters of business, which most gentlemen would not dream of discussing with their wives and he was attentive to what I had to say. As a rule, we were in accord, whether satisfying our carnal desires, or entering into serious discussion, or entertaining each other with jokes and nonsense, or simply being quiet and comfortable together.

I cannot disguise that James had characteristics which might, by some, be considered faults. There were times, when we were alone together, when he took a schoolboyish delight in making vulgar and indelicate remarks. Had he done so in company I might have been embarrassed, but he did not, and though I knew other ladies might be offended by such naughtiness, I confess, I found it rather endearing.

Neither could I blame him for his little jealousies, upon seeing less deserving creatures moving easily and partaking freely in activities denied to him. He acknowledged this failing and struggled to correct it, but I could sympathize with him and I also resented those who considered themselves superior for no better reason than that he was obliged to support himself with a crutch.

Since marrying James, I had watched other gentlemen.

Of those who were married, my observations had taught me how many husbands were neglectful, more intent on making their way in the world than in considering the happiness of their wives. Others were indifferent, pursuing their own sporting or gaming interests. Worst of all were those (I suspected Lord Pangbourn was one of them) who pursued other female companions.

Some gentlemen were attached to their wives. Sir Nicholas had been attached to my aunt, but that attachment had not progressed beyond fondness and a willingness to indulge: he had never confided in her or sought her opinion.

Henry's attachment to Arabella was more substantial, but

Henry was pedantic and dull, and far too starched in his notions: he would not have pleased me.

I thought Charles Meredith was attached to Emma, and though I found him pleasing, I liked him less than James. He was agreeable and willing to enter into any scheme which would please his wife, but he was earnest where James was shrewd, and he was too easily embarrassed.

Of all the married gentlemen I knew, James pleased me best.

In London, a number of single gentlemen paid attention to me, always ready to say pretty things. I had been told it was usual for young married ladies to gather a set of admirers, so I accepted the more restrained compliments with good humour and discouraged those gentlemen who showed a tendency to be too extravagant in their admiration.

James had remarked their attentions, and was not altogether pleased about it. 'Where did you meet that puppy Roxwell?'

'Emma introduced him,' I said. 'She says he has attached himself to me because he is wary of paying marked attentions to unmarried ladies.'

He raised his brows. 'And you believe it?'

'I can imagine no other reason why he, or any other gentleman, should flatter me with their attention.'

James found that diverting. 'Oh, Sarah! Never have I met a woman with so little vanity!'

'I believe they practise the art of paying compliments to learn what is pleasing and so ensure their own success when they meet the lady of their choice,' I said. 'I confess, I find their demands on my attention something of an imposition, and more to do with their vanity than mine. Why are you laughing?'

'I am thinking how they would be offended, could they hear you speak so.'

That evening we dined with the Lyndhursts, and we were introduced to the gentleman who was betrothed to Miss Lyndhurst, Sir Martin Colworth, recently become our neighbour.

I saw at once that here was a gentleman I could admire.

Sir Martin was handsome in a wholly masculine way, with strong features and dark hair and eyes. He was tall, he carried himself well and he was impeccably dressed without affecting any of the extravagances of fashion. His demeanour pleased me, also; his manners were gentlemanlike, but he was not pleasant by flatteries, nor by fussing needlessly over one's comfort, but by a simple and calm civility. There was an air of steadiness about him and I was instinctively persuaded he was a man of sound principle and strong character.

He had recently inherited his title and estates from Sir William Colworth and said it seemed strange that he should do so, for his elderly relative had fallen out with his family years ago, and had never been known to him.

He had been into Derbyshire and found the estates had been mismanaged and the house neglected. James knew how much needed to be done, and upon discovering my husband was a man of sense, Sir Martin spoke of plans for restoring the house and improving the lot of his tenants. Moreover, he was willing to listen, and paid attention as James told him of men who could advise him with advanced notions on agriculture.

His manner to Miss Lyndhurst pleased me, also. He was calm but attentive, clearly devoted to her, but not allowing his affection to embarrass her or the company. There was good understanding between them and I thought Miss Lyndhurst was a very fortunate young woman to attach such a man.

Listening to all the talk, I remained silent, regarding him and reflecting, absently, that he was the kind of gentleman with whom I myself might have fallen in love, had I not first had the great good fortune to meet and marry James.

This feeling was agreeable, but the thought was no more than an indistinct murmur and might have passed without my paying it any more attention had it not been given a sharp nudge when a loud and indignant denial echoed through my mind.

'He is crippled, ungainly, wholly repugnant! You cannot wish to marry him.'

But I had wished to marry James! Crippled and ungainly he was, and sometimes I was pained on his behalf, but never did I find my husband repugnant. In fact, he pleased me better than any other gentleman, better even than this handsome young man with whom I could not, at first sight, find fault.

I looked at Sir Martin again, now awakened to the knowledge that though I could like and approve him, neither he nor any other gentleman could ever be as dear to me as James.

Astonished by the power and strength of my own feelings, I was inattentive to most of the conversation.

I looked at James and saw he was regarding our new acquaintance with less enthusiasm, though I could not imagine why. Then I saw a fleeting sulky expression and understood. Once again, my husband was envious of a gentleman who had that ease of movement which he was denied.

I felt tears prickle behind my eyes. I longed to be alone with him, to tell him all my love.

Good manners demanded I should exert myself to please the company, but I confess, I recall little of that evening. I could not forbear from the occasional brief withdrawal, letting my mind become occupied with rehearsals: how I would comfort James, tell him my love, and anticipating his reaction.

Yet I was quite unaccountably awkward and nervous when, after we had taken our leave, I was alone with him in our carriage. James was quiet and it did not seem altogether appropriate to make a sudden announcement of that nature: better, I thought, to wait a little while, until a suitable opening presented itself.

So, instead, I made some trifling remark about the Lyndhursts and said I thought Sir Martin was a pleasing gentleman and would be an agreeable neighbour.

'Oh, yes, I saw how you were taken with him!'

I stiffened. Usually, James had the sense to recognize his own jealousy and dismiss it, but today there was a harsh note in his voice, a hint of anger and I turned to him in surprise. 'Why, whatever is the matter, James? Did you not like him?'

'How should I, when it was manifestly clear how you liked him well enough for both of us? I saw all the sheep's eyes you were making at him! I declare, I was never so mortified!'

I went hot, squirming with embarrassment. Had I been making sheep's eyes? Had I, in the delight of realizing my feelings for my husband, so far forgot myself as to fix my gaze intently on the gentleman who had brought me to that realization?

'James, I am sorry!' I said quickly. 'Was I staring at him? Well, if I was, I assure you it was in absence of mind. My thoughts were otherwise occupied.'

'Yes, I saw how your thoughts were occupied! A most agreeable neighbour indeed, and how much opportunity for knowing him better!'

'That is not what I was thinking.'

'Oh, come now! How do you think to deceive me, when I have seen all your interest in other gentlemen? Right from the start,' he went on, with a raging bitterness, 'almost as soon as we were married, you were looking about you! There is not one gentleman of our acquaintance who has escaped your notice!'

I was silent: I could not deny it, though I was appalled to discover what construction James had placed upon it, even more appalled to see how I had pained him.

We reached home. Indoors, I followed him into the sitting-room and said, 'James, you cannot believe I would—'

'Enter into liaisons with all of them? No, no, you are far too nice in your notions. But now I see what you have been about, I see what you have been looking for! A gentleman to take your fancy, a gentleman with wit enough to be discreet! He is handsome, my dear, is he not? And very conveniently situated, so soon to be our neighbour! So many opportunities for meeting, so many opportunities for teaching him to appreciate your undoubted charms! What could be better?'

'How can you be so absurd!'

'Absurd?' he repeated. The word seemed to strike him forcibly. 'But I am absurd, am I not? What could be more absurd than an

142

ill-favoured cripple, tempting a beauty into marriage with promise
of riches! Capering around, doing everything in his power to
please, nothing too much trouble! To be sure, I do not wonder at
your encouragement! Such a constant source of amusement, so
very diverting, how you must have laughed!'

'James, I beg you, do not torment yourself so! Come now, put
this nonsense out of your mind, for I promise you, it never entered
mine!'

'Oh, spare me your cajolery, it is wasted on me now! Every suspicion forced on me during the few months of our marriage has,
this evening, been confirmed! Well, Madam Wife, I will tell you
now, however tolerant society is of such discreet little affairs, you
will not find me so complaisant! I will have no scandal in my
household. Do you understand?'

'I had no thought of such,' I said coldly. 'And I doubt I could
seduce Sir Martin if I wished it, which I do not! I have not forgotten, sir, even if you have, that there is another lady in the reckoning. Sir Martin is betrothed to Miss Lyndhurst and he is devoted to
her, he has no wish for me!'

'Pshaw! A poor little dab of a female such as she? She has connections and fortune also, I do not doubt. Good reason for all his
devotion to her at this present, but it will evaporate as soon as his
ring is on her finger!'

'That is nonsense and you know it!'

But he was in black humour, his judgement warped and blind to
truth. I stared, flinching at the antagonism in his eyes.

At last, I said, 'Well, if you cannot believe me virtuous, at least
believe I am no fool! As you point out, Miss Lyndhurst has connections, powerful connections. who would very quickly rally to
her cause should I betray designs on her husband!'

I waited, but he was still watching me with hard, angry eyes. It
hurt that he could so misjudge me, but I could not think of blaming him. Rather, I was dismayed that my own thoughtlessness had
brought him such pain, for I knew how he had to bear many careless slights in addition to his lameness.

'I am sorry,' I said in a milder tone, 'if any conduct of mine has brought you to this misapprehension. I would not willingly pain you so. Indeed, James, you have mistaken me.'

He showed no sign of relenting and I saw no persuasion of mine would avail, not until this mood left him. I sighed and said, 'Well, you are angry, too angry to be rational, and I cannot make you understand. I shall leave you now. We may discuss the matter when you are calmer.'

I went towards the door. but his words halted me. 'We shall never discuss this matter again, never!'

There was a broken note in his voice, which almost had me rushing towards him. But when I turned, I saw his expression and thought better of it.

'We will not speak of it again,' he repeated.

I smiled at him. 'Oh yes,' I said gently, 'we will!'

Thirteen

I lay awake for many hours, hoping he would come to me and be comforted, but he did not. From time to time I was tempted to go in search of him and I was prevented only by my instinctive knowledge that, after such an episode, a declaration of love would not be kindly received.

'He would not believe it, not now,' I murmured aloud. 'But he will come to it. I shall prevail!'

It was late when I fell asleep and late when I woke and when I went downstairs to the breakfast-room I was wholly bemused to see Harriet there, happily drinking cocoa and eating plum cake.

'What a slug-a-bed you are, Sarah! You must hurry to be ready in time, for the Merediths will be here very soon.'

'The Merediths? What is this? Where is James?'

'Surely you have not forgotten?' she said. 'We are to watch the balloon ascent in Hyde Park!'

'Oh, that! Well, I had forgotten as a matter of fact, and I am by no means – where is James?'

'He is with Sir Nicholas,' said Harriet indifferently. 'I understand they have some business to discuss, he said you knew that. He was obliging enough to send me here in your carriage. I have sent it back, for the Merediths will convey us to the park. Do you wish for breakfast?'

My heart sank. What interest had I in balloons at such a time?

I wished nothing more than to see James and put right all the mis-understandings between us. Now I must resign myself to waiting, for I knew his business would take some time to arrange. I had no excuse for crying off, however little enthusiasm I felt for the excursion.

I sat down and took some tea and bread and butter, unable to occupy my mind as I wished because Harriet was demanding my attention with her chatter.

Her mind was once again occupied with Thomas. He had paid a morning visit yesterday, and had made himself agreeable, saying he was delighted they had come to town but he was shocked to find Mama laid up with a sprained ankle.

After enquiring how the rest of the family did and asking for news of all his Northampton acquaintance, Thomas had then expressed some disapprobation because Sir Nicholas could not bring them to a more genteel address.

'Had my father not insisted on selling our own house in town, this would not have happened,' he said. 'It is a great deal too bad of him! My dear Aunt, Cousin, you will not take it amiss if I venture a word of warning? The kind of people in this part of town are, I fear, all too likely to encroach on your good nature, should you allow yourselves to become friendly. You would be well advised not to encourage them, for most of them are not at all genteel, you know, and their acquaintance will do you no good in polite society.'

'So I told him not to make himself uneasy,' said Harriet brightly. 'For there is but one of our neighbours who has so far ventured a word, and he must be sixty years old, at least! I cannot abide an ageing coxcomb. I was very short with him, I can tell you. But Sarah, can you guess what Thomas intends?'

'How should I?'

'He means to take up a commission in the Guards! Is not that a famous notion? How handsome he will look in regimentals.'

So it seemed that Sir Nicholas had taken my husband's advice. I said nothing to Harriet. Instead, I ventured a little malice, saying it was to be hoped Lady Julia Cardew thought regimentals becoming.

'Oh, no, Sarah! All that is at an end, she cannot hope for him now! To be sure, I quizzed him and he admitted he had been taken with her, but had later discovered she was by no means as pleasing as he first thought. I believe there is hope for me yet.'

She continued with her prattle but I let my mind wander, impatient with the circumstances which separated me from James at a time when I most needed to be with him, and calculating how long I must wait before I could get him alone, let him know the truth, comfort him, make him happy and be happy again myself.

'Sarah, what is the matter with you, you are not usually so dull-witted.'

I roused myself. 'I beg your pardon, what did you say?'

'You should go upstairs and put on your outdoor clothes if we are not to keep the Merediths waiting.'

I sighed, wishing it would rain again and put a stop to the entertainment, but the weather was most disobligingly fair. So within a very short time I was in one of the four carriages conveying our party to Hyde Park.

The atmosphere was a little unpleasant, filled with a mix of smoke and steam escaping from an engine which was used to work the bellows. Billowing on the ground, growing larger all the time. lay a strangely shaped silken object, a profusion of scarlet and silver.

Men were running around, looking important and busy, some attending to the steam engine, others checking ropes and somewhere close by I heard a small boy pleading with his papa to ask the men to take him when they made the ascent in the balloon's basket.

The request was refused. Someone quipped 'Balloonatic!' and others laughed. The balloon continued to be inflated, eventually rising from the ground: the red and silver globe described an arc, and halted, straining at its moorings.

I heard Harriet declaring that she perfectly understood how the balloon was made to ascend, but she could not comprehend how it was brought back to earth.

Three gentlemen competed with each other to explain how a valve could be opened to let out the air in a gradual way, so the balloonists would float gently down to the ground.

I was feeling unwell, a consequence, I suppose, of forcing myself to remain awake for the greater part of the night. Overtaken once more by that lassitude which I had so constantly experienced since coming to London, this time I felt queasy, also. The strange mixture of steam and smoke in the atmosphere did not help, neither did the incessant clatter of the engine or the press of people around me.

Wishing myself alone, I turned and pushed my way to the back of the crowd and retreated to where the carriages stood waiting. I found a tree to lean against and felt inside my reticule for hartshorn. The sharp salts revived me a little and I was scanning the crowd with the design of returning to my companions when I caught sight of a certain gentleman.

Today, he was wearing a grey caped driving coat and a curly brimmed beaver, but even without the silver buttons, I could not mistake him. Certainly, he was the Harley Street gentleman: I remained in doubt as to whether it was my Mr Benjamin.

He moved and was lost to my sight. I started forward, meaning to encounter him and resolve the matter. But finding him amongst that crowd proved difficult: twice I thought I had a sight of him and lost him again.

Cheers from the crowd drew my attention another way: the balloon was beginning its ascent, rising slowly into the air, a huge, silent, pretty thing carrying men aloft into the skies.

It was then, when all eyes were watching the balloon and not one amongst the crowd to observe what happened to me, it was then that I was kidnapped by my cousin Thomas.

He crept up from behind: one hand closed over my mouth, his other arm encircled me, pinioning my arms beside my body. 'I have you!' he said triumphantly, and laughed. 'You shall not escape me now!'

If exertions were always rewarded by results, I would have escaped within a minute, but Thomas had taken me by surprise, I was unbalanced, and wriggle and struggle as I might, I was quite unequal to his strength. I was dragged backwards, stumbling, struggling, panting, unable to call out, and even my attempt to bite the hand over my mouth was frustrated, for Thomas wore leather gloves.

I was lifted and thrust into a carriage. I screamed then, but he was upon me in an instant, clamping his hand over my mouth again and the carriage jolted and we fell together into one of the seats as we began to move.

He kept his hold on me for some time, and not until we had left the park and turned into the Edgware Road, did he release me. By this time we were going too fast for me to escape the carriage. Thomas pulled down the blinds over the windows so I could not attract the attention of passers-by, and he restrained me when I attempted to pull them back.

I was panting with bitter fury. 'What mischief are you about now? How dare you abduct me? Take me back, this instant!'

The carriage turned and turned again, so often I lost all sense of direction. We were taking a roundabout route, perhaps to avoid pursuit and perhaps to avoid the turnpikes, also. Whatever Thomas meant, all this had been planned.

Thomas was leaning back, laughing, pleased and satisfied with the success of his scheme. And if I knew nothing else, I at once understood how he had known I would be in Hyde Park: he had visited Mama and Harriet to some purpose.

I tried again. 'What kind of folly is this? How can it avail you? Take me back, Thomas.'

'How can you be so foolish, Sarah?' He smiled at me, and spoke in a cajoling voice. 'Do you imagine I will believe you wish to be with Foster? What a tease you are, to be sure; I would not have thought it of you! Well, very soon you will be married to me, then we may forget him and be happy at last.'

'Thomas, you are ridiculous!' I said in some asperity. 'How do you imagine I can marry you? I am married already! Even at Gretna Green — is that where you think to take me? Even there, they will draw the line at two husbands!'

'Gretna Green? Why should I wish to go there? No, no! They understand these matters better in France.'

'France?' My voice came out in a squawk. 'You think to take me to France? No! I will not go! Tell your coachman to stop. Take me home instantly!'

He began to speak soothingly, as though I were a child: I would like France, he told me, and if my grasp of the language was not perfect I would soon become accustomed. We were to go there because the French were far more liberal in their attitudes than the English, and they were sympathetic to lovers. They would be especially sympathetic to me, a lady who had been persecuted by a cold and tyrannical husband.

I stared at him. Had he so settled the matter in his own mind? Did the notion that I preferred my husband so displease him that he refused to believe it? If that was so, then clearly it was not the smallest use trying to persuade him otherwise.

'Foster will pursue us, I do not doubt,' said Thomas loftily. 'But he will not find us. In the end, he will be obliged to divorce you. Then we may be married and return to England.'

The very thought of it was abhorrent to me, but I only said, 'There will be scandal and your father will not like it.'

'The scandal will die down, scandal always does. As for my father, I shall tell him he has only himself to blame. He should not have compelled you to marry Foster.'

Sir Nicholas had done nothing of the sort, but I did not say so. I was quite unequal to hearing how Thomas had arrived at that conclusion.

I was silent, wondering what I could do: I knew I could not hope for rescue, for I had been whisked away in an instant, and no one had seen what had happened to me. When my disappearance was noticed by my friends, time would be wasted waiting for me, becoming impatient, wondering what had become of me, searching, discussing what to do next.

Eventually, I thought with a wince, someone would inform James, who might easily draw a conclusion of his own to account for my disappearance!

Even if he came to suspect Thomas, it would take time to establish what had happened and to discover our direction. We could be in France before pursuit even began.

'What are you thinking, Sarah? Do you scheme to escape me? You will not succeed.'

I said, 'No, but Thomas, I have been considering the matter and I am persuaded you would do better to forget me and look for happiness with some other lady. Do take me home.'

'What, back to Foster? Can you be happy with that repulsive creature? He is nothing himself, so he bolsters his own conceit by taking a beautiful wife, someone he can flaunt in society. Besides, why should he have everything I want?'

I did not answer this. I could not suppose Thomas had any real regard for me. He had shown not the smallest interest in me until I became engaged to James. Now I thought his dislike of my husband was such that he would go to any length to deprive him.

Thomas was not in love with me. Even now, when he had me alone in the carriage, he made no attempt to kiss me, or fondle me, he had attempted nothing which might be expected from a man long thwarted in love. It had not even occurred to him! He simply meant to take me away from James.

Appeals on my part would not persuade him to release me, but my conjectures led me to suppose I might succeed with provocation. If Thomas could be brought to see me as a disagreeable, quarrelsome, complaining creature, he might come to feel that James was welcome to me!

So I began to sulk. 'I do not wish to go to France. Even though Napoleon is defeated and we are no longer at war, I cannot feel the French have any great liking for the English!'

'They are kind and sympathetic to lovers,' said Thomas with a grin. 'Even English lovers!'

'Well, I think it is very thoughtless of you to abduct me without warning! I dare say you have portmanteaux with you, but I have nothing, not even a hairbrush! What am I to do? How long do you imagine I can wear these garments?'

'They will serve until we reach France. You may purchase what you need when we reach Calais. And when we have established ourselves in Paris, you may send for Matilda, too,' he added handsomely. 'She will bring your things.'

'Matilda hates the French,' I grumbled. 'She will not consent!'

'Then you may engage a French maid,' he said, 'and be all the more fashionable for it.'

'And what are we going to use for money?' I demanded, believing I had hit upon a difficulty he would admit. 'I have nothing, and we cannot live on fresh air.'

'I have money!' said Thomas triumphantly. 'I have enough to keep us in comfort for a long time! Ten thousand pounds, as a matter of fact! There! What do you think of that?'

'Ten thousand—?' In my astonishment, I forgot my intention to provoke him. 'How did you come by such a sum?'

'Earl Cardew's daughter took a fancy to me,' he said. He must have seen something in my expression, because he went on, 'Do not look at me like that, Sarah, you need not be jealous of her! You must see that we could not elope on the beggarly allowance my father gives me! I had to have money, so I made up to her, just enough to have Cardew thinking I might upset his own schemes. He paid me off. I knew he would!'

'You—?' Words failed me. I stared at him incredulously, swallowed, and tried again. 'You paid court to a lady, with the design of getting her father to buy you off?'

Thomas nodded, laughing, pleased with his own cleverness. He seemed to have no notion of how unprincipled was such conduct, no notion, either, of the insult he had swallowed.

'Cardew is such a cheapskate,' he said, astounding me even more. 'He thought to fob me off with five thousand, but I was not having that! I drove a hard bargain, I can tell you.'

I felt a fleeting pity for the lady he had so deceived, but I could not sustain it. Her folly was, in part, responsible for my own predicament.

'I declare, I could scarce keep myself from laughing when my father called on me, accusing me of extravagance, and sermonizing and demanding to know the extent of my debts,' continued Thomas. 'He had wind of it from Foster, of course. I knew the little rat was spying on me! He told my father I was borrowing from the money-lenders.'

'And were you?'

'Of course I was; how could I be expected to live on the paltry six hundred a year my father gives me?'

I was about to point out my whole family had lived on less for many years, but Thomas was now feeling grievances against James. 'I would have settled the matter and no one the wiser, had not Foster interfered. My father threatened to cut off my allowance unless I engaged myself in a useful profession. He said I must take up a commission in the army.'

'What is wrong with joining the army?' I asked. 'My brothers enjoy it and regimentals would become you admirably.'

He smirked, pleased by my flattery, but whatever he might have replied was lost, for the coach horn sounded.

We had reached a turnpike at last, but the blinds were over the windows, signalling the coach was unoccupied. All hope of alerting the gate-keeper to my trouble was lost, for Thomas was upon me instantly, his hand over my mouth, holding me down.

The coachman must have paid the toll because the gate was opened and we passed through and we went some distance beyond before Thomas released me. I sobbed, because I had been pinning my hopes on gaining assistance from a toll-gate-keeper.

'Tears, Sarah? But you cannot really wish to escape me. not now, not after I have been to all this trouble?'

I recollected my design of provoking him with ill humour, and complained that he had hurt me.

'Pouncing on me like that!' I said peevishly. 'Did you have to be so rough?'

He shrugged and did not answer. After a minute, I added pettishly, 'Are we to make the whole journey to Dover in this disagreeable half-light? I wish you would put up the blinds, and let daylight in.'

Still he said nothing and I continued my grumbling: I wished for my clothes; I wished for my dressing-case; how tedious this journey was; and why must we have the blinds drawn over the windows?

'I will let up the blinds if you promise to behave yourself.'

'I seem to have no choice in the matter.'

He did as I wished and when my eyes were accustomed to the light, I looked out: we were out of town, in cultivated countryside. I had to suppose we were somewhere in Kent, though this part of the country was unfamiliar to me.

The weather was sunny and warm. I complained how stuffy the carriage was; I said I hated travelling in hot weather; I told him I was thirsty and wanted some tea.

'Tea?' His voice was raised in exasperation. 'How can I supply you with tea?'

'Well, coffee then. There must be an inn nearby, surely we may stop and take some coffee?'

'Oh stop your complaining, do! Can you not see I am doing my best for you?'

I shrugged and lapsed into silent sulks, and since he was no longer inclined to talk I began to consider how I might escape.

Whilst I was in a moving carriage, this was impossible. But we would have to stop sometime, we would have to change horses, and I might then find an opportunity.

Thomas was quick and strong: should I make an attempt to run away from him he would overtake me and capture me again. I might have a chance to hide from him, but this was uncertain. My best hope was to throw myself on the mercy of strangers and beg assistance.

He might have determined I was not to get down from the coach, but from now on, I would so exasperate him that he would be only too willing to alter this resolve.

I opened my mouth to complain, once more, of thirst. What I said was very different. 'Thomas, I am feeling unwell, you had better stop the coach, I think I am going to be sick.'

It was true, but Thomas did not believe me. 'Do you think to take me in by a ruse such as that? What are you doing?'

I was feeling inside my reticule. 'My hartshorn! I have lost my vinaigrette! Now I remember! I was feeling faint when you seized me, and I had it in my hand. You made me drop it! I have lost my hartshorn and it is all your fault! Thomas, please, you must stop the coach.'

It was too late. The carriage lurched and so did my insides, and Thomas yelped and flung himself away from my side into the seat opposite.

I had soiled the carriage floor, but his boots had not escaped and neither had my petticoat and his exclamations would have been diverting had I not felt so wretched.

'What a disgusting mess!'

'Well, cover it with some newspaper,' I snapped.

'I have none.'

'Then you will just have to endure it,' I said. 'You have only yourself to blame; you should have stopped the coach when I begged you to.' I found my handkerchief and scrubbed at my tears. 'Do you have anything useful? Some hartshorn or lavender water?'

'No, of course not, why should I?'

'Well, that is just what I would have expected of you! You scheme to kidnap me but you give not the least thought to bringing along anything I might need!'

'I have some brandy!' he said suddenly. He felt in his pocket and brought out a flask. 'Here you are, take a sip of this.' He was smiling now, pleased with himself again. 'That will set you up. Is that better?'

The spirit burned in my throat, but my head cleared and it took away the sour taste from my mouth. Thomas took a pull from the flask himself before corking it again. 'There, you see! I do know how to look after you.'

I felt better, but I had no intention of telling Thomas so, and I said, 'I have a pain.'

I put up my feet on the seat, leaning into the corner, sobbing. With evidence of illness before him, Thomas could no longer suspect a ruse, but a ruse was what I now intended. If I had my way, and I meant to, he would soon be looking for a doctor.

I discovered in myself a talent for theatricals. I took my time, wincing, stiffening, stretching, as though to ease a pain. Moaning, I clutched my hand to my side. I moaned again asking if he had, by any chance, brought along some laudanum.

He offered me brandy again, but I waved it away with a sob. I subsided for a while, then gave a great groan. I whimpered, gasped, groaned again, clasped at my middle, letting out my words between panting breaths.

'Thomas, I cannot go on! Oh . . . the pain! You must do something! Thomas, I am frightened! Oh, oh, it hurts so much! Is there a house nearby? Someone may have some laudanum? Oh. . . .' I let out a wail. 'I cannot bear it! I am ill, Thomas, really ill! You must help me to a doctor! You must!'

Thomas was sweating now, and red in the face, attempting to press more brandy on me, which I refused. And after another ten minutes of wailing and groaning on my part, he eventually leaned out of the window and shouted for the coachman to stop.

He alighted immediately and turned to speak to me, but I remained in my seat, doubled up and still groaning. 'Come, Sarah, get out. It is colic, that is what ails you, just a touch of colic! It will pass if you walk around for a while. Come, I will help you, you will feel better directly. It is only colic, Sarah, walking will help.'

'Oh dear! I cannot think it will.' I gasped and panted and sobbed and let him see what a struggle it was just to get out of my seat.

I kept my reticule: I had a few guineas, enough to buy assistance, should I encounter a farmer or some such person.

'Oh my head is swimming,' I moaned, clinging to the carriage door. 'Oh, the pain!'

He lifted me out of the carriage and I kept him occupied, staggering, clinging to him for support and wailing and complaining and all the time my eyes were coolly taking stock of the situation.

It was not what I had hoped for. We were now in what appeared to be uncultivated countryside, wooded land to the left and to the right a steep bank, overgrown with grass and brambles and hemlock. I could see no sign of habitation.

'Are you sure it is colic?' I gasped. He flung my arm across his shoulder and held me around the waist, supporting me and trying to get me to walk. I reeled and staggered and let him take my weight. 'I cannot think this is colic. You are not a doctor, you may be wrong. I am frightened, Thomas. Never have I known such pain! You cannot know what it is like.'

I wailed loudly, in the hope that someone was within hearing, but none came to investigate. Thomas tried to make me walk but I told him I could not and begged him to put me down. At last, tired of supporting my weight, he did so.

Now, I sought delay. If this was the road from London to Dover, it was reasonable to suppose there would, at some time, be others passing along the route, from whom I might beg assistance.

So I lay in the grass at the side of the road, doubled up, continuing my pretence. I begged Thomas to look for a house, a village, a shop, to procure for me some laudanum. I let my voice rise in panic. I begged for a doctor; I thought I might be dying.

'Oh the devil with it!' he exclaimed, and left my side and began to walk back to the carriage. I watched him, still wailing, wondering what he intended, and when he shut the carriage door and walked past, I thought he was about to speak to the coachman, sending him to bring assistance.

Even as I watched Thomas climb up on the box, it did not occur to me that I was to be abandoned. I truly believed he was going to find help. Only when I heard a brief protest from the coachman, quickly silenced, did I come to the truth.

The coach moved off.

'Well!' I exclaimed aloud. I was torn between indignation at this cavalier treatment and astonishment at being so unexpectedly free of him. I watched the coach until it was out of sight, and scrambled to my feet, and turned and began to run in the opposite direction, back towards London.

Panting and trembling, I stopped eventually and took a hold of myself, calming myself, knowing I must give proper thought to what I could do. A glance at my watch taught me we had been travelling for about an hour and a half, so I calculated I must now be some fifteen or twenty miles from town. I could not walk the distance: I must wait until a carriage came along, and beg to be taken up.

Twenty minutes later, the sound of horses had me in a panic in case Thomas was returning, and I hid myself among some bushes and watched a coach pass, exasperated with myself because it was not Thomas and I had missed an opportunity. Yet Thomas was unpredictable: I would not dare hail any traveller going in my direction, in case it proved to be my cousin.

Still, I had money in my reticule, and there must, somewhere, be a conveyance for hire. I sighed, beginning to feel the results of my adventure. I had been sick and now I was once again overtaken by lassitude. I rested for a few minutes, reflecting how this would not do and began to walk.

Before me, the road was level and straight and some distance ahead it appeared to run downhill. I stopped when I heard the sound of horses. They were galloping, a man's voice urged them and he appeared to be in a hurry, but it could not be Thomas because they came from the other direction.

I stood in the middle of the road so the driver would see me, but ready to fling myself to one side if he showed no signs of halting. And, as the horses breasted the rise, I saw a handsome pair of bays pulling a light open carriage, a curricle.

He had seen me; he was going to stop. And when he did and I saw the gentleman in the curricle staring down at me, I had that strange feeling of *déjà vu*, as though all this had happened to me once before, a long time ago, in a dream.

'Why, Mr Benjamin,' I said. 'I might have known you would come to my rescue!'

Fourteen

I was trembling again, and my teeth were chattering. Despite the warmth of the afternoon, I was cold. He took off his driving coat and put it around me and when he had turned the curricle round he helped me into the carriage, climbed up beside me and tucked a rug around my knees.

'Eynsford,' he said, naming the nearest village. 'First things first, Sarey, my dear: you need hot coffee and food, and the horses need to rest, for I have used them hard today.'

I nodded and leaned back in my seat, too weak and confused to ask even one of the hundred questions which presented themselves. I closed my eyes and did not open them again until we crossed a narrow hump-backed bridge into the village.

At the inn, he sent me upstairs with the landlady whilst he saw to the horses: I washed my face, tidied my hair and sponged my soiled petticoat. I felt better, and better still when I joined him downstairs and saw cold chicken and tongue and apple pie laid out on the table.

'Come, Sarey, my dear. You have sustained a good many shocks today, but you will feel better after some nourishment.'

We ate in silence, but I stole a few glances at him, seeking evidence to support the suspicion which had come to me when I first realized who had given chase.

160

I said nothing. Talk did not begin until I poured out my second cup of coffee and he was the first to speak.

'I confess I had no expectation of finding you had escaped your cousin. I meant to overtake you, but I was delayed, because I lost your direction at first. Such a tortuous route you took! Well, I promised your husband I would restore you to him before night-fall. And indeed, I shall!'

'You promised my husband. . . ?' I repeated in stupefaction. 'James knows what is happening? How? I confess, I am confused. . . .'

'I was in Hyde Park,' he explained, 'searching for you in the crowd, because I knew you were there.' He saw my expression and smiled. 'When you know me better, Sarey, my dear, you will discover I have many ways of knowing things. Well, I heard you scream, and when I looked, I saw the scoundrel wrestling with you in the carriage. I would have prevented, but I could not. So I ran to my curricle meaning to give chase, then bethought me to scribble a note to your husband. I told my tiger to take it to Harley Street. Yes, I know!' He held up his hand, silencing me when I would have spoken 'I knew your husband was there for I happened upon him this morning.'

'Indeed? And did he see you?'

'He did; we spoke together. You had told him about me, Sarey, my dear. And I quite thought you had forgotten me!'

'No, I thought about you often. I own I did not immediately recognize you when I saw you again, so fine you are become! It came to me later. Do you live in Harley Street, sir?'

He nodded, but evidently he thought he had told me enough, because now he wanted to know how I escaped Thomas.

'I was sick in the carriage,' I said. 'A little queasiness, but I took advantage to pretend I was very ill indeed. I asked for laudanum, or a doctor, for I thought either would assist my escape. Laudanum, I might sometime slip in his drink to ensure he slept, or a doctor to whom I could confide my predicament.'

Mr Benjamin chuckled. 'You have your own resources, have you not, Sarey, my dear?'

I smiled. 'Almost, I could feel sorry for my cousin!'

He was excessively diverted when I told of my sulks and my pretences, but when I explained the outcome he stopped laughing and got to his feet to pace the room in indignation.

'Do you tell me he abandoned you, left you to die by the roadside?' he exclaimed. 'Well, I never heard the like! I do not feel sorry for him! Deuced scoundrel!'

'But it was all pretence on my part,' I reminded him. 'And I achieved my end, which was to escape him.'

'Which does not excuse his conduct,' he declared. 'He thought you were in extremes, and yet abandoned you! Should he come within reach of me, you may depend upon it, I will have him horse-whipped!'

'That is not the worst of his villainy,' I said soberly, and I told how Thomas had extracted money from Earl Cardew. 'Not only that,' I added indignantly, 'he has left his father and my husband to settle all his debts! Poor Sir Nicholas! This will break his heart! How,' I demanded, 'how can a man so kind and honourable produce such a son?'

'Should I know? Tell me, Sarey, how should your husband be involved in settling your cousin's debts?'

'Why, only because he is friend to Sir Nicholas and offered assistance should he have need of it,' I said. 'My uncle has been burdened with expense this last half-year, ever since Kilburn Hall was burned down. I expect you know of that, too?'

He slanted a quizzical glance at me. 'How should I?'

'You seem to know a great deal about my affairs! I would not be astonished if you knew more than I do.'

'Do you know me, Sarey, my dear?'

I stared at him and thought about the implication in that question, and conviction came to me and I nodded.

'Never were you a tramp,' I said. 'I know not why you saw fit to disguise yourself, but certain I am our first meetings were not mere happenstance, as I then supposed. They were contrived, by your design.'

I waited, but though he smiled, he said nothing.

'I do not perfectly comprehend how it can be so,' I went on, 'but I now believe you are related to me.'

'And when did you arrive at that conclusion?'

'Today, when you happened upon me. I looked up at you and, just for an instant, I saw Papa. It is no very striking resemblance,' I added slowly, 'but something is there, something about the mouth.'

'The Holroyd chin! You have it yourself, Sarey, my dear.'

'So who are you, sir?'

'Did your papa never speak of his brother Benjamin?'

I stared. 'You are my uncle? How can this be? I knew Papa had a brother, but he believed you dead! You were thought to have perished at sea!'

'I did not go to sea,' he said, 'but I meant to, and I suppose my father thought I had. No doubt he made enquiries. I know not how he came to presume me lost, but such mistakes occur.'

'What did happen to you?'

He had seated himself in the window, but now he got up and stretched. 'It is a long story,' he said, 'and we should be on our way, Sarey. We can talk as we go. I will have the horses put to.'

He went to the door, but another thought occurred to me and before he could go outside, I said, 'Tell me, sir, do I have an aunt and cousins besides?'

'No, I was never married.'

I let him go then, and not until he had settled the bill and we were in his curricle travelling the road to London, did he come to explain himself.

'It was my father's wish that I should succeed him as game-keeper,' he said. 'But I wished for adventure and it did not seem right the master would assist Daniel, your papa, in his soldiering yet expect me to remain on the land. Well, Daniel had what he wanted, and soon after he went, I took myself off.'

'I was told you ran away to sea,' I said.

'I ran away,' he admitted, 'but my intention of putting to sea was never fulfilled.'

Intending to make for Portsmouth, he had been set upon and robbed of his money. Rather than make a shame-faced way home, he had walked as far as London and worked, for a time, as an errand boy. Deflated by the consequence of his escapade, he had determined to disappear, keeping his family uninformed of his whereabouts and his true situation.

Later, he found office work with the East India Company. He had adventure in the end, most of it deuced uncomfortable, he admitted, for he had been sent to India and he had been caught up in fighting, acquitting himself well enough to be entrusted with the administration of a large district.

'A daunting task,' he acknowledged, 'and one which took all my energies, for the French would stir up trouble given the smallest opportunity. I may congratulate myself,' he added modestly, 'for I kept the peace and managed the trading, silks and spices, and gemstones besides, and thereby increased the prosperity of the district. And somehow, Sarey, my dear, in a fit of absence of mind, I became a rich man.'

I laughed, diverted by the notion of absent-mindedly becoming rich, and laughed again as I was struck by another idea. 'Are you what is known as a nabob?'

'I am.' He stole a glance at me. 'I am too wealthy and too upsprung to be popular in polite society,' he said. 'And you have married gentry. Will your husband be displeased to find himself with such a vulgar relation?'

'I think you are not vulgar. A little eccentric, perhaps, but not vulgar.' I laughed at his expression. 'James will not object, but I know of one who will!'

I laughed again at the pleasing thought of Lord Pangbourn's elegant displeasure. And then I stopped laughing, because it occurred to me that when His Lordship had spoken of my uncle with such disdain, it was not Sir Nicholas he had in mind.

'Do you know Lord Pangbourn?' I asked.

'The old lord was my father's master,' he said. 'The present lordling was still in long skirts when I left home. What has he to do with you, Sarey?'

I told him and he nodded. 'Aye, he knows me,' he said. 'I sought him out upon my return to England, wishing for news of my family, and I had ado with him. Very high in the instep, that one, and not half the man his father was. I told him so.'

Lord Pangbourn had told him how his father had died and his brother's family was in Nottingham.

'I discovered it was not so,' he said, 'but I must suppose he believed it, for whatever else he is, the lordling is not a liar!'

I now learnt it was no coincidence that Mr Benjamin had appeared in my life so soon after Papa had died.

'I was searching for Daniel almost a twelvemonth and only discovered his whereabouts when his death was announced in the *Morning Post*. Imagine how I felt! Oh, heavens! You are crying again!'

'I am s-sorry,' I sobbed. 'I was thinking how Papa would have been so happy to have his brother restored to him.'

'We shall meet again in Heaven, do not doubt it,' he said.

I wiped my eyes. 'But why disguise yourself so?' I asked. 'Why did you not make yourself known to us directly?'

'I would have been welcome, I know,' said Mr Benjamin drily. 'A long-lost brother, a single gentleman with wealth at his disposal would have been like manna from Heaven to your mama! I am sorry if it pains you, Sarey, but the first thing I learnt of your family was that I had no wish for her society!'

I was silent, not wishing to be disloyal to Mama, but I could easily comprehend.

'I had other ways, other disguises, for learning of the others. I have encountered each one of them, in my way. It was your papa's idea,' he went on, with an air of innocence. 'He came to me in a dream and told me what I should do.'

'Such a scheme sounds most unlike Papa to me,' I said. 'You must forgive me, sir, if I say it is more in keeping with what I know of Mr Benjamin! When I spoke of you to my husband, he said you had a taste for theatricals and he was right.'

'Perhaps he is,' said Mr Benjamin. 'I learnt how Arabella had taken you to Kilburn, so I went and took a peek at you, though you did not see me. Black as night, I was, driving the coal cart, and a kitchen maid gave me a mug of ale and we had some gossip about the family. Since I was persuaded you were happy, I would not disturb.'

'My uncle and aunt were very kind,' I said. 'Thomas was rarely at home and paid little attention to me in any case.'

'Well, so! Always I read the *Morning Post*,' he said, 'and always I look at the announcements, and I learnt of your aunt's death thereby. I suspected your circumstances would be reduced, and I thought it time to reveal myself, little knowing what a scoundrel your cousin is! I blame myself, Sarey, for much of what has happened! Thomas is no kin of mine and I had no thought of making myself acquainted with his character.'

'I do not understand you, sir?'

'I wrote to you. I meant to make provision for you, find a genteel lady chaperon for you, bring you out, do what I could for you. And after weeks of waiting I received a very curt note saying you wanted none of me!'

I was shocked, exclaiming my indignation. Then his meaning became clear. 'Are you saying Thomas intercepted your letter and withheld it from me, and answered it himself?'

'I fancy it is exactly what he would do, and seek to profit himself with the intelligence he gained thereby. Because what he well knows, Sarey, my dear, and you have, as yet, no notion of, is that my will is made out entirely in your favour.'

I said in a small voice. 'May we stop a while? I am feeling a little unwell.'

He pulled up and for the second time that day I was sick and for the second time I was fortified with brandy. The world was spinning and I steadied myself by leaning against the curricle.

At last, I said weakly, 'Why choose me? I am but one of your relations, I have brothers and sisters, why not divide between?'

'Because you were the one who won my heart,' he said simply.

'Do you remember me, Sarey, my dear? A ragamuffin tramp, and
you so polite, calling me sir, barbering my hair, bringing little presents. I have encountered each one of your family and none
moved me as you did. How could I help but love you?'

I brushed away the tears in my eyes and said, 'I have married a
wealthy man, I want for nothing. Perhaps you should now reconsider, sir?'

'Well, I will not!' He laughed. 'Do not look so perturbed. Were
any necessitous I would provide, but none of you are in desperate
need. You shall inherit and you may make dispositions for the others as you wish.'

I smiled and told Mr Benjamin I thought he looked healthy and
likely to live long. He laughed, but I resolved to put his fortune out
of my mind: should it ever become mine, James would have the
right of it and he would know what to do.

'Are you feeling better now? Shall we resume our journey?'

We did so, and I returned to the shocking intelligence of my
cousin's perfidy.

'My aunt's death must be accountable for your letter falling into
his hands,' I said. 'There were many letters of condolence at that
time, so I may suppose it was given to him by mistake. Well, if he
learnt I was to inherit a fortune, that explains why he wished to
marry me! Never did I believe he had any regard for me!'

I was pained to learn how Mr Benjamin received such a cold
reply to his letter, believing, at first, that it came from me.

'How did you come to learn it was Thomas's mischief?'

'Soon after your marriage I chanced on your cousin in
Brighton. He heard my name was Holroyd and enquired if I was
related to you. I knew who he was, of course, and willing enough
to talk with him, for I wished to know more of you and I was
desirous also of gaining some intelligence of your husband.
Thomas was sour about your marriage, saying it was all for
advancement and he did not believe you could have any regard for
an ungainly creature such as Foster.'

'Thomas does think that, but James is very dear to me.'

'I am very happy to hear it,' he said. 'Well, your cousin's account of you did not resemble the Sarey I knew and loved, but I confess, I was confused. Do not forget, I was perturbed by the answer I received to my letter.

'Had Thomas copied my hand so exactly?'

'My dear, never did I see your writing,' said Mr Benjamin, 'so how should I know? I thought three years at Kilburn must have changed you, taught you false values. And I knew a connection to such as I might be unwelcome to your husband.'

'James knows of my family, I told him myself before we married,' I said. 'He is not as prejudiced as some.'

'Aye, well, I have his measure now,' said Mr Benjamin, smiling. 'But then I did not and neither did I suspect Thomas until he began to say how very different you were from your sister Harriet. So much I knew, but I was surprised to learn how Harriet was an excellent creature with the sweetest disposition imaginable!'

'Thomas said that?' I was puzzled. 'For what purpose?'

'I believe his design was to deceive me, if he could, to persuade me my will should be changed. With that accomplished, I think he would quickly make her Mrs Thomas.'

'Ah, now I understand!' I did not mention my sister's designs on Thomas. 'Poor Harriet!'

'I knew Harriet,' said Mr Benjamin, 'by not knowing her! My humble disguises were not successful in approaching her, for she is short with servants and tradesmen. I saw her in church, most inattentive! and I spoke with others and heard something of her doings. I heard, also, the opinion others had of her, so I was not as ignorant as Thomas supposed.'

When Kilburn Hall was burnt, and Thomas recalled to Leicestershire, Mr Benjamin had returned to London and there he learnt enough of my cousin to comprehend how he sought to increase his fortune by whatever means he could. So, when Thomas was back in town and was once again speaking ill of me, Mr Benjamin was very short with him.

'Were you indeed?' I glanced at the profile beside me in the curricle: I had his measure now. 'What disguise did you use when you came to Foster Leigh?' I enquired.

'I never came to Foster Leigh.'

'Really? You astonish me!'

'Well, I took a peek at your house, and very fine it is, my dear! But I stayed at the inn, in Ashbourne. There, I learnt how your husband is well regarded. And over a tankard of ale, I fell into conversation with one of your footmen.'

When I stopped laughing he went on, 'Baines had much to say on the subject of his new mistress. How beautiful you were, how elegant, how civil and gracious to all, and how you wept to see the master in pain and did everything in your power to ease his cramps. I knew then my Sarey had not changed!'

'Baines?' I was startled, for of all our servants, he was the most correct. 'I had no idea he was so devoted to me.'

'You have a way of winning hearts, Sarey, my dear.'

'Well, I—' I shook my head, not knowing how to answer.

I recalled how Mr Benjamin had seen me in Harley Street. 'I was puzzled, not immediately knowing you,' I said. 'But you knew me! Why did you not speak to me then?'

For the first time, Mr Benjamin looked a little awkward. 'I had not known you were in town,' he said. 'And when I came out of my house and saw you, I thought at first I must be dreaming, I could do no more than stare! I collected my wits when I saw your husband was with you and I thought – well, that letter had put it into my mind that I could be an embarrassment!'

'Nonsense! By then you knew I never wrote it!'

'Aye, and though you had been much in my thoughts, I also knew you had received no intelligence of me! To you, I was still a ragamuffin tramp. It has been many years since you and I had open dealings and I had no notion that you remembered me. In any case, Foster is gentry, and should he know anything of me? Why would you speak of me to him? Do you see, Sarey?'

'I suppose I do,' I said slowly.

'Never was I more startled than when he spoke to me, this

morning. "Would your name be Mr Benjamin, by any chance?" he said. He asked if I remembered you, and said you had told of our meetings and spoke of me with affection! We conversed for a few minutes only, of course, no time to divulge everything, but he said you would be delighted to renew your acquaintance with me, and just happened to mention you were going to watch the balloon ascent, this morning. Which I took for permission to seek you out, Sarey, my dear.'

He seemed moved by my husband's interest, and I told how James had attempted to get word of him and promised me to make provision, should it ever become possible.

'We believed you necessitous, of course.'

I told more of James, of his childhood agonies, of his generosity and his humour and the way he was so often diverted because I could not rid myself of the habit of economy.

I recalled how he had been attacked just before our wedding, and I told Mr Benjamin of that, too.

'James was fearful of making false accusation,' I said. 'So was I, but today I am perfectly convinced it was my cousin's doing. What do you suppose Thomas will do now?'

'If he has any sense at all, he will continue his journey to France, and stay there,' he said. 'Good riddance to him, say I! What a day you have had, Sarey! You look pale, and I am sure it is no wonder. Take heart! You will very soon be home again.'

We had crossed the river at London Bridge and were passing through Cheapside towards St Paul's. Mr Benjamin was silent now, giving his attention to driving through the city traffic.

As we continued westwards, I fell to wondering what James had been doing since he learnt of my predicament. And my nerves received a jolt, for I had forgotten, in all the pressing concerns of the day, that my husband was very seriously displeased with me!

I wondered apprehensively what my reception would be when I was restored to him.

Fifteen

James was outside and struggling down the front steps even before Mr Benjamin had pulled up the curricle: he looked up at me with an expression I could not fathom and said not a word.

I ventured a wan smile and apologized for his anxiety. 'I understand you have become acquainted with Mr Benjamin?'

Sir Nicholas had followed James outside. 'Sarah, thank heaven you are home safe,' he said. 'Now where is that rascally son of mine?'

Mr Benjamin took charge. 'We cannot discuss these matters on the doorstep and Sarah is exhausted.' Then, to me, 'Best if you go to bed, Sarey, and leave me to tell the story.'

So, like a child, I was sent upstairs with supper on a tray and Matilda came and fussed around me and at last I was settled comfortably between the sheets. I slept so long into Sunday morning that I missed church.

Mr Benjamin was in the breakfast-room with James. I had to suppose he had been home in the meantime, for he had changed his clothes: today he wore the silver-buttoned coat. I was told that Sir Nicholas had set out in pursuit of Thomas and, should he need to, he would follow him to France.

'Never have I seen him so distressed,' said James soberly, 'as when he heard how unprincipled was his son's behaviour. He seemed to age ten years in an instant.'

171

'The extraordinary thing is, Thomas appears to have no notion of his own wickedness,' I said. 'Did Mr Benjamin tell how he extracted money from Earl Cardew? Thank heaven my poor aunt did not live to see the day; it would have broken her heart. Poor Sir Nicholas! He is the one worst affected. I suppose there will be a scandal?'

'I fear there must be, it can scarce be avoided.'

'I have been considering the matter,' said Mr Benjamin. 'A story there must be, for your disappearance, Sarey my dear, quickly became a matter of public knowledge and already it is rumoured that Thomas was accountable. But we may pass it off as mere folly: the world shall be told he did it for a wager, and meant to bring you home safely, no harm intended.'

I looked at James. 'Would it answer, do you think?'

'Thomas is known as a gamester and somewhat foolhardy besides: I see no difficulty there. Can we account for your return with Mr Benjamin? You were seen driving through town in his curricle.'

'I came upon them on the road,' said Mr Benjamin promptly. 'With a horse gone lame, in ill-humour with each other, and Sarey abominably queasy through travelling in a closed carriage. I offered assistance and Thomas prevailed upon Sarey to return with me. Thomas remains in the country until his horse is recovered.'

'No one will believe Thomas remains in the country for the sake of a horse,' said James drily. 'Let us invent an accident for him.'

'Very well,' Mr Benjamin conceded, 'a coach wheel ran over his foot. We fear he may be indisposed for some time to come.'

'We may account for his absence in any way we choose,' I said. 'Most will believe he stays away until the gossip has died down. Well, I do not care for deception, but it will spare my uncle a scandal, if not distress. Oh! What of Mama and Harriet? Do they know the truth?'

'They do not,' said James.

James had received Mr Benjamin's note before Harriet returned from Hyde Park with the Merediths. She was angry, the Merediths uneasy, and James told them only there was mischief of Thomas's, which he and Sir Nicholas were about to check.

Sir Nicholas had seen the note, for he was with James when it was delivered. Unwilling to accept his son as the culprit, Sir Nicholas had first preferred to suspect Mr Benjamin. At James's suggestion, he had then gone to Thomas's lodgings only to discover the rooms vacated and his belongings gone.

Forming the intention of pursuit, the two gentlemen had found themselves unable to discover our direction. They were obliged to return home and wait, hoping Mr Benjamin had better success and hoping they could trust him to fulfil his promise.

'And Sarey rescued herself!' said Mr Benjamin with pride. 'No doubt she would have brought herself home too, had I not happened along.'

'I had only to walk to a place where a conveyance was to be hired,' I said.

Mr Benjamin had spared Sir Nicholas the full account of my escape. Now he began to entertain my husband with how I had schemed to escape Thomas, and James smiled and appeared to appreciate the story and agreed I had been resourceful.

I watched James carefully, and felt easier, for there was no sign of that angry, wounded man who had so jealously accused me of preferring another. I thought he must have reasoned himself out of ill-humour, and we could be happy again.

So it was a grief to me when, after Mr Benjamin had taken his leave, my husband's countenance lost its smile and became aloof and austere.

'So, *Sarey, my dear*,' he used Mr Benjamin's form of address with hard and bitter emphasis, 'you are heiress to a fortune of your own. There is irony, is there not, in that Thomas deprived you of that knowledge? Really, one might almost say he compelled you to marry me!'

'Such was not his intention,' I said absently. 'No, James, Thomas did not compel me and neither did you. And if the circumstances have changed, I have not! I do not repent it.'

I thought I might go on to tell him how I loved him, but he turned away to stare through the window and there was a sulky note in his voice as he said, 'You would not have married me had you known of your expectations!'

'As to that, I cannot say. Does it matter now? So far, we have been happy together, have we not?'

He did not answer and it occurred to me that perhaps he had been less happy than I supposed.

I remembered a sour witticism I heard long ago. 'Of course it is possible to be happily married,' an acquaintance had said. 'My husband has been happily married for years!'

Reviewing the months of our marriage, I wondered if I had been too complacent. I had watched other gentlemen in a spirit of self-congratulation, happy to find, in all, some failing or mannerism to advise me of my own good fortune in marrying James. It was thoughtless of me not to realize how he might suspect such observations, for I knew how he felt his disadvantages.

Now, I said, 'I have been happy. If any conduct of mine has pained you, I am sorry for it, because I would not willingly cause you distress. Come, James, are you still troubled over that gentleman whose name I cannot, at present, recall? A pleasing gentleman, I do not doubt, but I am content to leave him to the lady who chooses to make him her business.'

'He is handsome,' said James, as if it mattered.

'So is Thomas,' I retorted.

I allowed silence to say the rest. We stared at each other and I truly believe I would have prevailed had not someone rung our doorbell.

Harriet errupted into the room without waiting to be announced, flinging her bonnet and gloves on to a chair.

'Well,' she exclaimed, 'a fine to-do you caused yesterday, and all of us wandering around Hyde Park in search of you! And now Sir Nicholas has taken himself off to France without so much as a word of explanation, and a strange gentleman has called, claiming

to be a relation! I can make no sense of anything! Give me a plain
tale, I beg you.'

'Ah, you have met Mr Benjamin, have you?'

Harriet regarded me with disfavour. 'He says he is brother to
Papa, in which case I would suppose his name is Holroyd.'

'Indeed it is, but I have always called him Mr Benjamin.'

'You have always called him Mr Benjamin?' repeated Harriet.
'How long, then, have you known him? And why,' she demanded
accusingly, 'have the rest of us never been informed?'

'Do sit down, Harriet,' said James. 'A plain tale we cannot give,
for it is full of twists and turns, but if you will give us time to collect our thoughts we may satisfy your curiosity.'

I gave her warning of the story we concocted to avoid scandal
and then, between us, we told the true version.

James, to my surprise, was not inclined to spare Harriet any of
the details. He told how she might have become a favourite with
Mr Benjamin had she not been short with him, and he told also
how Thomas would have married her, had he successfully persuaded Mr Benjamin to alter his will in her favour.

For Harriet, this was not comfortable listening. 'Well, I shall not
make the mistake of repining over Thomas,' she said. 'But I do
think you are sly, Sarah, to keep our uncle to yourself all these
years and to cozen him to favour you!'

'We have explained, Harriet, that I learnt of these particulars
only yesterday.'

'Indeed?' Harriet raised disbelieving eyebrows. 'Well, my dear
sister, I now know of them also and you may depend upon it, I
shall do my best to cut you out. I shall charm dear Uncle Benjamin
into transferring his allegiance.'

I laughed, but James's voice was tinged with annoyance. 'You
may discover, my dear Harriet, that your uncle is too shrewd to be
taken in by such a scheme.'

'Should my sister want his wealth, having made such an advantageous marriage?' she enquired sweetly. 'Or could it be, sir, that
you are not so well-to-do as we have supposed?' She smiled at

him, her eyes sparkling with intent to make mischief. 'Could it be you have hoodwinked Sarah, knowing better than she how she was situated? Thomas once said you had wind of Holroyd's scheme, and now we know what he meant.'

'What a spiteful cat you are, Harriet,' I remarked.

'And what a credulous ninny you are, Sarah,' she said in a pitying tone. 'Previous knowledge would not be impossible for your husband, him being related to Lord Pangbourn. Indeed, the more I think of it, the more I am persuaded—'

'Harriet, that is quite enough!'

James said nothing but he was very white about the mouth and I, sensible of other discords, tried desperately to stem the flow of her malice.

'You are talking nonsense and you know it.'

'You said yourself, I distinctly remember you saying it, that few gentlemen in his position would accept a lady with neither birth nor fortune to recommend her!'

I walked across the room and tugged at the bell-pull and when a footman answered the summons, I said, 'Miss Harriet wishes to leave, now. Be so good as to procure a hackney carriage, if you please.'

Harriet gave a brittle laugh. She picked up her bonnet and sauntered towards the looking-glass, preening herself as she tied the ribbons. As she pulled on her gloves, she turned back to me with a sharp little smile.

'Did you think he had been captivated by your beautiful eyes? No, no, my dear sister, even your undoubted charms would not avail you, were it not for your expectations.'

'You grow tedious. Harriet, do go away.'

There was a hackney carriage waiting, the footman returned to tell us so and Harriet took her leave with one parting shot. 'A gamekeeper's granddaughter? Too ramshackle by half!'

'Little termagant!' I let out my breath as the door closed behind her and then subsided into a chair and began to laugh.

'Excessively diverting, I make no doubt!'

James was white, his mouth a straight uncompromising line and his eyes were dark with anger.

'What, do you imagine I believed that faradiddle? Even Harriet herself does not believe it!'

'Indeed? Why then would she speak so?'

'She was angry, she wished to wound. You annoyed her, James, by telling how Mr Benjamin had determined against her. And, I may say, you surprised me, too. There was no need to disclose that part of the story.'

'Indeed? Then it has been all my own doing, as I understand?'

'Well, as a matter of fact, I think it has.'

It was the first time I had occasion to venture any reproach to my husband and I saw how he was taken aback. I said, 'Do not repine too much. A mere family squabble, I promise you. You have no sisters of your own, James, so perhaps you do not understand how we can rip at each other, on occasion. Harriet does not expect us to take her seriously.'

'I may say, I find it very hard to forgive!'

'Harriet has ambition, you know that. It must seem quite intolerable to her that having made a good marriage, I am to inherit a fortune besides. I must say it seems strange to me, too.' I laughed. 'Mr Benjamin said he became rich in a fit of absence of mind. I begin to understand what he meant!'

I hoped to ease the awkwardness, I hoped he might laugh but once again, at a point of high promise, our discourse was interrupted by visitors.

This time it was the Merediths, as much anxious about me as curious for information. We gave them the story we had concocted, and throughout that day we recieved a steady stream of visitors, all our acquaintance, curious to know what had happened to me.

When the last of them had departed, James seemed morose, answering my remarks in monosyllables. I recollected he had taken no exercise that day, but when I ventured to suggest we should go for a walk, he said he would prefer to go alone, if I had no objection.

I let him have his way, thinking he might reason himself into better humour. I took up a book, but I soon gave up my half-hearted attempts to read and began to reflect on the various causes of discord between us, uncertain which of them most occupied his mind.

I could not believe he retained his suspicion that I had looked at Sir Martin Colworth with wanton intent, neither could he think I gave any credence to the suspicion that Harriet had started, though he might now be regretting having married into a family such as mine.

That, and Mr Benjamin's fortune seemed to be the cause of his present disquiet. Thanks to Thomas, I had married James knowing nothing of an uncle who meant to provide for me.

James had expressed the opinion that, had I been properly informed, had I known of my expectations, I would not have accepted his proposal. And he had reason, for I cannot, with any truth, say that I would.

When James proposed marriage, he urged his suit by making much of the material advantages to me and I had been moved by his offer to provide comfort for Mama. And though I had given consideration as to how well we would suit, I cannot disguise that my decision had been influenced by promise of comfort.

Small wonder then he should believe my character to be wholly mercenary. Others certainly did, and James was too shrewd to be ignorant of the fact. I recalled what Arabella had said of Harriet's opinion.

'She does not admire your husband and she cannot believe you have a particle of regard for him.'

I sighed, knowing very well how it was difficult to avoid having doubts when the rest of society adhered firmly to a contrary opinion. James had his doubts assisted by my own foolish thoughtlessness. How could I hope to convince him of my love?

As I brooded over the matter I took no account of passing time. Only when a footman came to enquire about dinner did I become alarmed, for James had not returned.

I stifled thoughts of accidents and foot-pads: instead, I determined he had met some acquaintance and accepted an invitation. For all my exertions, James was in no good humour with me and might well have determined to dine elsewhere.

So I ate a solitary dinner and waited for him to return, uneasy, but still reluctant to send out servants to look for him, knowing from my brothers how gentlemen were careless and exasperated by feminine anxieties.

I waited until past bedtime, anxious, but also angry, because really, I knew very well he was doing it on purpose and he could easily have sent a message. I took myself upstairs at last, rang for Matilda, and whilst I was being prepared for bed I heard him return.

Relief that he was home safe made me angrier still and I did not go to him. Neither did he come to me. He spent that night in one of the other bedrooms and when I went down to breakfast the next morning I was feeling a sense of grievance on my own account.

I waited for him to tell me where he had been. He did not. I determined not to ask and said only that I would be obliged if, on future occasions, he would be so good as to inform me when he meant to be absent, because I had not known whether or not to wait dinner for him.

Unable to visit us, Mama sent for us to wait upon her in Harley Street. We went, and I was not displeased to see Harriet looking embarrassed and a little silly.

Mama favoured us with her opinion of Mr Benjamin and his methods of acquainting himself with his family. She thought it freakish behaviour on his part and she was sure she did not know why he had chosen to favour me above any of the others.

Her discontent was not on Harriet's account: always, Mama liked her sons better than her daughters and she thought the boys should benefit.

'You must allow the gentleman to dispose of his fortune in the way that best pleases him, ma'am,' said James.

179

Mama's colour rose and I recognized the signs and spoke hastily to avoid whatever broadside she was about to deliver. 'You may be certain, Mama, that I will always do anything in my power to assist my brothers and sisters.'

Mama subsided. She looked at me and seemed to be undergoing some change of mind. Then she nodded and said, 'Well, I have to admit even now, you have done more for your family than you would have done had you married Thomas.'

James stiffened and looked aloof in a manner which reminded me forcibly of his cousin, Lord Pangbourn. I had to acknowledge it was not a felicitous remark, for it reminded him of my other not very complimentary reasons for marrying him.

Mama had meant no ill, however, and his response increased my annoyance. Yesterday, I had struggled to break the discord between us: he knew very well, he could not fail to know it was what I wished and he had dashed my hopes by going out alone and leaving me to grow ever more anxious! And this morning, not one word of apology or explanation had I received!

Recalling his cool manner at breakfast, I determined that if James would prefer to pay attention to others than respond to my attempts at peace-making, he was perfectly welcome to do so.

We spent the next few days in an atmosphere of cold civility, though we kept the engagements we had made previously and our acquaintance observed nothing untoward.

I had convinced myself it was his responsibility to make the first move, but I watched for signs that I might move towards him. There were none, and I confess I found it upsetting.

Much of our time was occupied with other people. We visited Mr Benjamin, who requested my husband's permission to take me out, saying he hoped he did not appear selfish but he would so like to indulge himself with my company.

Mama's ankle mended: she took her first tentative steps with the aid of a walking stick and declared that with a little careful exercise, she would do very well. We took her in our carriage for an airing in the park and the next day we took her and Harriet to the theatre.

Sir Nicholas returned to London on Saturday. He had been as far as Calais, where Thomas had certainly been, but there the information was conflicting. Some said he had returned to England, others said he had set off towards Paris, and another declared Thomas had stated an intention of travelling to Italy.

'So I have no means of knowing which direction he took,' said Sir Nicholas heavily. 'I must resign myself to waiting until he chooses to make his whereabouts known.'

'Will he do so, do you think?'

'He will, though I fear it may be many months before we hear from him.'

Sir Nicholas was grateful for our exertions to spare him a scandal, though nothing could improve his spirits and we, in our knowledge of Thomas, could find no comfort for him.

'Were it not for Mama and Harriet, I believe he would return to Leicestershire,' I said.

'He would, but it would not be good for him to do so,' said Mr Benjamin sagely. 'Here, in London, there is much to distract his attention. At home, his mind would be too occupied with his trouble. It does not do to dwell on trouble when there is nothing to be done about it.'

My mind was most frequently occupied with my own trouble. Convinced there was something to be done about it, I sought to resolve it. In this, I was hindered by the obligations of society and also by that lassitude which had been overtaking me ever since I first came to London. I no longer mentioned this to James, but it was getting worse and was sometimes accompanied by bouts of nausea.

I longed for a return to Foster Leigh, to be away from the smoke and noise of London, to be no longer obliged to keep engagements. I was persuaded I needed the quiet, the country air and a return to keeping regular hours to make me feel better.

There, away from the constant demands of other people, I felt

I might reach James: here, I could not determine which of our particular discords most occupied him, but I was persuaded that if we had some time alone together, I would penetrate his mind. Once, we had been happy. I was persuaded we could become happy again.

So I was shocked beyond measure when, one morning, James announced that he meant to return to Foster Leigh. He had no thought of taking me with him. He meant to return alone.

Sixteen

'And what,' I demanded frigidly, 'have you determined for me?'

I was, to own the truth, very frightened indeed, for I knew that if he had his way in this, there would be no reconciliation, ever.

'You may remain here, in this house, should you so wish it,' he said, 'though you may prefer to join your mama in Harley Street, for there you will be close to Mr Benjamin, also.'

'I do not wish to remain here in this house, neither do I wish to join my relations in Harley Street,' I said. 'I am your wife, sir, and even though you have grown tired of me, I will not be put aside as though I were of no more account than a worn-out coat. You have married me and now, however inconvenient it may be, you are encumbered with me. I would advise you to make the best of it. I shall accompany you to Foster Leigh.'

'Indeed? Would this be on account of our handsome new neighbour?'

I did not immediately comprehend. When I did, I flushed and said, 'Do you accuse me still? I shall not demean myself by repeating all I have said on that subject.'

'Then might I enquire what you mean by it?'

'I am your wife, sir, and I am carrying your child. Even though—'

'What? Can you be certain of this?'

'Certainly I am carrying no other child,' I said drily.

James flushed. 'I meant – are you certain you are with child?'

I was certain of it, though I had surprised myself as much as James by my announcement, for until then I had no conscious knowledge of it.

'I have the symptoms,' I said. 'Even though you no longer wish for me, I make no doubt you will wish for your son, and you have the right of him. But I will not be separated from my child! If you wish for him, you must accept me also.'

'Sarah. . . .'

'So I go to Foster Leigh?'

'You had better see a physician before we leave.'

'What?' I was angry. 'Do you doubt me?'

'I wish you to have the best possible care.'

'I need rest, country air, and better milk than this wretched stuff we have in town.' I said coldly. 'But send for a physician, by all means, if it makes you happy.'

The physician was younger than I expected and I was rather embarrassed to submit to his examination, but he was businesslike, and told me what I already knew and agreed that I would benefit from a return to the country.

'A little exercise would be good for me and the child, no doubt?' I suggested and perhaps he heard something in my voice, for he looked at me with more attention, and said it would do no harm.

'Nothing too strenuous, mind. But why do I tell you? You ladies have ways of knowing what is best for yourselves at such times.'

'Do we?' I was astonished, for all the doctors I had previously encountered seemed to hold contrary opinions.

'I have frequently observed it to be so, madam.'

'I beg you will not say that to my husband,' I said. 'When you speak to him, perhaps you will be so good as to tell him I should take gentle walks, daily, if possible?'

He stiffened. 'If you have a scheme to deceive your husband, madam, I cannot—'

I laughed. 'I have a design of my own, and no harm to anyone. Nothing like that, I promise you.'

I schemed a return to our former ways, which James now seemed unwilling to pursue. I would accompany him on his walks and talk with him and hope to come to a closer understanding. Even quarrelling with him would be better than this cold distance between us.

James invited Mr Benjamin to accompany us to Foster Leigh. Leaving him was my only regret, but I was thankful when he declined the invitation for I wished no company, however agreeable, to come between James and myself.

Whether Mr Benjamin guessed at anything amiss I know not, for he only said, 'I have engagements at this present which I cannot break. But I will be pleased to visit you in August, should that be convenient to you.'

It was agreed and later he said to me, 'Sir Nicholas is pained by his son's conduct. I have no right to interfere in his concerns, I know, but no man should have such troubles without a friend to lean on. Since he is dear to you, Sarey, I shall preserve acquaintance with him and have a care for him.'

'Oh, Mr Benjamin!' I said gratefully. 'I cannot tell you how relieved I am to hear you say so. He is in poor spirits, I know, and I cannot feel—'

I broke off in some discomfort, for I had been about to say how Mama and Harriet would be little comfort, disloyal and improper sentiments, though unfortunately close to the truth.

'Well,' I said lamely, 'I shall be easier in my mind for knowing he has someone to turn to.'

We began our journey into Derbyshire the following day: we had a second carriage for our servants, though on the journey to London, Matilda had travelled with me. Now, I wished to be alone with James. Telling her we had private matters to discuss, I ordered her into the other coach.

So I was half amused, half annoyed to see how James had provided himself with a newspaper, burying himself behind it as soon as the carriage began to move. I said nothing. Even he could not spend all day reading the *Morning Post*.

For the first hour we travelled in silence. For the next ten minutes, I did not care. I had armed myself with hartshorn, lavender water, brandy and a large basin, prepared for the nausea for which I held my condition to be accountable.

Now, though I had many unkind thoughts about my husband, the infant in my womb and the unfair arrangement nature had made for my sex, I had no opportunity to give voice to them.

James stopped the coach, and I was grateful for the cessation of movement but in no fit state to step outside. Someone emptied the basin at the roadside, and I wiped my mouth and gasped for breath and leaned back in my seat and allowed the tears to trickle down my cheeks.

I opened my eyes when I felt the sharp aroma of hartshorn under my nose. 'Can you take a little brandy?' he asked, and I nodded, and he poured a measure into the silver beaker and held it for me as I sipped.

I was encouraged to see how he could not be indifferent to my distress, and when, after a short turn in the fresh air, I was recovered sufficiently to resume our journey, he no longer seemed interested in the newspaper.

After I had advised him that I did not, as a rule, suffer from travelling sickness and this was merely a symptom of my condition, I said, 'Shall you like to be a papa, James?'

He did not answer directly, but said, 'Do you know when the child will be born?'

'Early December, or thereabouts. But I think I shall not spend the whole time suffering this sickness. I have heard other ladies say it becomes easier after three months. Though I confess, I am a little apprehensive of giving birth: I fear I am by no means as brave as some ladies of my acquaintance.'

'You may rest assured I shall engage the very best people to attend you. Shall you wish your mama to be with you?'

'No, certainly not. I could wish for Arabella, but she will be nursing her own infant then, if all goes well. Is Mrs Clegg experienced in confinements?'

James thought not, but he knew of a physician in Derby who had a good reputation and spent some time telling me of his qualities and how he would engage a woman experienced in midwifery to be present at Foster Leigh, ready to assist at the very first signs of labour.

This was the most agreeable interchange we had had for some time. I smiled and thanked him and by way of prolonging the goodwill, I asked how he wished the child to be named.

'You have determined to have a boy?' he said, after we had considered several masculine names without making up our minds. 'It might be girl, you know.'

I was feeling queasy again. 'No daughter of mine,' I pronounced, 'would put her mother through this torment!'

We stopped again as I endured another unpleasant interlude, set off again when I felt better, and continued in this fashion until we reached Dunstable, where James decided we would put up for the night.

We had intended to spend the first night at Mama's house to see how Edward and Joseph were faring, but James said, 'You have had quite enough. We may reach Northampton tomorrow.'

I washed and tidied myself and James ordered some tea. When I had drunk it I declared that a stroll in the fresh air would give me an appetite for dinner.

The landlord gave directions for a pleasant, easy walk through country lanes. We set off, myself doing most of the talking: I avoided conversation of a personal nature and confined myself to observations about the scenery. James answered me, seeming awkward rather than hostile and I noticed he directed a few puzzled glances at me.

I had not yet told him how I loved him: with the troubles between us, and myself by no means certain what was in his mind, I felt the time was not yet right for any such declaration on my part. My present determination was that we should be easy together and as happy as possible.

Dinner was a tolerable meal: afterwards I took up some sewing and when he took out a book I asked if he would be so good as to read aloud to me. So we occupied ourselves pleasantly until the light faded.

In providing accommodation for ourselves, our servants and other guests besides, the inn was full. We had the best bedroom, but here, there was no question of sleeping in separate rooms, a notion which had first occurred to me, if not to James, as soon as he announced we would stay.

I had been in bed for half an hour before he joined me and when he did he merely murmured 'goodnight' and turned away. I was disappointed but not surprised, and I had no intention of allowing this state of affairs to continue.

Wishing I knew a little more about the art of seduction, I snuggled close to James and put my arm around him. I felt him stiffen, which was painful to me, but I did not withdraw. I kissed the nape of his neck, stroked his hair, and raised myself on my elbow to nibble at his ear.

He moved then, turning on to his back and though I could not read his expression in the darkness, I fastened my mouth on his in a long slow kiss, and felt a tremor run through him. I moved my lips to the hollow of his throat, heard him gasp, and drew his hand to my breast.

There was a sound which was suspiciously like a sob and he rolled towards me, and his hands were on my shoulders, pinning me back against the pillows.

'Why?' he demanded.

'I love you.'

'Do you?' There was pained scepticism in his voice. 'Do you know what it means?'

'Yes!' I took his face between my hands and brought it down to fasten my mouth on his again. I wriggled myself beneath him, pulled up his nightshirt, clamped my hands on his buttocks and took him to me, accepting a dark, angry coupling which was over too soon to heal all his wounds.

*

'I love you.' I said the words again, but I knew they were not enough. Without understanding me, with no knowledge of how I had come to it, they were mere words, easily said, and too easily suspected.

Afterwards, he rolled away from me and I felt him give a sudden jerk. 'The child! Sarah, what of the child?'

'Do not make yourself uneasy. He will come to no harm.'

'Well, then.' As far as I could tell in the darkness, he seemed a little disconcerted. His hand touched my face, briefly, gently. 'Sleep now.'

The next morning James determined we would break our journey whenever I needed respite and since we did not need all our servants, he sent them ahead. Matilda remained with us, travelling in our carriage. Her presence made all but the most meaningless conversation impossible, but I voiced no objection.

The second day of travelling was no better than the first and I was thankful when we arrived in Northampton.

The house which James had provided for Mama was larger than I had expected, with a long saloon, elegantly furnished, used for entertaining and forbidden to the boys. The housekeeper informed me they had a room upstairs which was called the schoolroom but was filled with boyish playthings.

The boys were at school: we took tea and afterwards I plucked some blooms from the garden and asked James if he would accompany me to visit Papa's grave.

On the way, I spoke of Papa with no design other than making use of a natural subject for conversation, but it occured to me, as I was talking, that what I was saying might bring James to understand that, to me at least, his infirmity was no cause for disrespect, no barrier to love.

No source of amusement, either. I recalled his angry, bitter words.

'I am absurd, am I not? An ill-favoured cripple, capering around, doing everything to please. So very diverting, how you must have laughed!'

That was one resentment I could remove. For, like James, Papa had been crippled.

I thought James already knew of the deep affection in which I had held my papa, though I had never before spoken of it at length. Now I did so, telling how he got his wound at Toulon, before I was born, and how he had told me it had taken him a long time to become reconciled.

'He was used to being quick and agile,' I said. 'And he had to invent new ways of performing simple tasks and discover a new sense of time, for what had before been a ten-minute walk now took half an hour! He had to be patient with himself, and also patient with the impatience of others. I should imagine you have had something of the same experience?'

'I have never known what it is to be quick and agile,' said James soberly. 'It may have been harder for him than for me, how can I tell?'

'When Papa was asleep and dreaming,' I said, 'he was always whole. He said it was often a shock to wake and find himself crippled.'

James winced.

'What troubled him most,' I went on, 'was that he had no money of his own. Mama brought her fortune to the marriage and though it became his, he was always conscious that he himself had brought nothing, and we were not well-to-do. So Papa did everything he could to make himself useful.'

I told how we needed no masters, Samuel, William, Robert, Arabella and I, for Papa had taught us our letters and numbers and a good many other things besides.

'And I declare, a more patient and gentle teacher one could not hope to find anywhere,' I said. 'Though he always insisted we should pay attention to Mama in the matter of genteel behaviour!' I laughed. 'He meant well, but it was the only thing I could not agree with.'

We came to the churchyard and found the grave well tended, for Mama paid the sexton to cut the grass and clean the headstone. James uncovered his head, whilst I knelt and placed my flowers on the grave.

'Dear Papa,' I said. 'I wish you could have known him, James. You would have liked each other, I think.'

'We have learnt from Mr Benjamin how your grandfather was gamekeeper to my uncle,' said James. 'I might have met your papa but it was so long ago, I was but an infant, then.'

A hollow opened up inside me, as I recalled his cousin's disapprobation of my birth. A gamekeeper's granddaughter! James had been indignant with his lordly cousin, but that was before he knew how he had entered into a marriage with one so close to home. And now, I had an uncle to remind him of it!

Did he regret our marriage on that account?

On the way home, I talked of Papa again, rather defiantly telling how, to assist our finances, he kept poultry and bees and tended the garden, growing vegetables and fruit. Occupations which could hardly be considered genteel, but when I stole a glance at my husband's countenance he was smiling.

I saved the best, or the worst, till last. One day, Papa came home with a cobbler's last: he meant to save the family the expense of purchasing boots and shoes by making them himself. In this he acquired some skill, but when he ventured to make shoes for profit, Mama had been furious. She was a gentleman's daughter, she would have no tradesman for husband!

'Which always struck me as strange,' I added, 'since a good many tradesmen were far more well-to-do than we were.'

'Your mama is of a different generation,' he observed. 'You should not blame her for what she was taught as a girl. She would feel it to be a disgrace, especially since her sister was married to Sir Nicholas. The tendency to look down on people engaged in trade still persists, but it is changing.'

So it was not that which troubled him. I breathed a sigh of relief and said, 'Papa always made excuses for Mama, he said she deserved better. But I think she could have had no kinder or more considerate husband, even if society did say she had married beneath her. I know girls are thought to be attached to their mothers, but I always felt closer to Papa.'

We were home and the conversation ended there. I was not dissatisfied: James had been attentive and his answers were thoughtful and considered, more like the man I had married than the distant creature he had recently become.

So I could congratulate myself on making some progress and I hoped James had been reassured that his infirmity could not affect my regard.

My young brothers were in good health and lively spirits: they kept us occupied with accounts of their doings, and they were excessively diverted to learn of Mr Benjamin.

'I do not wish for his fortune,' said Edward. 'I shall make my way in the world. But I think our uncle should have given thought to Emily. Well, she shall not want if I can prevent!'

I was touched by this boyish concern for his sister and hastened to assure him that I would not forget Emily. 'Or any of you, for that matter.'

Later that evening, I became ill again and quite exhausted with retching. Matilda and the housekeeper put me to bed and when James joined me, he said, 'I fear the travelling has knocked you up more than you realize: we will remain another day in Northampton to give you a respite.'

'But we travel only as far as Kilburn, tomorrow,' I said. We had planned to visit Arabella and Henry after leaving Northampton. 'The journey is no more than twenty-five miles!'

'Kilburn on Thursday, and only if you are well enough,' said James firmly. 'After that, we will see.'

I rested and took only invalid food the next day and it seemed to set me to rights for I was sufficiently restored to make the journey to Kilburn on Thursday. We set off, bearing messages for Emily from the boys, and I made the journey without a hint of nausea. Though I confess I felt a little dour to see how Arabella was blooming.

Her condition was just beginning to show, and I had never seen her looking so well or so happy. For her sake I was pleased, for she had previously suffered two miscarriages and she deserved her present good fortune.

I said nothing, but the difference between us was so marked that I came to have misgivings about whether I would carry my own child to a successful confinement.

The last few days seemed to have brought about an easing of James's manner towards me: he was concerned with my sickness and did what he could to help me. With my brothers, he had been agreeable, as indeed he was with Henry, Arabella and Emily, and in trifling matters, he was very much himself. But apart from my talk of Papa, there had been no opportunity to advance understanding, and he made no attempt to open up any discussion.

It seemed to me that something had been settled in his mind, but he did not choose to speak of it. And in puzzling over it, I recollected my own cold words: '*I make no doubt you will wish for your son and you have the right of him, but I will not be separated from my child! Should you wish for him, you must accept me, also.*'

It would be like James, I thought, to determine that, since there was no help for it, he would accept me. He would observe that I was taking pains to be agreeable, and exert himself to be equally amiable, reflecting, no doubt, that such behaviour would make life tolerable for both of us, and would certainly be the best for our child.

My apprehension of suffering a miscarriage was now increased. I had the cold feeling that should I lose the child, I would also lose my husband.

Seventeen

I would not lose the child if I could help it.

Having observed how invalid foods had given me respite from being sick, I apologized to Henry and Arabella for refusing the rich meats and pastry on their table and took only a few vegetables and some calves-foot jelly.

'You are supposed to eat for two,' remarked Emily.

'I cannot feel the child receives proper nourishment from food I cannot keep down. If you have some arrowroot, Arabella, I will take a little at supper-time.'

No more was said, for my relations had other matters to occupy them when we told what had occurred in London.

Henry seemed just as dazed and shocked as Sir Nicholas. 'I knew,' he said, 'how my cousin was selfish and sometimes forgetful and careless in matters of principle, but never before had I thought him intentionally wicked!'

Arabella, on the other hand, seemed irritated by the stratagems of Mr Benjamin. After dinner, when we ladies had withdrawn from table, she said, 'So this enigmatic uncle of ours made a point of investigating me, too? Which of his humble disguises did he use for that purpose, I wonder? Such a ramshackle notion. I cannot approve of it.'

Emily said nothing, but Arabella continued to voice disapproval, pointing out that, for all I was Mr Benjamin's avowed favourite, I had so far received no benefit whatsoever.

'He knows I have no need.'

'You married James because you were in need!' snapped Arabella. 'You would not have done so had you known of your expectations.'

Arabella's observation echoed a remark James had once made, and I thought, not for the first time, that he might have come to resent my original motive.

One could not wonder at it: I had married him, as Arabella pointed out, because I was in need. Yet he had known it from the outset and never before had it appeared to trouble him.

I sighed. How much better, for both of us, had I been in love before I married him!

To Arabella I said only that I did not repent my marriage. 'In any case we can hardly blame Mr Benjamin for our cousin's perfidy.'

'We should be thankful Sarah did not marry Thomas,' said Emily quietly. 'Really, by withholding your letter, our cousin might be said to have defeated his own design.'

'His design was defeated before it was begun.'

The two gentlemen did not remain long in the dining-room and there was time, after we had taken tea, to walk the half-mile to Kilburn Hall to see how far it was rebuilt.

The original hall was gone: in its place stood a house which was about half the size, the stonework complete, the roof added, but no glass in the windows, no doors, and inside, only bare walls divided the rooms. Much remained to be done.

'Sir Nicholas cannot meet the expense of building larger,' said Henry. 'But the design will allow for extension by future generations, should the family increase and prosper.'

We were all silent, thinking of the heir to Kilburn on whom the future rested: if the family was to increase and prosper, a miracle was needed. I brushed away a tear and saw Arabella do the same and we returned to the parsonage in sombre mood.

Later, when we retired for the night, I again made advances to

James. He responded and took me in a gentle coupling, treating me with affection. I was heartened but I knew too little of what was in his mind to speak again of love.

We left Kilburn the next day, but travelled no further than Leicester. I was not sick, but for my sake James had determined on making the journey in short stages.

'There is no great hurry, after all,' he said.

Matilda's presence prevented any talk of a personal nature until we arrived. I again determined we should take exercise and we found a park and walked along a broad avenue under some mature elms. It was fine and warm and pleasing in the shade, but my mind was too occupied to look about me.

James talked easily and naturally of trifling matters: he was relieved and pleased that my sickness had abated and hoped I would soon feel able to partake of more appetizing food. We would reach Nottingham tomorrow, and the next day, providing all remained well with me, we would defy those who disapproved of Sunday travel and cover the remaining miles to Foster Leigh.

The rest of his discourse was equally unexceptional, but it was clear he had no thought of opening his mind on the subject which most occupied me. I was confused, for he now behaved as though he had wholly dismissed those suspicions and resentments which had so recently emerged with such bitterness.

If he had dismissed them, he had given no assurances to me. Our affairs were unsettled; I felt there was no confidence between us and I could not penetrate his mind.

'Sir Nicholas,' he was saying, 'has charged me with a matter of business on his behalf, which I shall attend to before we resume our journey. Since we travel only as far as Nottingham tomorrow, we may delay our departure until after noon.'

'I see no difficulty there,' I said. 'Is this business of a confidential nature, or may I know of it?'

'It is merely to do with the rebuilding of Kilburn Hall.'

'Oh, I see.'

I began to speak of the new building, wondering how soon it

would be finished and making some comparisons with the old hall. From there, I felt it was natural to reminisce and I spoke of all my astonishment when first I had been received at Kilburn.

I had a design in speaking so. I could not deny I had some mercenary motives for marrying him and I could not blame him for his present resentment, but I thought he might come to better terms if I could give him a notion of how necessity could burden the mind.

So I spoke of Kilburn as a contrast to my former life. I did not speak of obvious luxury such as large rooms and elegant furniture and beautiful ornaments: instead, I told how Kilburn, gracious, lavish, extravagant Kilburn, had shocked me exceedingly with what I then considered profligacy.

James appeared diverted, but he was startled when I said Kilburn would burn enough candles in one night to supply my former home for many weeks.

He was more startled when I spoke of hot water. At Foster Leigh and at Kilburn, one spoke to a servant and hot water would appear as if by magic. Before, when I wished it for washing or for tea, I would often be obliged to make up the fire, fetch water from the pump and set the kettle to boil.

I could swear James himself had never worked a pump in his life. He looked his astonishment. 'Did not you have servants?'

'A pair of maids, yes, but they were lackadaisical creatures, and no amount of scolding would alter them.'

I told how amazed I was to discover my aunt's dressing-room full of beautiful garments. I told how, unable to decide between two hats, she had purchased both. I had been shocked by such extravagance, because each of them had cost enough to purchase a complete outfit.

'We did not lack essentials,' I said, 'but we had to make contrivances. We purchased material when we could afford it, to make up gowns for ourselves and shirts for my brothers.'

'How did you find the time?'

'Sometimes, I wonder myself,' I said. 'Making up garments was one of the more agreeable tasks. Most of the time, our needles were busy with mending and patching and darning. There was always a prodigious amount of sewing. We never came to the end of it.'

I did not point out how my aunt had occupied her time just as she wished: James had seen her knotting fringes and making embroidery and indeed he had admired her handiwork. James himself took such pastimes as reading and card games and backgammon for granted, but now I let it be known there was a time when I had but little leisure for such occupations.

James slanted a quizzical look at me. 'How then, did you learn to dance?'

'We all went to dancing class,' I said. 'Mama insisted upon that: one sixpenny lesson each week, and woe betide us if we did not learn! We had to practise at home, humming the music, partnered by our brothers.'

I spoke next of small mundane items such as scissors and inkwells and penknives, which we had to share and which were frequently mislaid. When we wished to use some such thing we had either to search for it or wait for some other family member to finish with it.

'You must have found that vexatious.'

'Sometimes we would fight over things,' I admitted ruefully. 'We all thought our own need was greater. There was no such trouble at Kilburn, of course.'

Kilburn had an inexhaustible supply of such things, other useful items which we did not possess at all, not to mention the luxury of so many servants, the choice of dishes at table, and the calm, ordered course of the day.

The greatest gift that Kilburn gave to me was space. There was room to breathe, to spread out my work, to be organized. Never did I have to move myself or my things to accommodate someone else.

'It may be there is something odd in my nature,' I told James, 'for I know others do not feel as I do. But at home, I felt stifled. I could not walk across a room without treading on someone's feet, or squeezing past someone in a chair, or asking someone to let me by. And, of course, others had to get past me, too. I felt I was perpetually in the way.'

James shook his head, but he had nothing to say. I was encouraged to hope that some part of my discourse had found its mark, however, because he was wearing his vacant, foolish expression which always meant he was thinking deeply.

I said no more, because some of our contrivances had been revealed earlier, when I spoke of Papa. Had he wished to know more he could have questioned me, but he did not, and I did not discover what conclusions his reflections brought him to, or how far he took my meaning.

I continued with my self-imposed diet of invalid food and the rest of our journey home progressed as intended, with only occasional lurches of queasiness on my part. At last, on Sunday afternoon, we reached Foster Leigh.

'I know you disapprove of Sunday travel, Mrs Clegg,' I said, 'but I beg you will not be cross. I did so long to be home!'

Our lives settled back into a regular train, receiving our neighbours, paying calls and attending to our domestic duties. James made arrangements for the doctor to visit at regular intervals and after a month I found I could go for several days with no sickness at all. Though I was careful what I ate, I gradually began to take more enjoyable foods.

We received letters occasionally from London, Mr Benjamin's being the most informative. Nothing had been heard of Thomas and Sir Nicholas remained out of spirits.

Harriet was enjoying the amusements, behaving prettily to all. There was a young man paying attention to her, but he, Mr Benjamin, could not tell how well she favoured him.

Mama, whenever Mr Benjamin saw her, would oblige him with annecdotes about Papa and tell him what fine young men my brothers were.

At Foster Leigh, James continued as he had been throughout

our journey, always agreeable and considerate, even showing me some affection. We shared a bed, coupling when I was well enough. Never did he speak of those matters which had come between us. One might suppose nothing untoward had occurred, but I felt something was lost.

In my attempts to guess what was troubling him I had spoken of Papa to teach him his crippled state was no cause of repugnance to me, and I had spoken of my early life to teach him my view of how money assisted well-being.

I had hoped he would pursue these matters and reveal his own mind so that we could settle it between us. But he did not take me into his confidence and though I knew he was not quite happy, what he felt was a mystery to me.

In June, Mama and Harriet returned to Northampton and Sir Nicholas to Leicester. Emily remained with Arabella and Henry and these three were also concerned with Sir Nicholas. Arabella wrote a very strong letter, telling me exactly what she would like to say to Thomas, if she could get near him.

Also in June, Miss Lyndhurst married Sir Martin Colworth. After a short honeymoon, they came to Derbyshire and in July, James and I were obliged to pay our bride visit.

I confess, I went in some trepidation, not only because I was uneasy as to what James was thinking but also because I was embarrassed on my own account. James had accused me of staring too much at the gentleman: such conduct could not have escaped their notice and I felt some apprehension as to what they thought of me.

I was relieved when we arrived, for they greeted us with genuine warmth and pleasure. After some conversation, we touched upon the subject of my own interesting condition.

'Have you determined how the child shall be named?' asked Lady Colworth, smiling.

'Sarah is convinced of a son,' said James, 'and if she is right, I think his name should be Daniel, for her father. Would you like that, Sarah?'

'Oh! Oh yes! Daniel James Foster! That is exactly right!'

We remained for the usual half-hour and after we had taken our leave, I had some thought of remarking to James that neither Lady Colworth nor her husband appeared to recollect anything untoward in my previous behaviour.

I said nothing, for he was pale as a ghost and his eyes were very bright. It could not be because I had looked at Sir Martin more than was necessary, for I had taken particular care to guard my behaviour. I thought he was recollecting our quarrel, possibly feeling a resurgence of anger.

I felt it prudent to remain silent, and waited to hear what he had to say.

He did not speak for some time and when he did, it was nothing to the point. 'Since we have now determined on a name for our son, perhaps we may consider how we should name a daughter? That possibility remains, after all. Do you have any preference?'

'None of my sister's names, for choosing one would offend the others. Your mother was named Elizabeth, was she not? That will do very well. It is a pretty name, and I like it.'

At home, he remained pale and unhappy: I ventured to enquire if he was ill and he said not. I suggested we take exercise, but rain threatened and he refused on that account.

Since my presence did nothing to help him, I thought I might assist him by my absence. Making my condition my excuse, I said I felt tired and wished to rest.

I slept for two hours that afternoon, unwisely, because later, when we retired for the night, I was not tired and could not sleep. I lay quietly so as not to disturb him and again applied my mind to the vexed question of why he was so unhappy.

Today, I was brought back to the possibility that James was distressed by what he imagined were my feelings for Sir Martin. Three times I had attempted to reassure him on the matter, and done so no more because I was persuaded that labouring the point would assist his suspicion. But if he could not believe my assurances, what could I do?

I was half determined to have it out with him, even to quarrel with him if necessary, when I noticed his sleep was restless: he tossed and jerked and began a few incoherent mutterings.

I sat up, wondering whether to wake him from this troubled sleep. As I was still debating with myself, he spoke very clearly, one word: 'Trapped!'

It was like a blow in the face. Was that how he felt? And it seemed it was, for after another incoherent phrase he spoke clearly again. 'Selfish! I should not have married her.'

I no longer thought of waking him. I stumbled out of bed and groped towards a chair and I sat down clutching at my aching midriff, choking back my sobs.

My agitation was severe indeed. That he considered me self-ish was mortifying enough, but even more mortifying was that I could easily comprehend: I had married him and taken every-thing he had to offer, and I had repaid him by looking at other gentlemen. That I had done so preferring my husband rather than with any wanton intent, was no excuse: it had been done in a spirit of self-congratulation which was, in itself, open to that suspicion.

And now, he felt himself trapped! Married to a woman who had wounded him with the worst insult he had had to bear in his life, and nothing to be done about it. There was to be a child, he had obligations, a duty, he had to face a lifetime with a wife for whom he could no longer feel respect. Small wonder he had not opened his mind to me.

I saw the truth of it, now. The coming child left him no alter-native but to accept me. At some point, when I was ill, he had determined the course of the future: he would play his part to make our lives tolerable by treating me with consideration. And, since I had shown myself willing, I would be the woman in his bed, the mistress of his house, the mother of his child, but no longer the dear companion of his life.

I had not thought it possible to feel such pain. Even when Papa died, I had not been so overwhelmed with grief as I was now. I was doubled over, gasping, stifling my sobs so as not to wake him and my very bones ached with misery.

It was growing light before I crept back to bed. Exhausted with all my grief, I at last found respite in sleep and, upon waking, I discovered James had risen before me. I could not bring myself to rise and join him until I had made some attempt to compose myself.

Compose myself I must, for I knew there was nothing to be done until I had given birth. James was the father, he had the right of decision in everything to do with the child.

Even after the birth, I could remain: I must reconcile myself to a marriage which had lost its delight but which was, after all, no worse than most and better than many. Even if I left, I could not feel that James would wish the scandal of a divorce. We would remain married, but separation would relieve him of my presence.

When I thought of leaving my own child, my firstborn, I was overwhelmed with despair, and when I thought of staying I despaired again at the thought of James trapped forever with a wife he no longer cared for.

Knowing I had nothing to hope for, I was, nevertheless, confused by some deep urging, a false conviction that this state of affairs could be remedied. I saw my own reluctance to accept the truth more evidence of selfishness, and I put it aside, but I was no closer to reaching a decision.

In the days that followed I was careful not to inflict myself on him. I remained a willing partner in his bed, and at other times I was there when he wished for me. I accompanied his walks on the occasions when he suggested it, but never did I suggest it myself. I consulted him on domestic matters as usual; I accompanied him on visits; I was a gracious and smiling hostess when required; I was civil and agreeable at all times, but I would absent myself when I was not obliged to be with him and when I was so obliged I would sit quietly with my sewing and leave him to determine the conversation.

This seemed to be what he wished and expected, but it was

anguish to me. It was a relief when August brought with it the promised visit from Mr Benjamin.

Sir Nicholas came with him. Mr Benjamin had broken his journey from London to call upon him and had urged him to the visit. He appeared to be in good health and was occupying his mind with managing the Kilburn estates and rebuilding the hall.

Nothing had been heard of Thomas. 'To own the truth,' said Mr Benjamin, 'I feel your uncle now dreads learning anything of his son, for fear it can be nothing good. He finds consolation in knowing he cannot be in England. Whatever mischief he is about, he is, at least, out of the country.'

'Can you be certain of that?'

'I would hesitate to swear to it on the Bible,' he admitted, 'but I am as certain as may be.'

We took them on excursions, showing them the curiosities and beauties of Derbyshire and on one occasion, finding ourselves near the hilltop village of Stanton-in-the-Peak, James suggested we should pay our respects to the Nine Ladies.

'The nine ladies? Who are the nine ladies?'

James led us across some moorland until we came to a circle of stones, each about three feet high, placed there in ancient times by our pagan ancestors.

I stared, and even in the bright August sunlight I felt the chill of a dark mystery and goosebumps rose on my arms. I shivered and placed my hands across my belly to protect the child within. And though my companions appeared to notice nothing, I could have sworn I heard those stones singing.

Sir Nicholas appeared fascinated. 'Who put them here? How long ago? And for what purpose?'

'A long time ago,' said Mr Benjamin. 'Before the gospel of Christianity was preached, when superstition was rife. This is a place of pagan rites and human sacrifice.'

'You cannot know for certain,' objected James. 'There are other theories.'

There was an area of woodland beyond the stones and something there, perhaps a magpie, set up a chattering screech. I felt I was looking down all the years into a chasm, dark with secrets, with fires burning and swirling figures with torches and mistletoe and branches of oak. I shivered again.

'I do not like this place,' I said. 'May we go home? James, do not step within the circle, I beg you!'

'Come, Sarah, these ancient superstitions cannot harm us now.'

Sir Nicholas was already within the circle and James was about to follow, but I clutched at his coat and held him back, unable to explain my dread but sensible of it all the same.

'Do not go within!' I sobbed. 'I want to go home!'

'Better humour her, sir!' That was Mr Benjamin, hearty but serious. 'She is in a delicate condition and at such times ladies are subject to odd fancies which we gentlemen do well not to question. Let us leave this place and these secret stones.'

We left and, as we drew further away from that place of ancient magic, the dread left me to be replaced by the uncomfortable feeling that I had been very foolish indeed. I said so, rather apologetically, to James and he answered more seriously than I expected.

'Well, I do not know that you were wrong,' he said. 'Some of these ancient sites have power we cannot account for.'

Our guests left at the beginning of September, in spite of our pressing them to remain. At the end of September, we heard Arabella had been safely delivered of a son, named Nicholas, for my uncle.

I wrote to her all my congratulations and delight. I would have liked to go to her, but I was grown large with our own child and I began to suspect I would be confined earlier than we had thought.

One morning in mid-October, I was with Mrs Clegg in the upper part of the house, supervising all the refurbishing of the nursery when I chanced to look from the window, which overlooked the courtyard.

I stiffened: a visitor had arrived alone, on horseback, and

though I could not see his face, I knew by the set of his body who it was and I cried out in alarm.

For whatever reason my cousin Thomas was here, I could not feel it boded well.

Eighteen

I pushed a maid out of my way and ran from the room, cursing the three flights of stairs. I stumbled, narrowly escaped a fall, recovered, and took myself more carefully. At last, I reached the ground.

'Baines!' I spoke urgently to the nearest footman. 'Where is he? Where is my cousin?' Then, as he looked uncomprehending, 'The gentleman who arrived a few minutes ago?'

'He is with the master in the library, mistress. There is a matter of business, as I understand. He said he was not to be disturbed.'

I was already halfway along the corridor, still gulping my breath after my flight downstairs. When I reached the library, I stopped outside the door to listen.

Within the room there was laughter, a strange laughter, and the sound of it raised goosepimples on my arms. I faltered, braced myself, and opened the door.

How I kept myself from fainting, I know not. I walked into the room and James spoke in alarm, 'No, Sarah, go back!'

Thomas held a pistol, threatening James, who was seated, upright, very steady, but pale.

Clearly, Thomas was deranged: he giggled and squirmed and waved the weapon to and fro. I thought he must have been mad for some time. James knew it, too. Once again, he begged me to go back.

207

He was in more danger than I, for I knew how Thomas hated him, but I thought I might distract my cousin where James could only provoke.

So, I sailed forward. 'Why, Thomas!' I said, sounding surprised. 'This is most unexpected! Why did you send no word of your coming?'

Thankfully, my cousin's early training took effect: the pistol was lowered, pointing to the floor when he turned to look at me. As he took in my condition his laughter died.

'A brat!' His features contorted and his voice seethed with repugnance. 'Do you mean to tell me you let this little rat have his way with you? How could you be so disgusting? Well, I shall know what to do with that, when it is born!'

I did not allow myself to dwell on what fate he intended for my child, for we were all in peril now. I saw at once that no rational talk was going to serve.

'Thomas, where have you been all this time? No one knew where to look for you.' Then, I added plaintively, 'Why did you leave me? I do think you were unkind to leave me, when I was so ill. I would have died had not some kind people come to my assistance.'

'You—' Thomas shook his head, looking confused. 'You were not ill!'

'But I was!' I insisted. 'Do not you remember? We were eloping, you were going to take me to France. But then I was ill and it all came to nothing because you left me.'

Thomas flushed, angry again. 'You were not ill! It was a ruse, to escape me! My father said so.'

'Did he?' I frowned, looking puzzled. 'Well, I do not know why he said that, or why you believed him. You saw how I was sick; you saw how I was ill. And you left me. After promising I would have a French maid, too!'

It was fortunate Thomas did not see James at that moment, for in spite of our danger, a hint of amusement crossed his features. Praying he would remain silent, I gave my attention to Thomas. I sat down sobbing and, as I pulled out a handkerchief, I surreptitiously poked myself in the eye to ensure a flow of tears.

'You s-said we would live in Paris!' I wailed. 'You said I could b-buy new clothes and have a French maid! I th-thought you cared for me, but you left me at the roadside, to die!'

'You did not die,' said Thomas sulkily. 'You returned to Foster, and now look at you, you are carrying his brat!'

'It is not my fault!' I protested. 'What could I do? The people who came to my assistance were so starched in their notions, how could I tell them we were eloping? I had to return with James, because they sent for him. Besides, I did not know how to look for you. Where were you, Thomas? Did you go to France? Why did you stay away for so long?'

'I will not have it, I tell you!'

This answer seemed to have nothing to do with anything. And as I looked at him, uncomprehending, he began to blink very rapidly. Agitated and disturbed, he paced the room, muttering under his breath, 'I am the one who gives the orders, here! Presumptuous puppy! Do not tell me what to do! How dare you speak to me like that!'

I quailed: his mind was confused as well as unbalanced and I guessed he was going over an argument with some previous opponent. Thomas was in a worse case than I thought.

Thankfully, James knew that any speech or movement on his part was likely to inflame Thomas. He was pale and strained, but he resisted the temptation to interfere. He remained silent and still but he was watchful.

Thomas went on pacing the room, his arm hanging loosely, the pistol pointed at the floor. Then he raised his hand and seemed surprised to discover what he held there. He laughed and looked about him.

I felt pity and fear at the same time. I said kindly, 'Thomas, dear, you do look tired. Come, sit down and rest yourself. Shall I order some tea?'

'No time for that, Sarah!' His voice was decisive now. 'I have remembered why I came here. I am going to shoot Foster!'

He was close enough for me to catch his arm, but not, unfortunately, the one which held the gun.

'You are going to shoot James?' I contrived to sound puzzled. 'But why, Thomas, dear?'

'So we can be married, of course.'

'Married? Are you sure you wish to marry me, Thomas?'

'Of course I do! That is why I have to kill Foster, you see.'

This present determination was not even for Mr Benjamin's fortune, he had forgotten that. I thought his mind was so fixed upon it because he had been thwarted.

'Must you kill him?' I clung to his sleeve as I stood up. 'Cannot you think of some other scheme? You could make him divorce me. We can elope again, go to France, or Italy if you prefer. . . .'

I gabbled on, talking of how I would like to live in Paris, how I longed to wear French fashions and be attended by a French maid, saying anything which might distract him.

I moved in front of him, thinking to put myself next to his gun hand, thinking I could make him discharge the weapon safely if I could bring my weight to bear down his arm.

He was strong! He lifted me with his free arm and put me aside. Thankfully, he had no suspicion of my design and he attributed my action to feminine ignorance.

'Foolish, Sarah!' He waved an admonishing finger. 'You should know better than to stand in front of a loaded pistol.'

'I wish you would put the gun away, Thomas.'

There was an ornamental pitcher in the corner by the fireplace. I had looked at it three times, with a vague idea of throwing it at Thomas, a temptation I had resisted, fearing to show my hand and fearing to raise his anger.

Now I remembered it was one of the pitchers I had placed around the house after Kilburn Hall was burnt down: it was filled with water!

If I threw water over the gun, would it make the powder damp? I thought it might, but I did not know enough about firearms to be certain. But Thomas would not suspect there was water to hand and a drenching might disconcert him long enough to get the gun away from him.

I edged round a sofa to get closer to the pitcher. Then I saw he was once again blinking and looking confused.

'Are you very tired, Thomas?' I spoke soothingly. 'Would you like to sleep? I am sure you would feel better if you slept for a while. This sofa is extremely comfortable. Would you like to take a nap?'

'I am tired,' he admitted. 'But I cannot rest now. I have some business which cannot be delayed.'

'Oh, you gentlemen are always about some business!' I said archly. His eyes had stopped blinking but they were clouded and confused. I thought he was not at all certain where he was. 'Surely,' I went on, 'surely your business can wait until you are rested? You need to sleep, Thomas, dear. Later, we can all consult together to determine what is to be done.'

For a moment I thought I would prevail: Thomas wavered and looked tempted as I patted the cushions invitingly. But just as he seemed about to settle himself, he blinked again and he straightened. 'It is perfectly clear what is to be done, and I have not an instant to lose!'

'Why, Thomas, what do you mean?'

'I have to kill Foster!'

'But we decided against that, do you not remember? Because we thought the law would say it was murder and we did not wish you to be taken and hanged!'

'The law officers will not take me,' he said.

'Oh yes they will! I know they will! They are cunning, Thomas, very cunning indeed; they will hunt you down.'

'I shall be safe enough in France,' he said indifferently.

'Thomas, wait! You do not understand. James has many friends, powerful friends. Did you know he is related to Lord Pangbourn? He is rich; he can afford to send his own men after you, and he will bribe people to betray you.'

211

'Why would he do that?'

'He is a dreadful man and that is what he is like! I can see how it will be. They will kidnap you and smuggle you back to England and make you stand trial and then you will be hanged. So you see, Thomas, you had better not shoot James.'

'I want to shoot him!' He was aggrieved, like a child denied a treat.

'I know you do, Thomas, dear.' I tried to sound sympathetic. 'But you had better not, because you do not wish to be hanged, do you? Can you not think of some other scheme?'

'No, I cannot and I shall not attempt to do so, because I have remembered now how I shot my father. So you see, they will send men after me anyway. I had better shoot him quickly and get away.'

I sustained a very severe shock and I saw James was looking stunned. 'Thomas!' I whispered, appalled. 'Did you shoot Sir Nicholas? But why?'

'There was nothing else to be done,' he said. 'He would not listen. He would go on talking. He kept saying how I behaved abominably; how I was a disgrace to my name and I had better mend my ways or he would disinherit me! He would not listen to me and he made my head ache with his prosing. So I shot him!'

'Is he – is he dead?' I had a faint hope that my uncle was only wounded and might recover.

'Of course he is dead!' said Thomas impatiently. 'I told you, I shot him. Why are you crying, Sarah? You cannot grieve for that old curmudgeon!'

'He was kind to me,' I said.

'He was not kind when he compelled you to marry Foster. Well, that can be changed. But mind, Sarah, you must get rid of the brat! I will have no spawn of Foster's in my house.'

Now he was once again occupied with his intent to murder James and marry me. He seemed to have forgotten his earlier realization that already he was a hunted man.

I put aside my grief for Sir Nicholas for fear of a worse grief to come. I spoke quickly, telling him we could make up a story to pass off his father's death as an accident.

'But you must not shoot James as well. We cannot explain two shootings, they will not believe us. They will say you did two murders, and they will take you and you will be hanged.'

My voice broke and the tears flowed, for even my best endeavours could not prevent me picturing the horrid scene of my uncle's death. But I turned my distress to good account. 'I do not wish you to be hanged, Thomas! But if you shoot James, they will make me say you did it!'

'Calm yourself, Sarah, you need have no fear of that, for we shall be married. You must know a wife cannot speak against her husband.'

'But if you kill James, you will make me a widow and I shall have to go into mourning. We cannot marry until I put off my weeds and by then it will be too late!'

'I had not thought of that,' he admitted. The blinking began again. 'You would not speak against me, would you, Sarah? I thought you cared for me.'

'Of course I do, Thomas, dear. But you know how it is, the judges will make me swear an oath on the Bible! I shall have to tell them.'

'What are we to do then?'

'I think you should put the gun away, Thomas, dear. Shall I ask my butler to look after it for you? Then we can sit down and discuss the matter sensibly.'

'Sensibly?' Thomas jerked and I realized my soothing words had quite the opposite effect. He was now in a state of extreme agitation. 'Oh no! No! I know all about discussing matters sensibly! You mean to talk and talk until you get your own way. I will not endure it! I refuse to discuss matters sensibly. I am going to shoot Foster!'

He levelled the gun as he spoke and he was too close to James to miss. Sobbing, desperate, all hope of persuasion at an end, I turned and lunged for the pitcher.

I lifted it and flung it with all my might and from behind my tears

I saw a cascade of water and breaking crockery and someone shouted, 'No, Sarah!'

I know not whether it was James or Thomas, but in the noise and confusion I saw something flash. Shadows leapt, there was a crash, a searing pain, and the floor tilted and rocked before spinning me into the dark.

Commotion was all around. I was tired, very tired indeed, but my sleep was disturbed because people would talk! I tried to wake up. I wished to wake, for I had been dreaming a terrible dream. Besides, James was there, I could hear his voice, and he sounded upset.

'Sarah, my love! Oh my dearest, how could you do it, how could you put yourself in such peril? Sarah, please do not die! I cannot bear to have you die!'

That was James, and he called me his love! I tried to wake up and tell him I would not die, but I could not struggle out of my sleep.

It did not signify. Another voice told him, 'No fear of that, sir. The bullet has touched no vital spot: a flesh wound only, she will be right as rain in no time.'

A bullet? Had someone been shot? I had dreamt something about a gun, and it was James who was shot!

'Sarah? Sarah, my love, can you hear me?'

That was his voice, so he had not been shot. It had been a dream, just a terrible dream. I was still asleep. Why could I not wake?

'Leave her be, sir, until I have the bullet out.'

It was Thomas, he had a knife; he was stabbing me; he was hurting me! I wanted James to make him stop, but he did not and I could not wake up to complain about it. Something pushed me down, back into the dark.

Vigorous movement from the child in my womb brought me to awareness and when I opened my eyes the room was lit with candles. Confused, I tried to sit up: hot knives cut into my shoulder and I fell back, moaning.

James was instantly by my side. 'Be still, do not attempt to move. How do you feel? Can I get you anything?'

I tried to speak and at the second attempt I managed to say I was thirsty. 'Tea?'

Matilda came and so did Mrs Clegg and I winced as they lifted me up against the pillows. I asked the time and when someone said it was ten o'clock at night, I looked around in surprise, because that seemed odd.

'You have been insensible these many hours.'

Memory came to me in fragments. James held a cup for me as I drank some tea, and I smiled at him, overjoyed because he was here and no longer in peril.

'Do you have pain? I have some laudanum, will you take some?' I shook my head, and he said, 'Do you recall what happened?'

'He was going to shoot you so I threw the pitcher. The gun went off.'

'You were hit! You might have been killed. At first, I feared—' He trembled and gulped. 'Why did you do it? Why put yourself in such peril?'

'I had no thought of danger to myself. He meant to shoot you, should I stand by and make no attempt to prevent? He is quite mad, is he not? Indeed, I wonder how we did not recognize it sooner, the signs were there. Poor Thomas! What will happen to him, now?'

'He is dead.' James spoke curtly and, as my mouth opened in surprise, he burst out, 'I killed him! Dear heaven, Sarah, I have killed a man!'

He was white-faced, anguished, and after all that had happened, I could not wonder at it. I used my good arm to pat the space next to me. 'Come, sit beside me.' When he was settled I said, 'How did it happen?'

Thomas had been distracted by my movements when I lifted the pitcher, the gun went off when I threw it and James had reached for his crutch and swung it with all his might. It hit Thomas across his shins, causing him to crash to the floor.

215

'He hit his head,' said James, 'on the fender.'

There were ornamental brass bosses at each corner of the fender, one of which Thomas had struck. 'His head was broken,' James told me. 'There was nothing we could do for him.'

'An accident, then. Well, I cannot be sorry.' I lifted my hand to his cheek. 'Do not take on so, James. He was mad, dangerously so. While he lived he would have been locked up, he had no hope of happiness. It is better for him this way.'

I was ill the next day, with a dreadful shivering weakness and frequent vomiting. My wounded shoulder hurt so abominably I was persuaded to take laudanum. I was looked after by Matilda and Mrs Clegg and these two gave the orders. James was allowed to come near me only for half an hour in the afternoon.

'The master worries too much,' said Mrs Clegg. 'Besides, he has business to attend to, and nothing useful he can do here.'

'Mr Henry is here,' Matilda said later. 'Sir Henry, I should say, because he becomes master of Kilburn, now. Well, it is not what we expected and he was not brought up to it, but he is conscientious and will do better for Kilburn than Mr Thomas.'

'Heavens!' I was diverted from my troubles. 'Arabella is Lady Kilburn! Well I never!'

Henry was very shocked. 'This is a sad business, Sarah. I wonder we did not realize poor Thomas was in such a case. He must have been deteriorating for some time.'

'I thought wickedness, never thought of madness until it was all too plain to see,' I admitted. 'No one did.'

Days passed: thanks to some herbal lotion applied by Mrs Clegg, my wound began to heal without festering. The child continued to make his presence felt, but showed no inclination to enter the world before his time.

Henry had Thomas coffined and hired a hearse to convey him to Leicestershire. Father and son were to be buried together. I persuaded James to attend the funeral. 'I cannot go, I am not well enough to venture, but you should be there.'

I grieved for my uncle, but I could not grieve for Thomas. My principle sensation was relief: relief because there would be no further trouble from that quarter and relief because the future of Kilburn was in safe hands.

Our neighbours came to call, most of them out of curiosity. Amongst those who showed real concern were Lady Colworth and Sir Martin. I took pleasure in their visit, but I could not help being reminded how their acquaintance had brought about the distance between James and myself.

During that brief period when I was only half-unconscious, I had heard him call me his love, his dearest! And later, when he reproved me for putting myself in danger, his distress had been plain to see.

Ever since, in spite of my pain and sickness and in spite of my grief, I had a return of that comfortable feeling which had been absent these last long months.

I was not mistaken: I heard him, I remembered quite distinctly. But I remained perturbed by those other words, spoken in sleep, which had advised me how he felt himself trapped. Selfish! That was what he said and the recollection pained me.

I had leisure to ponder during the three days he was away, and though I pondered long, I was no closer to understanding.

Every day, I got out of bed and took a turn about the room. My legs were weak, but I was supported by Matilda and Mrs Clegg. Satisfied I was on the mend, I thought it not beyond my power to take a bath.

So I was clean and powdered, cool, between fresh lavender-scented sheets when he came and his countenance lightened to see how I was getting better. We took supper together and there was sober talk of the funeral, and more optimistic talk of the future at Kilburn.

He gave me messages from Arabella and said, 'Your mama was at Kilburn. She had formed the intention of coming here, but we persuaded her against it, Arabella and I. I hope you do not object? Do you wish for her? I could write. . . .'

'No, indeed! I wish to have you to myself for a while.'

His eyes flickered with surprise and when I demanded kisses he was surprised again. I put my good arm around him, ran my fingers through his hair, drew my knuckles down his cheek. And when we parted, he looked at me with an expression which brought an ache to my throat.

'You know why I married you,' I said.

He flinched and looked away. 'Must we discuss it?'

'I believe we must.'

'Very well.' He swallowed. 'I do understand. It was to benefit your family, no thought for yourself. Henry said your manner concealed a strong sense of duty, and he was right.'

'Good heavens, have you been discussing me with Henry?'

'Indeed I have not! But he said that, and it struck me most forcibly. A strong sense of duty! It told everything about you.'

'My sense of duty is strong indeed,' I said with a smile, 'but only when it agrees with my inclination.'

'Aye, I knew you would laugh, but Henry is right. You never had ambition for yourself, did you?'

'I had ambition to be provided,' I said. 'I had no expectation of wealth, therefore I saw no sense in greater ambition, though I was quick to seize opportunity, as you well know. Not only for my family, for myself as well! I confess, my years at Kilburn had taught me to value the comforts money could provide. Why James, what is the matter? Is it cramp?'

'No, no!' But he had heaved himself out of his chair and was hauling himself about the room, too distressed to be still, and there was grief and pain in his features when he turned to look at me.

'Had we but known it, you had no need to marry. You had Mr Benjamin.'

'We did not know it, thanks to Thomas.'

'And now you are trapped!' he burst out. 'You might have had your own establishment, with all the comfort you could wish, and be married to a man you could admire! I blame myself, indeed I do! When I heard of your situation I pressed my own material advantages, for how else should I hope to win you? I snatched what I wanted! I should not have been so selfish.'

'Selfish?' I was all astonishment. 'You? You are the kindest, most generous husband anyone could wish for!' Then, when I fully took in what he was saying, 'Trapped? I? Good heavens, is that what you meant?'

James, of course, had no recollection of talking in his sleep. When I explained, he looked incredulous. 'You thought I felt myself trapped? You thought you were selfish? When have you ever been selfish? Answer that, madam, if you can!'

I told him then of how I had looked at other gentlemen without admiration, finding fault, and congratulating myself on my own good sense and good fortune.

'It was all folly and vanity,' I said miserably. 'And it was selfish also, for I gave no thought as to how you might be pained; it did not even occur to me!'

James shook his head, speechlessly. I looked at him and said hesitantly, 'That evening, when we dined with the Lyndhursts . . . er . . . may I speak of Sir Martin?'

'I suspect,' he said in resignation, 'I am going to discover I made a fool of myself. In fact I know I made a fool of myself! Such things as I said to you—'

'Oh, hush, James! It was my fault you were so pained.'

'Well, go on. I shall be interested to learn what manner of fault you found in Sir Martin.'

'I found no fault in him,' I said calmly. 'No doubt he has faults, but I have not discovered them. I found him handsome and pleasing. I liked him but I had no wish for him.

'Indeed?' James frowned, not displeased, but puzzled. 'I find that insufficient explanation for why you were staring at him so constantly.'

'He struck me as the kind of gentleman who wins the heroine in the popular romances,' I admitted. 'Yet I knew straight away that I did not wish for him. If I must account for staring at him, it can only be because my mind was occupied with the truth. For, absurd as it may seem, it took that to teach me how very dear you are to me.'

219

'I can scarce believe I am hearing this! Do you say you saw him, found no fault in him, and decided you preferred me?'

I nodded, blinking through my tears. 'I have come to love you, James. I cannot deny I married you for a less worthy reason, and I am sorry now that I did. You may feel my love has less value for that. But I do love you.'

'Are you—? Can you—?' Unable to finish his sentences, he gazed at me, his eyes full of question. When he found his voice at last, he said, 'Can you be happy with one such as I?'

'If I could make you whole, I would do so and rejoice,' I said. 'But for your sake, not for my own vanity. I do not repine upon your infirmity, James: I see only your beauty.'

'My what?'

'Look!' I said. I reached out and took one of his hands. 'See your hands, how shapely they are, how skilfully they produce music. Now take a looking-glass and see the expression in your eyes! Look into your heart and mind, sir, and do not dare tell me there is no beauty there.'

He looked at me with undisguised wonder. 'Your admiration has me quite puffed up in my own esteem,' he said at last. 'From now on, I shall be forever preening myself!'

I had to laugh. 'Will you spare the time to love me, too?'

'I may condescend to notice you.' He kissed me. 'Just once every so often.' He kissed me again. 'Do not expect too much, mind. Beautiful gentlemen like myself are such favourites with the ladies, you know.' He took my hand, clung to it and laughed. 'Upon my soul, Sarah! I have heard how love is blind, and you have proved it!'

We kissed each other and teased each other and we laughed for joy in our blessedness, and the child leapt within me, joining in our laughter.